The Value of Miss M

By

Diana Johnson

Diana Johnson

to: Linda

Enjoy the Read &

always

- Diana

For Mom and Dad.

Thank you. I love you.

To Amy, Amanda, and Judy thank you!

You each answered the call and helped shape this project
with your love of a good story and an eye for
the third thing.

Summer

1999

Melinda folded the hem of her good black dress behind her knees and knelt down in front of the credenza in the foyer of her Aunt Helen's house. The bottom drawer opened sluggishly, picking her pantyhose before resting in her lap. She reached in and lugged the dried leather Bible from its musty bed. She rose, muscled the drawer half-closed with her stockinged foot, and headed for the dining room table. Brady was clearing away the last of the coffee cups. She picked up *The Sun Press* from atop the pile of papers in front of her and cut out her aunt's obituary.

"It was a nice service, wasn't it, Brady?" she stated rather than asked. "It was simple, and that's what she wanted. That's what she was, just simple, no-frills-kind-of-people. She always told me, Melinda, keep it simple."

"It was fine, honey," he answered with a kiss to the back of her head and a quick squeeze of her shoulders. "She would have approved." He passed through the dining room and lumbered upstairs, banging his big square head on the rickety wooden trim… again. "Damn it to hell!"

"Watch your head, Brady!" his wife jibed.

She held the clipping in her hand and read out loud to the empty room.

"Francis Helen Harper, 70 of Cleveland, died at her home on Thursday, August 5, 1999. Miss Harper, born February 5, 1929, was the daughter of Pete and Margaret 'Peggy' Morely-Harper, formerly of Chillicothe. She was a 1947 honor graduate of Cleveland Heights High School and attended Cleveland Business Academy, where she achieved the esteemed Isaak Lowell Maxwell Award for Excellence in Business Communications and several ribbons in local and national typing tournaments. She worked for Higbee's Department Store (later Dillard's) for 54 years, starting as cashier at the lunch counter at sixteen, retiring as supervisor of the switchboard and public address systems earlier this year. Miss Harper leaves behind her great-niece Melinda Tennant-Garlow and her husband Brady, both of Cleveland. She was preceded in death by her parents, her sister, Polly Harper, her niece Lucille Harper-Tennant and her husband Red, and her cat and constant companion of 18 years, Phinehas. Funeral Services will be held Sunday, August 8th at Cummings and Davis Funeral Home on Euclid Avenue. Viewing from 11am to 4pm, followed by a brief service. In lieu of flowers, please make donations to the Cleveland Animal Protection League."

She let out a long, low sigh and whispered, "Cleveland Business Academy, we *are* a legacy."

She opened the Bible and the glossy, gold-lined pages split to uncover another newspaper clipping safely tucked between the parchments. She let a clump of pages cover it now and placed her maiden aunt's obituary smack in the middle of the Psalms.

"Hm… 116; verse six. 'The Lord preserveth the simple; I was brought low, and he helped me.' Yes, ma'am," she thought aloud, "Good spot. And that'll be enough reading for one night."

She closed the book and pushed away from the table, checked the doors, and flipped off the downstairs lights, then ascended the creaking stairs to the bedroom.

Brady was already in bed, flipping through TV channels. "Hey honey, we have to send that Private Ryan movie back tomorrow. You want to watch it? I know you like Tom Hanks and that Afflack guy."

She giggled from behind the bathroom door, "It's not Afflack, goofy! And (A) he's not in that movie and (B) it's his friend that I love. And you know he's the reason I wanted to see that." She emerged from the bathroom, her tiny figure covered to the knees in one of her husband's many Cleveland Browns jerseys, pulled her thick amber hair back in a low ponytail, and crawled into bed.

"Oh, is that so?" he teased, pulling her close under the covers.

"I mean, I like Tom Hanks, like the boy next door."

"Yeah… like me… sure."

"But I like Private Ryan like your best friend's older brother you try to get a peek of walking out of the bathroom wearing just a towel, when you sleep over."

"Oh, you tramp! Whose brother did you ever spy wearing nothing but a towel coming out of the bathroom?"

"Susan Rogers'."

"What? Wally Rogers! You lusted after Wallace Rogers?"

Brady busted out in his signature bellowing laughter, and Melinda laughed hard at him laughing. Then her laughter turned to tears. He didn't say a word, he just held his best friend and now twice-orphaned-wife until dawn.

Melinda woke to the sound of Brady brushing his teeth, readying for work. He looked around the bathroom door to see if she was awake. "Good, you're up." He spat and toweled off, then parked his heavy carcass on the side of the bed. "Sattler said he had a big announcement today." She looked worried. "Before you go all 'half-empty' honey, I think he might promote some people." An expanding grin spread across his freshly shaven face.

"But the overseas trends are…"

"Nope," he interrupted. "I will not let you do this. Not today. We are due some good news and I'm believing that this is the day." He grabbed her face and mashed her mouth with a hard kiss. "I love you. Call me after the meeting with the lawyers." Not giving her the chance to argue back, he leapt from the bed, bounded down the stairs, bashed his head again, "Damn it to hell!" and was gone.

Melinda showered and dressed and was out the door with her coffee in hand. Running down her to-do's she would stop at the apartment and pay August's rent, that was now nine days late, then drop by the funeral home, pick up the death certificate and settle her accounts with them, and finally end up at her two o'clock appointment at Gallagher and Ferris, attorneys at law.

Dave Gallagher and Nick Ferris had known her all her life.
They had facilitated her mother's adoption by Aunt Helen
when Melinda's grandmother, her aunt's only sibling,
Polly, lost her mind and ended herself. And they were there
after Melinda's parents died, for Act II, when Aunt Helen
adopted her. She was almost looking forward to seeing
them. They were like family. It might provide a moment of
respite from her perpetual loneliness.

At precisely two o'clock, Gallagher and Ferris came out to
the lobby and in unison began chatting her up.

"Melinda, so good to see you. How are you bearing up?"

"Brady ok, is he?"

The two shrinking, gray men flanked her on either side and
grabbed an elbow, escorting her through the double doors
into their inner office. What she mistook for chivalry, she
quickly recognized as the tug of their ancient bones and
weak joints, and soon knew they were using her to steady
their own gaits. They deposited her at the head of the long
mahogany conference table and collapsed in the seats on
either side. Julia, their equally ancient secretary, followed
them in and placed an antique silver tray bearing a pitcher
of water and three glasses just beyond the neat stack of
documents before them.

"Thanks, Julia." Gallagher acknowledged. "Shut the door,
please."

Once Julia disappeared and the three of them were alone,
the partners exchanged a worrisome look.

Then, taking her hand in his, Ferris began, "Now Melinda,
we know you've been through a lot in the past year with

Helen getting so bad after her fall. You know she loved you. And she wanted the very best for you. She wanted you to have every one of her worldly possessions."

Gallagher took over, "So of course as her only heir, you have inherited everything."

Melinda couldn't help but pick up on their mixed signals. She knew her aunt had worked all her life at a good-paying job and that she spent little. She was fairly confident there would be a good chunk of money and, of course, the house. But these guys were behaving as if they were about to deliver bad news.

"I know Aunt Helen invested some and there's the equity in the house, but just shoot me straight, gentlemen. What have I inherited? A silver mine in Argentina?"

The two laughed nervously and then began explaining. Back and forth like a long volley, they laid out all the details. Helen had invested poorly and lost most of her savings. What remained liquid, Melinda and Brady had all but exhausted to take care of her in the months since her fall. They could sell the investments for a couple hundred dollars after fees and penalties, but she'd be better off just leaving them alone and seeing if they were going to do any better in the coming months. But the real gut punch was the house. Even though she'd paid off the initial mortgage years ago, she had refinanced several times to keep some capital moving into her waning stocks. They had also discovered that she neglected to pay her income tax for the better part of the last decade, somehow evading an audit, and apparently accrued roughly $58,000 worth of tax liens against the place. Melinda's mind wandered while the lawyers conjectured and theorized. She helped fill out those tax packets herself. Aunt Helen had expressly asked for her help with that. They went over every line item, exemptions, social security. She even asked her niece once if she could claim Phinehas as her dependent.

"Wait, gentlemen, with all due respect, this makes little sense. I did her taxes with her every year. I helped her file them myself."

"Did you file them, Melinda?" Ferris asked.

"Did I file them?"

"Did you put them in the mail? Did you file them yourself?" he repeated.

Stricken, Melinda looked beyond the conference table to the window at the far side of the room as if she saw her diminutive aunt on the other side, shrugging at her.

"I'll be damned," she whispered. "No sir. She always insisted on sending creepy Kevin from next door. He was slow or something and she liked to pay him to do simple chores, like…"

"Like taking her mail to the post office," the old men chimed in sync.

"They were never filed, dear," Gallagher said. "Now, you're not in trouble per se, Melinda. We just have to sell the house and pay the taxes. Now surely you and Brady have discussed selling that house."

"Well, we've discussed…"

"Of course, you have. Now we want you to call Mary Rutherford at Home At Last Realty. She is a colleague of ours and we serve together on the Committee for a Better Cleveland. Known her for years. She's the best." Ferris opened a folder on the table and produced a business card. "Now, Melinda dear, don't you worry about a thing. You call Miss Mary and she will get things going in a heartbeat."

And then, in what seemed like a mad rush to get her out of their office, the two men continued on while shuffling her off.

"We'll probate the will and let you know when we need you to come sign off on everything."

"And again, dear, so sorry for your loss. Please give our best to Brady."

She suddenly found herself in the hall outside their offices, frowning in disbelief as the doors latched shut behind her.

"What now, Melinda?" she asked herself. Then it hit her… she knew someone else to ask.

She pulled into the parking space in front of the unmarked purple door. She looked up and down the street to see if anyone she knew would spy her entering. When the coast was clear, she jumped out and went through and up the steep stairs. She rested a moment to catch her breath and took in the signage on the door. 'Clara Voyant * Seer-Psychic' painted in Algerian script on the privacy glass; but covering the message 'BY APPOINTMENT ONLY' spelled out in self-adhesive mailbox letters below that, was a handwritten, paper sign, Scotch-taped to the glass that read 'Walk-ins Welcome'.

"Business must be booming," she said sarcastically and turned the knob.

The room she entered was unremarkable. Cheap brown paneling covered the walls, worn indoor-outdoor carpeting, the floor. Fluorescent overhead lighting cast a greenish tint on the space, while a couple of metal folding chairs flanked some potted plants in what looked like an attempt to soften the harshness just a touch. The single wooden door into the next room opened suddenly and out popped Clara!

"Melinda! Oh, my Goddess!"

Melinda jumped.

"I'm not in the least bit surprised to see you here today, sister. I've been dreaming of you every night for a week."

"Really? Well, you've manifested me here, so let's get to it, Clarissa."

The psychic held up her hand and cleared her throat.

"Melinda, I'm not Clarissa in this realm. I am Clara. Please. That is my professional name, and I would ask that you respect my position."

"Of course, Clara. I beg your pardon."

The two women bowed to one another, and Clara led her client through the door. This room was remarkable. Blackout curtains blocked nearly all but a sliver of light coming in through the single window, dark purple walls hung with tapestries, and the brown painted fiberglass ceiling tiles were draped with yards of sheer aubergine fabric that suspended strings of tiny twinkle lights to resemble the starry sky. Candles and incense sat atop a long chest of drawers on one wall and a small round table took up the middle of the room, with four wooden chairs pulled up to it. A shimmering crushed velvet throw with silky fringe along its hem covered the table, and one unlit candle and a book of matches sat in an amber bowl in the center.

Clara pulled a chair out to seat her client and continued around the room, waving her hands to waft the incense smoke toward her face. She sat down opposite Melinda and began.

"As always, I invite you, Melinda, to this space to connect you to the spirit world for all it has to offer. Will you please accept the invitation and light the Candle of Belief to open the channels?"

Melinda took the matches, lit the candle, then placed them back in the amber bowl. Clara wafted the scent of the candle and caught a ribbon of sulfur rising from the head of the match and choked just a little before exhaling and closing her eyes. She laid her arms, palms up, across the table and wiggled her fingers to prompt Melinda to take her hands. Melinda freely obliged and closed her eyes. Clara addressed the spirit world.

"We are open, spirits. We are here in heart and mind. What wisdom do you have for this one who seeks to know?"

The room remained quiet.

"Melinda, think of three questions you have for the spirits and concentrate their importance into my hands."

Melinda concentrated, and Clara squeezed her hands in response.

"You are not where you thought you'd end up after a long task has been completed. No?"

"No. I'm not."

"And you are not sure about the future with an additional burden you've gained. Am I right?"

"Yes, Clara. That is right!"

Melinda opened her eyes just a slit and Clara tugged at her hands to signal her to stay focused. Melinda resumed her concentration.

"And your love will be far from home when you begin your journey."

"Brady? Umm… no. Brady and I are fine."

"This is a part of the puzzle that has yet to be revealed."

"Really?" Melinda's eyes were open again. Her patience with this stuff was spotty. Like most *believers*, she only bought in if the future sounded relatively good. She was always quick to reject any seriously negative vibe. Nothing in her life with Brady indicated he would leave her side… ever. "You might be off on that one, Clariss- sorry, Clara."

"Yet to be revealed. Yet to be revealed. And not a bad thing, just a unique thing, a distant thing."

Melinda shrugged.

"And…OH!"

They both jumped.

"There is someone trying to come through, Melinda!"

"Is it my mom?" Melinda hoped.

"No. It is female."

"Is it one of the babies?"

"Melinda, I've told you the souls who've turned back before they're born don't have the strength to connect through me."

"Don't tell me it's Aunt…"

"It's your Aunt Helen!"

"Tell her I don't want to hear it!"

"Melinda, she is coming near… sheepish… no, penitent."

"Let me guess. She's sorry."

"Yes. Regret, remorse. She is feeling sadness and sorrow. She loved you very much, and she's sorry for the way she left things."

"If she's really sorry, tell her to give me the winning lottery numbers so I can pay my way out of this financial hole she's left me in."

"She says she's paved the way to easier days. Just look back to the place where you both learned the way."

"Look back? What? Ok, Clara. I'm done."

Melinda snatched her hands out of Clara's grip and blew out the candle.

"Melinda! She was trying to tell you something."

"I said I didn't want to hear it! Do you have any idea how much crap I'm going to have to wade through because of my dear departed Aunt Helen? A ton!"

"All the more reason you should have listened to her wisdom. But it's alright. She'll return if she has more to say. That's how the spirit world is."

"Whatever. Let's just do my numbers and I'll write you a check."

"Whatever you say, Melinda."

Clara reached for a tarot deck and a leather-bound journal on the chest of drawers and flipped on a floor lamp just behind her chair. She fanned the cards out on the table and then opened the book. She turned to where a pen held the place of the next blank page.

"M-E-L-I-N-D-A. So, 4-5-3-1-5-4-1. So… 23."

"No. Do Mindy Jo."

"Melinda, I've known you since junior high and I never heard anyone call you Mindy Jo."

"It's what my mom called me. It's just about the only thing I remember about her."

"Ok then. M-I-N-D-Y-J-O. 4-1-5-1-1-7. So… 19. Oh, that's the Sun!"

13

The woman panned her hand across the deck, then pushed the Sun card toward her client.

"The number 19 reduces to the Original Force number 1, as you know. This is good, Melinda. This is the energy of creation and new beginnings. You know it represents repeated endings and beginnings; setting, rising, over and over again."

"I seem to be the queen of the do-over."

"Yes! Well, apparently, you're in for something new. Something full of light and new life!"

Melinda's core warmed at the prospect of a new life. Her cheeks reddened, and she felt a breath of hope in her lungs where anxiety had been just minutes ago. She looked her psychic in the eye.

"Thank you, Clara."

"My pleasure, dear friend."

"Twenty today?"

"Sorry no. It's twenty-five now. They raised my rent."

Melinda wrote the check and, with a slightly lighter heart, headed for home. She pulled up in front of the house, just as Brady's friend Riffle was pulling out. They beeped and waved. Then she glanced at her watch and realized he was home too early for this to be good. Inside, she found her husband sitting in the middle of the couch with what remained of his second beer in hand, staring out the window. She tossed her things onto the coffee table and lowered herself into a chair opposite the man.

He leaned toward her intently and asked, "How'd it go, honey?"

"Well, Mr. McQuain took our rent check, shared his condolences, and asked if we wanted to keep the place since Aunt Helen has gone on to meet Jesus and we have the house now. I paid the funeral home with what I've learned may be the last of Aunt Helen's savings because I found out from old 'Uncles' Gallagher and Ferris that the late, great F. Helen Harper owed over fifty-seven grand in income taxes, which results in a lien in that approximate amount against this very address!" She took another long deep breath, huffed it out, and asked, "How was your day?"

Brady slowly reached into his uniform shirt pocket and presented a thin folded pink paper, then announced, "You were right! I have been downsized. The decline in foreign production is making the Ford Motor Company, THE FORD MOTOR COMPANY nervous and, to pre-empt massive shutdowns, they are closing the smaller plants and focusing their attention on increasing production in the biggest ones."

"Brady! What the hell?"

"I know! But don't start worrying, honey. Me and a bunch of the guys are calling around the other plants. I will not be out of work!"

"Ok. Other plants? What other plants? Is there anything else around here? I don't want to move to Detroit!"

"Me neither. Johnson and Riffle know a guy from a GM plant in Delaware."

"G… M? General Motors? Brady, that's like switching from the Browns to the Ravens. Do you really want to do that?"

"Art Modell lost his mind! It doesn't matter, we're finally back this season. And we agreed never to mention the other team in this house!" Brady was easily side-tracked by his Browns. "I have no choice, Melinda. I have to go where the work is."

"Well, I am free to work now, too. I could come with you and find a job wherever you are. Maybe we could move away, away!" she hoped.

"Yes! You loved the Carolinas when we went to the beach that time, right before we got married. And Virginia is nice with the farms and the fields. Remember when we went there after the…" he stopped short.

Melinda's face froze, and her eyes instantly filled with tears. "Oh yeah, sure, I remember… after the next to the last miscarriage. Could this day get any better, I ask you?"

"Oh my God, Melinda, I am so sorry, honey. I'm an idiot! Please forget I said anything. Brady Garlow, you're such a horse's ass!" He rocked back against the couch and covered his face with his big mitts.

A single tear escaped and slid down to the corner of her mouth. She licked it off and reached across the coffee table to place a comforting hand on his giant knee. "I'm ok. We will be ok. We just have to figure this out."

He looked directly into her wet, hazel eyes with all the empathy in the world.

"Besides, Clara says we're in for a new beginning. She said, 'new life' and I'm excited about what that could mean."

"Melinda, you didn't go back there."

"I know you don't believe in it, Brady. But it's the closest thing to faith I have left."

"But Clarissa Hendershot was just a couple of years ahead of us in school. She dropped out of Cleveland State her freshman year and joined a commune! Her brother said she was never right after that."

"Or maybe she was more right than any of the rest of us. Either way, I don't care. You don't have to approve, but I'm going to keep seeing her as long as it serves me."

"I don't want to fight about this now, honey."

"Good. Neither do I. Now go change your clothes and take me to an early dinner."

After dinner, the couple returned to Aunt Helen's and Brady began delegating.

"Ok. I'm going to the apartment to square things with McQuain. I'll call Riffle and Johnson and see what they've come up with. You call that Rutherford woman and make an appointment to list the house tomorrow! I don't want to move without you if we can help it."

"I never thought about that, Brady. What if things don't line up that way? I can't hardly think about staying here by myself."

"Honey, you'd be fine. It might only be for a couple of weeks while I get settled somewhere and we get this house on the market." He held her shoulders, looked into her eyes, and smiled. "You'll be fine. It's only temporary."

He kissed her and walked out. Melinda watched him drive away as a soft summer rain fell.

She repeated the psychic's words, "Yet to be revealed."

She walked into the kitchen, retrieved a beer, and sucked the escaping foam off the top of the can. She went through her purse to find the realtor's card and dialed the number.

"Home At Last Realty, this is Mary."

"Miss Rutherford, hi. I'm Melinda Garlow. I got your number from Nick Ferris and Dave Gallagher. I have a house to sell."

The questions began with the address and asking price, which included the information about the tax lien. Mary Rutherford filled out an initial contact form as she quizzed Melinda on what she knew of the property. They inventoried the number of bedrooms, bathrooms, and closets. They covered the yard, the garage, the attic, and the basement. Melinda wasn't sure about the square footage, but Mary would bring a tape measure tomorrow and size the whole thing up.

"How's ten tomorrow morning work for you, Melinda?"

"That would be great."

"Good enough. See you then. And thank you so much for calling Home At Last."

Melinda hung up the phone and downed the beer. A rattling belch bubbled up from her throat and she giggled at the eruption.

"That beer tasted like another one."

Brady was gone until after dark and when he returned, he found his sleeping wife curled in a ball on the couch, three empty cans crushed on the coffee table. He crept in and, sliding his hands underneath her petite frame, lifted her effortlessly to his chest. He tiptoed up the stairs, ducking his big square head to miss the trim, and tucked her into bed. She didn't stir until morning.

She woke again to the sounds of him in the bathroom and opened a squinty eye in his direction.

"Where are you going, Brady? You got laid off."

"I'm meeting Johnson at Riffle's place this morning to call their guy at that GM joint."

"The New Jersey plant?"

"Delaware. That's the only one we could find that needed people. The other operations in Ohio have either frozen hiring or are downsizing too. The Rust Belt is no joke."

"How far away is that?"

"A little over four-hundred miles. It maps out at about a seven-hour drive."

She rubbed her hands over her face to rouse herself more awake.

"That's awfully far away, Brady. What if I can't come with you?"

He sat down next to her on the bed.

"What if? What if? Honey, what if the house sells and we get to leave? What if our dreams come true? What if things actually work out for the best this time, huh? What if that happens?"

"Ok. Ok! What if it does? I get it. Think positive."

"If the great Clara Voyant told you to look on the bright side, you'd sure as hell do it, right?"

She glared at her husband.

"You're just cranky because you're hungover," he ribbed.

"I am not! I had three beers. I wasn't even drunk last night. I'm just exhausted."

"I know, Melinda. I know. And we'll rest… and soon. But for now, I really need you to stay positive and help me get through this. I've lived in Cleveland all my life. My people are buried here. I've been a Ford man all… my… life. We'll get through if we keep reminding ourselves that it's only temporary."

"You're right, baby." She stroked his burly forearms and then shooed him away. "Go! Get out of here and go meet your girlfriends and hatch a plan. Tell Charlie and Roger I said 'hey'."

Brady kissed her hands and tore down the stairs, less carefully than the night before, and banged his head on the trim. "Damn it to hell!"

She giggled, laid still for another minute, then flung the covers off.

Toast and coffee satisfied her empty gut after she showered, and she busied herself tidying up before her ten o'clock date with the realtor. Miss Mary Rutherford was spot on time and rang the doorbell repeatedly.

"Good morning, Melinda!" Mary charged her hand into the foyer with all the zeal of an evangelist, backing Melinda all the way into the living room.

"Oh! Good morn -…"

"I just love these old houses," Mary said as she pushed past her new client and produced her tape measure. "I'd love it if you would just give me a sec to roam around. Is that alright? I like to pretend I'm a potential buyer. You know, see it through their eyes, walk a mile, so to speak. Do you mind?"

"Be my guest, Mary." Melinda surrendered to the woman's energy and wandered back to the kitchen to freshen her cup. "Can I get you a cup of coffee?"

"Not just yet, dear. Give me a minute to get my business out of the way and then I'll join you."

Melinda sat at the kitchen table and watched and listened as the agent opened doors and windows, counted steps, photographed and measured everything. She heard the 'slide' and the 'snap' of the tape measure over and over as

Mary worked diligently to record every detail of the place. Once in a while she uttered a 'Hmm' or an 'Oh my!' and while it tempted Melinda, she didn't dare interrupt to question the process. She sipped her coffee and reminded herself to stay positive. Mary blew by her to go down the basement steps, where more, 'Oh mys!' were uttered, then she heard her thrust herself out the downstairs door into the backyard. Melinda parted the cotton daisy curtains at the back window to peek out where Mary was walking off the width, heel-to-toe, from one side of the property to the other.

Looking up toward the kitchen windows, she bellowed, "To the clothesline in back?"

Melinda nodded. Mary answered with a salute and began pacing off from the back stoop to the alley just beyond that marker. When the realtor doubled back to check herself, Melinda opened the back door and welcomed her to a seat at the kitchen table.

"How about that coffee now, Mary? Cream and sugar?"

"Black please, Melinda. And thank you, dear."

The agent opened her portfolio and separated a couple of pre-printed forms from the pockets inside. Melinda carried the coffee to the table and sat down opposite her guest.

"Well, what's the good word?"

"Oof!"

"Oof? That's not a good word, Mary? What does 'oof' mean in the real estate world?"

"Well, from what I can see, you have a couple of really dangerous code violations with the current furnace and wiring in this old girl."

"Oof!" Melinda took another swig of coffee while Mary did some figuring. "Let's have it."

"So, cloth-covered wire, frayed and exposed at the fuse boxes in the attic and upstairs hall. It looks like your aunt had someone put a breaker box in the basement for her electric dryer, but they wired nothing else to that. And the furnace, which appears to be an old coal boiler converted eons ago, wasn't properly vented. Your chimneys will have to be redone. With the plant closing, selling anything is going to be a challenge, but no bank will loan a buyer money with these kinds of violations. It would never pass inspection. If you want it sold and you want even the skinniest of profits, you're going to have to update this wiring and furnace. Of course, the best is to have a qualified craftsman for a job like this, but I have seen folks do it themselves when they couldn't afford that. And I'm afraid it won't be cheap. Does your husband do that kind of thing?"

"He's the one who installed the dryer. But he may leave town to find work."

"Not to worry, Melinda." The realtor dug through another pocket in her portfolio and presented a typed list of contractor's phone numbers. "These are the guys I always recommend. They're all pretty busy but drop my name and you might just get a call back a little sooner. There are several outfits on this list. I suggest you call until you find someone who'll come have a look. Now, I would put you under contract today, but in all honesty, even if you had a bite, no one is going to put earnest money down until these issues are resolved."

Melinda sat dejected, staring at the list in her hand. Her disappointment registered with Mary who placed a caring hand on hers and said, "I've seen worse. We'll sell this house. I promise."

Melinda looked up and feigned a smile, then heard the front door open. Brady was home and lumbering toward the voices in the kitchen.

Mary gathered her things and prepared to exit. "You have lots to discuss. I'll get out of your way."

"Good morning. You must be Ms. Rutherford," Brady said with his hand outstretched to the visitor.

"Yes good morning, Mr. Garlow. So nice to have met you. I'm just going to leave the contracts, and the two of you can ring me back when you've decided how you want to go forward." She stood and strapping her bag over her shoulder, thanked Melinda for the coffee and offered to show herself out.

"What did she have to say about the place, honey?" asked Brady as he sat, picked up the loose papers, and began reading.

Melinda poured him a cup of coffee and let him study what the forms laid out.

"Rewire?"

She nodded.

"And the furnace, too?"

"She said that it won't pass inspection for any bank to loan money on it. We could list it, but it won't sell without the repairs." Melinda sipped at her cup while he continued to read. "I told her you wired the dryer; do you think you could do the rest of the house?"

"And the furnace? No. I don't know anything about building code. And even if I did..." He dropped his enormous hands to the table. "They hired us, honey. I need to leave this weekend."

"Oof!"

"Oof? That's kind of a weird response to your husband telling you he's leaving to work four hundred miles away. Oof?"

"That's what Mary said after examining this house. Oof. And that is what I'm saying about this entire year. A great big fat OOF!"

"Melinda, we knew this might be a wrinkle. We talked about it."

"I know, Brady. Can't I be a little upset? The house won't sell without work you can't do to it plus you're leaving me with the whole damn thing while you move to New Jersey!"

"Delaware."

"Wherever! I think I'm entitled to my oof and I'm going to take it!"

"Honey!"

"Don't 'honey' me now, Brady. Here's the list of contractors Mary gave me." She slammed the paper on the table in front of the man. "You have the rest of the week before you leave. Find someone you trust to do this work."

He reached for her and snagged her by the wrist to stop her from storming out.

"Hon-... Melinda, none of this is my fault. I'm doing the best I can."

"I know, Brady. Me too! Now let me go. I need to look in the paper for a job so I can help pay for this shit." She shrugged him off, and he let her go.

Brady and Melinda were good together. They'd been through a lot of life side-by-side with little tension between them. When they fought, which wasn't often, they fought fair and always ended up closer afterwards. But the compounding problems since Aunt Helen's decline earlier in the year had taken a toll on their ability to see the bigger picture. Each one withdrew to separate corners to do what came next. Brady cleaned out the garage, emptying boxes they could use to move the apartment things to Aunt Helen's and the few things he'd need to survive in Delaware with his buddies. The men arranged to rent a tiny furnished house and they would each have space for a couple of personal items and their clothes.

Melinda sat at the dining room table scouring the Want Ads for anything she could do to earn enough to help pay for the renovations. "Cleaning... cleaning... babysitting... nope. Part time... part-time... full-time trucker." She laughed a little at the image of her behind the wheel of a semi.

"Nobody needs that unholy mess." She folded *The Sun* in half and pressed it flat to concentrate. "Part-time accounting… part-time bookkeeping… part-time administrative assistant. Wait! What's this?" She picked up the paper and held it closer to read, "Wanted: full-time technical school instructor to teach Business Math and Beginning Accounting at the Cleveland Business Academy. Bookkeeping and managerial experience preferred. Interviewing August 9th thru 13th. Call Jeannie at (216) 541-1982 for an appointment."

She tore out the notice and sprinted for the garage. "Braaaadeeee!"

He heard his wife's call and dropped what he was doing in an instant to run to her. They met in the breezeway, both out of breath.

"What, honey? You scared the shingles out of me!"

"Sorry, baby. Sorry," she giggled. "Look!"

He took the shred of paper from her hands and read.

"The Academy? Oh my gosh, that would be perfect!"

"Right? Close, familiar, and I remember what it was like going as a student. It can't be that hard to teach there."

"What about the rumors?"

"What about them? That place has been standing as a fixture on Merrifield road since Christ was a corporal. If the man hasn't brought them down yet, he's not going to!"

They kissed through smiling teeth.

"Sorry about earlier. I feel much better now," she said.

"Me too. I hate it when we fight."

They kissed again.

"Go call and get your interview set up!" he prodded.

She ran back into the house, and he got back to his chore. He stood for a moment in the middle of the old garage and looked up to the rafters.

"Please God, let this be a good thing. We're drowning here. Our girl needs a win." He dropped his head and squeezed his eyes shut tight. "Amen."

She'd have two more days to prepare for her interview on Friday the thirteenth. What could go wrong?

They spent Wednesday moving and packing. They got everything out of the apartment and separated what Brady needed to take with him to Delaware. He asked around about the contractors on Mary Rutherford's list and called a couple to make appointments for estimates on Friday afternoon. They both decided they had enough to throw a quick yard sale before he left town. Melinda made the signs and called *The Sun* to put the ad in for Saturday morning.

Thursday they sorted and cleaned and buzzed about the bittersweet memories clinging to the brick-a-brack they were putting in the sale. The hours wore away with them wishing they had a dollar for every time they said, "Remember that time…?" Both of them nervous about the days and months to come, both of them putting that out of their minds for one more project together before the next big turn, they fell into bed too tired to dream.

Melinda woke Friday morning with a dull buzzing in her head. Conflicted, she felt excited to be pursuing full-time work again but uncomfortably anxious about where. Having taken both the basic and advanced course studies at the Cleveland Business Academy and learning valuable skills that enabled her to secure gainful employment, she felt uneasy about attending the school. She couldn't afford college but didn't have the attention span for four years of anything anyway, so Aunt Helen had insisted on the academy. Helen knew from her own experience they'd teach her great niece something she could use. But a family of questionable characters ran the school whose reputations in the community were sometimes less than stellar. The patriarch and founder of the organization was Isaak Lowell Maxwell, CPA. Before he died under mysterious circumstances at 74, he sired six ungrateful children in his forties who, along with their aging mother, now shared ownership and operating responsibilities of the academy. They were an apathetic group and, while mostly represented only on paper for payroll purposes, all were "employed" in some role at the school. Melinda had always felt that there were unseemly motives attached to the operation of the institution. This was in part because of reported allegations of the family's connection to organized crime. The fact that each one of the Maxwell heirs owned separate businesses left to them by their father that could easily have outlined a racketeering ring did nothing to quell the rumors. But theirs was the only ad in the paper she felt even remotely qualified to answer. So, Brady made her eggs and sent her off in her good blue suit. She made her way through town, turned onto Merrifield Road, pulled up in front of the timeworn building and parked.

Nothing much had changed outwardly at the school since her days as a student there. The six-story building loomed graying over Merrifield Road opposite the old barbershop and the other vacant storefronts on the block. A failed attempt at "modernizing" the façade in the early '80s had resulted in a cheaply applied white stucco finish that had stained and aged horribly. The old concrete urns flanking the main entrance sported plastic topiaries and the fading synthetic red and blue ribbons they'd forgotten to replace after the 4th of July. Young people too small for their mandatory suits huddled under the awning to take the last drags off their forbidden cigarettes before entering.

One more quick flip of the visor to check the mirror for lipstick on her teeth, she stowed her gum in a tissue in her purse, grabbed her resume, and crossed the busy street. She followed a group of students into the main entrance and watched them wander off into their respective classrooms. Melinda stopped short at the corner of a tiny booth to her right, just as its sentry called out to her.

"Stop!"

"Oh!" Melinda startled and caught her collar with her free hand. "I forgot there was always someone there. It was always Mrs. Maxwell. Oh, no... is she?"

The woman occupying the space behind the half-wall that separated the little room from the rest of the hallway grinned and giggled at the rattled guest.

"Oh no. Miss M is alive and kicking. She's just late. So, she's probably kicking her driver. Sorry. I love catching the kids off guard when I'm playing gatekeeper! But you're not a student."

"No ma'am. I'm here..."

"Oh, you're here for the interviews! Oh no. I am sorry!"
The woman scanned a list in front of her.

"No, no. It's alright. I'm sure it's good to get the bad mojo
scared out of you right before a job interview."

"Garlow? Is that you?"

"Yes ma'am. Melinda Garlow."

"You look familiar Miss Garlow. Have you applied here
before?"

"I attended as a student a little over a decade ago."

"Well, welcome back!"

"Thanks. Where do I need to go?"

"Straight down this hall to the elevators, up to the sixth
floor, and left to the end of the hall. The door will be open
and there should be a room full of people. They're loud!
You can't miss them!"

"Thank you…?"

"Jeannie. I scheduled you."

"Thank you, Jeannie."

"Good luck, love."

Melinda turned down the long hall and followed Jeannie's
instructions to board the elevator. She noticed a few
changes to the flow of the building, but it was mostly
familiar. As the rickety metal box chugged its way up, she

heard the faint din of activity on every floor, and as she neared the top level, a cacophony of raised voices grew louder. Jeannie didn't lie about the volume. Once off the elevator, she proceeded until she found herself a few paces from the open door to the room at the end of the hall. She stepped forward with her hand raised to knock on the door frame when a man appeared out of nowhere, scaring her for the second time since entering the building.

"Next!" he yelled into her face. "Oh, my God! I heard the elevator ding but had no idea you were already down the hall. Sorry if I spooked you. Are you here for the job?"

"I'm fine. Yes, I'm here for the job." She presented her hand. He ignored it and grabbed her resume instead.

"Come in and sit," he directed as he read the paper in his hand. "I'm Sam Maxwell. Everybody, this is… Melinda Garlow."

The group settled to a lower roar.

"Everybody listen up!" he attempted to command the room but obviously lacked the clout. They continued to talk over him as he and Melinda stood awkwardly at the end of the long table. He tried again. "We have another applicant! Listen!"

A booming voice came from just behind Melinda.

"Quiet!"

She flinched again and her eyes darted around to see a tall, sturdy silhouette charge by her toward the other end of the room.

"Thank you, Ike. As I was saying, this is Melinda Garlow." Sam gestured to Melinda to take the empty seat nearest her, and she did. "It says here, you're a graduate of our academy. When did you attend?" He passed the paper down the table for everyone to have a look.

"I came here right out of high school for the two-year program in '85."

"So that's graduating twelve years ago?" confirmed the woman seated to her right. Melinda nodded. "Before my time."

"Melinda, that's Kitt. She teaches Advanced Tax Prep and Audit Anatomy." Sam pointed to the woman who interjected and the only person of color, then went around the table introducing the rest. "At the end of the table is my brother Ike Maxwell, the Executive Director of the academy. To his right, my other brother, Manfred 'Manny' who teaches Office Etiquette and Pitch and Presentation. And to my left is Deidre. Deidre runs the whole damn place!"

A collective chuckle ran through everyone in the group except Deidre. She looked nervously at Melinda with dark-ringed eyes and attempted a twitchy smile.

"Deidre does Usage & Sales, B&O, and Advanced Accounting. Your beginning class would be a prerequisite for her advanced one."

Melinda and Deidre exchanged a courteous nod.

"Plus, she's the accountant for the school itself. She knows where they buried all the bodies, so to speak!" Sam bellowed, igniting another round of laughter and chatter.

Melinda surveyed the action until she located her resume again. It had made it around the end of the table to the director. She studied him, studying it. He looked at her for an uncomfortably long time, handed the resume off, then said, "I remember you."

The group quieted, waiting to hear more.

"You're Helen Harper's grand-daughter."

"Great niece, sir," she corrected.

"Right. Right. Helen was something. My mother and father talked about her like she was a legend at this place."

"She won quite a few typing titles and an award in communications."

"Yes. Yes. I'm remembering that now. People, this girl's a legacy."

The group nodded and hummed with approval.

"What have you been doing for the past twelve years, Melinda?" asked Deidre as Manny handed her the resume.

"I got married and worked part-time at the Richmond Town Square Branch of the Cuyahoga County Public Library."

"The one in the middle of the mall?" asked Manny.

"Yes. They closed it for that big renovation last year."

"I never understood why they put a library in a mall," Sam confessed.

"Probably to give those suburban white kids some incentive to actually read a book instead of wandering around the mall all damn day, spending their parents' money!" Kitt preached.

Rolling her eyes, Deidre sarcastically droned, "Oh Kit, please tell us how you really feel."

"When you grow up walking downtown to the library because you don't have the money to go to the movies or the arcade..." Kitt was off toward the deep end and the others dived in, some to her rescue, others to push her under.

The debate only lasted a couple of seconds more when Sam, reclaiming Melinda's resume, attempted another call to order. "Ok!"

Melinda waited for the quiet that only came after Ike, knocked his hand on the table, then yielded to his little brother.

"Ok. So, does anyone have any more questions for Melinda?" The lot shrugged and shook their heads. Turning to her, he asked, "Do you have questions for us? Anything you'd like to share about yourself?"

Afraid they'd reject her application if they knew she only intended to work in the area long enough to sell the house and join Brady on the coast, Melinda sat guiltily for a moment without offering that information. Then she thought of something to ask.

"How much does the position pay?"

"We pay more than minimum wage here," Sam defended. "We are a professional academy, after all."

"You'd start at eight," said Deidre. "All new hires start at eight. You'll get evaluated after ninety days for a five-cent raise, and once a year after that."

"Well, that's more than I made at the library. When do you think you'll be deciding?"

Sam piped in again, "We have one more interview this morning to finish them out, and barring any resistance from the other board members, we should make our decision this afternoon."

"Other members?" Melinda asked.

"My brother is referring to the rest of the family," Ike explained. "Our executive board comprises our brothers and sisters, our uncle, and our mother. We technically don't hire anyone for employment at the academy without a unanimous decision from the entire board."

"When I didn't see Mrs. Maxwell at her station downstairs, I just assumed she had retired." The staff laughed out loud. "Will I have to interview with them as well?"

Everyone around the table scoffed at the idea and met with an irritated eye from their Executive Director. "We are confident this panel's input will convince the board of the right man for the job."

"Great." Melinda was relieved. "So, I'll hear from someone this afternoon?"

Sam rose next to her and pulled her up by the elbow to escort her out. "Yes. We call all our applicants to let them know, one way or another. Thank you for coming in, Melinda. We'll be in touch."

She smiled and headed hastily for the elevator. As the doors opened, Jeannie popped out, flushed and flustered. The woman ran past her toward the conference room that had already begun simmering again. Melinda closed her eyes to imagine that kind of chaotic energy on a daily basis. As she descended to the ground floor, she comforted herself, "It's only until we get the house fixed up. It's only temporary." She darted out the back door to safety.

Brady was sending off the first contractor when she pulled into the drive.

"How was it, honey? Did you feel like a kid again?" He walked her into the house through the breezeway.

"It was weird. I felt like I was interrupting a political coup. Those people are intense!"

"But how do you think you did?"

She shrugged and tossed her purse onto the kitchen table, then plopped down in a chair. "How was your guy?"

"Oof!"

"Oh no."

"He told me everything Mary told you. She really knows her stuff." He poured them a cup of coffee.

"Thanks, baby." She blew on her cup. "So… how much and how long?"

"He thinks he can do it all in about three months, but he wouldn't be able to start until October!"

"What?"

"So many people have left the area, he can't keep good, reliable help."

"Well, how much?"

"He said about $20,000."

Coffee sprayed from her mouth. "Holy Mary, Mother of God, Brady!"

Her arms hung in the air as coffee dripped from her nose and chin. He smirked, then scrambled to get a tea towel and wipe up the mess.

"He said he needs half when we sign the contract and half when the job is done."

"So, we have six weeks to come up with ten thousand dollars if we want him to start in October?"

"We can do it. I'm going to be making fifteen an hour and Riffle said they give you all the overtime you can do. I'll have at least six or seven thousand by then."

"They pay eight dollars an hour at the academy, Brady. I won't even make two grand by then."

"Maybe the other guy will be a little more reasonable. He's due any minute." Reading the worry on his wife's face, he jumped into hero mode. "Why don't you go up and take a long bath and then lay down for a minute? We won't disturb you; I promise. I'll see what kind of deal this next guy's offering and then finish up the stuff in the garage."

"No. I'm fine. I can help with the garage."

"Melinda, there's not that much left to do. You go relax and when I'm done, I'll make you stuffed peppers and corn on the cob. Your favorite summer supper!"

She jumped to her feet, threw her arms around his neck, and kissed him.

"You're the best husband ever!"

The steamy water and Avon bubble bath left her limp and drowsy. She wrapped herself in a towel and snuggled down in the cool sheets and fell out. The phone woke her hours later.

"Hello," she cracked.

"Melinda, it's Jeannie from the Cleveland Business Academy. I'm calling to let you know the board voted to offer you the job."

"Really?" She was more awake now. "That's great."

"Yes. So please report to the conference room where you interviewed, Monday at eight am. We have a staff meeting at the beginning of every week before classes begin. Afterwards, you can get acquainted with your textbooks and your classroom. Seniors are finishing up next week, so we have a full week to prepare before the next session begins. That should give you plenty of time to settle in. Questions?"

Melinda thought for just a second, then answered, "I don't think."

"Terrific! See you Monday at eight."

"I'll be there."

"Congratulations!"

"Thanks again, Jeannie."

The sun was already low, and the room was glowing orange by the time the phone woke her.

"How long was I out, jeez?" she asked herself and stretched.

She dressed and peeked out the window just in time to spy Brady closing the garage door. They met at the foot of the stairs.

"Why did you let me sleep so long?" she scolded.

He glanced at his watch. "Holy hell, Melinda! I had no idea it was this late. I haven't even started the peppers yet."

"Let's not bother with that tonight, baby. You go get a shower and relax and I'll make us breakfast for supper."

"Pancakes and sausage?"

"Yep; your favorite. We can celebrate my new job!"

"You got it? When did they call?"

"Just now!"

He wrapped his sweaty arms around her narrow waist and lifted her off the ground.

"This is awesome! I'm going to get cleaned up!"

The couple sat at the kitchen table listening to the sounds of the night blowing through the open windows as they enjoyed their pancakes and speculated about their new prospects. Not until they both had seconds did Melinda ask about the other estimate.

"Who was the second guy today?"

"Caldwell from C & C Construction."

"And did he come in any lower than the first one?"

"Not lower, but better. He says it'll take him twelve to fourteen weeks too. He's only asking for five to start, but he is booked through the end of October."

"Who do you think we should go with?"

"Them. We can't save every penny we make for the next six weeks. We gotta eat."

"Agreed."

She giggled to herself, and he got curious.

"What's funny?"

"I was just thinking that maybe someone will come to the yard sale tomorrow and discover we have some priceless artifact that's worth millions and all this lower-class struggling will be a thing of the past. Wouldn't that be amazing?"

"Amazing? Yes. Probable? Not so much."

"I know, hence the chuckle."

They cleared the table and set the sticky plates to soak in the dishpan. They closed up the house and retreated to the second story. Brady opted against starting the attic fan to cool the house after his day with the contractors, so Melinda put a box fan in the bedroom window to keep the night air moving through while they slept. They lay beside each other in silent agreement, both too full of sugar and grease to attempt making love, and sleep overtook them quickly despite the August heat.

Melinda was up with the chickens and dressed and downstairs before dawn. Brady smelled the coffee and joined her as she was finishing the dishes from the night before. He slid his arms under her elbows and hugged her from behind as she rinsed the last pan.

"Morning, honey." He kissed her ear.

"Morning, sleepyhead," she answered.

"Man, I was out!"

"I know. You didn't even snore last night. Or at least I don't think you did. I was out too!"

"You ready for the day?" As he asked, the arc of approaching headlights beamed through the door to the breezeway; the first sign of the yard sale early birds.

Melinda dried her hands and grabbed her coffee cup. "Ready or not, here they come."

With fabricated optimism, she greeted the first customers. And though she didn't hope high that the sale would generate any real money, at least they'd get rid of some of their junk and have less to move when they sold the house and relocated. She knew nothing about Delaware except that it was a coastal state and growing up a flat lander made her ache for the difference that would make. She haggled with the droves at the sale, imagining waking up to the smell of sea breezes instead of the metallic air of Lake Erie. Brady came out to help mid-morning and proved a worthy salesman. He improvised long, impressive stories every time someone picked up some worthless knick-knack to make it sound priceless and one-of-a-kind. The two exchanged knowing grins throughout the day. She took a couple dollars from the till and popped out for a dozen hotdogs at around two and returned to a thinner crowd than the morning had produced.

"What do we do if we have a bunch of stuff left over, honey?" asked Brady.

"There are always the hyenas at the end," Melinda explained. "People come around sometimes even after dark and offer you five or ten bucks for the rest of it."

"That might be the best deal yet. I'm not sure all the stuff we started with was worth five bucks!"

"They know that. That's why they wait."

Their shadows got longer as the buyers trickled off and once the streetlights came on, a little rusty pickup with a homemade, wooden, flat bed rolled up to the drive. Melinda left Brady to negotiate the last of the sale items with the driver and went inside. She cracked open a beer and ate a cold, leftover hot dog over the sink. Brady followed behind her as the truck lurched away with its haul.

"Well, I got ten for the rest of it. But I had to throw in the card tables." He checked with his wife too late to matter, "That was ok, right?"

"We can get a new card table down the road if we need one. You did good, baby," she assured. "What was the final tally?"

"Let's see." He opened the cigar box and counted the bills first, and then the change. "Eighty-five, eighty-six, eighty-seven dollars and forty-two cents."

"Forty-two cents? I took nothing I didn't round off. How in the hell did you get forty-two cents?"

He puffed out his chest and beamed, "Hey! You're looking at a champion wheeler-dealer here, girl. Don't nobody get this man down below his bottom line."

"Not even two pennies?"

"Not even!" Brady declared to the open fridge while grabbing himself a beer.

Melinda laughed, "Are cold hotdogs ok for dinner?"

"I will pay exactly eighty-seven dollars and forty-two cents for three cold hotdogs please, ma'am."

"Coming up!"

"Let's eat in the dining room tonight, Melinda. I feel like celebrating our newfound wealth."

Brady was the best. Here they were gathering the good China and crystal (that they probably should have had in the yard sale) to eat in the formal dining room that Aunt Helen never even used. Melinda fed paper napkins through ugly brass rings she found in the drawers beneath the curio, while Brady tilted the crystal goblets they dusted off only once before for their anniversary and filled them with Miller High Life.

"To us!" he chimed.

"To our new adventures!" she answered. The glasses clinked, and they chugged the golden brew.

"Ahh!" Brady held his glass up to the light to examine the bubbles. "Ninety-nine, an excellent year."

"Agreed!"

They cut their dogs, buns and all, with the good silverware and mimicked stuffy aristocrats enjoying a gourmet meal. Pinkies out, dabbing the corners of their mouths, they played at the charade until the food was gone.

"We're the most ridiculous people ever!" he laughed.

"Agreed," she answered, and then burped out a toxic bubble.

"Oh, no! You've got the burps! Now that's not proper!" he feigned a British accent.

"Forgive me sir," another burp. "Now I'm afraid I can't stop it!"

She laughed, and the more she laughed, the more she burped. He was howling at her distress before he realized she was in real trouble.

"Oh damn, honey! Take a breath. Do you need a Rolaid?"

She shook her head as her laughter died down and her burps converted to hiccoughs.

"Great–HIC–that's–HIC–all I–HIC–need!"

"I'll get the dishes. You go get some Alka-Seltzer."

She struggled up the stairs while he returned to the kitchen to clean up. When he met her in their room, her bubbles had subsided, and she was bathed and comfortable in bed. He took a quick shower and joined her.

"I didn't mean to get so gross there, Brady."

"You've never been able to handle the bubbles, honey. It's ok."

"Why doesn't beer do that to you?"

"I don't think it was the beer as much as the combination of the beer and the cold hotdogs and the stress of everything lately."

"Can stress make you burp?"

"It can mess with your digestive system."

"I don't want to talk about stressors tonight." She snuggled close to her partner. "I want to pretend that we're six months down the road, living in a little beach house on the coast of Delaware, half-way through a viable pregnancy, with money in the bank, and the sounds of the ocean coming in the windows at night."

"You got everything in there, didn't you?"

"Why not? I said I'm pretending. You can put anything in a pretend."

"Can we pretend we're making passionate love to each other in this house by the sea?"

He kissed her hand.

"We could actually do the love-making part now," she teased. "We'd just have to pretend the beach part."

"Yeah?"

"Yeah."

The banter stopped, and their breath changed. Kissing and touching, the heat between them rose as he slid his hands under her nightgown and slipped it over her head. He scooped her up and slid under her, his hands reading every inch of her back, butt, and thighs. He gently pulled her legs apart until she straddled his waist. She could feel him swelling underneath her. Anchoring her toes under his hips, she began to grind. She raised up, her palms on his chest, and tugged at his tee shirt until he was free of it. Then she dipped her mouth to his and feverishly kissed him while his hands scrambled to wrangle his boxers off, past his knees. She rose again and planted him inside her, and he sat up to latch onto her breasts. While she held his thick brown hair in her fists, he playfully bit and sucked at her nipples. He was thick and throbbing, and she was sweet and hot and wet. They sweat and growled and cooed until he worked her up to that frenzied brink where she could drop off. She groaned, quivering, and caught her breath. He waited just a moment for her heart rate to settle, then flipped her onto her back and bent her at the waist to rest her ankles on his shoulders. She squealed, and he leaned into her with every thrust stronger and harder than the last, until he gave in to his own sweet, painful rescue.

They lay still as the sweat evaporated from their skin and their pulses returned to normal.

"Sorry, that was so quick. You got me really hot, really fast, honey."

"I'm not complaining, Brady."

He fished his arm under her hair and around her neck and pulled her close to his side. She laid her arm across his ribs, and he held it in place. He stroked her long hair to its ends, smelling her head in big deep breaths; trying to keep it locked away in his senses for the duration of their looming separation.

"How am I going to sleep without you in my bed, Brady Garlow?" she asked, tasting the salt of an inevitable tear.

"You'll be fine, Melinda. How am I going to sleep with Charlie and Roger?"

"I could easily sleep with your friends," she said emphatically.

He pulled her head away to look her in the eye. "You -. You could what?"

"I could see myself falling peacefully to sleep with both Charlie Riffle and/or Roger Johnson."

"Oh, falling asleep."

"Well... yeah. What did you think?" she played.

"I thought you meant *sleeping* with you know as in, sexing to sleep."

"Oh, yes, well. I guess that too, come to think of it," she teased. "I guess, you know, whatever it takes to get a good night's sleep."

"You trollop!" He squeezed and tickled at her waist, and she giggled and squirmed and then pushed back.

"Wait! Stop! I don't want to get the hiccoughs again, Brady. Quit!"

They settled back into each other.

"Aww. You're so funny." He breathed out a heavy sigh, then dozed away to sleep.

She stayed awake a little longer to keep his heartbeat in her ear. This was the moment she started missing him. She was aware of it and helpless in the knowing of it, she too gave up the day.

A horn sounded out front early Sunday morning and the two stirred just a little. Then a hard rap at the door made them both bolt from the bed!

"Holy Moses and the tablets!" Brady croaked, his voice still full of sleep.

"How could you not set your alarm, Brady? You knew they'd be here first thing!"

Melinda rushed to dress, and her husband hung his head out the window to signal his friends he was coming. He threw his bathroom bag together, tossed it into his packed duffle bag, and ran down the stairs, crashing into the trim and leaving it in splinters, ringing his bell. He dropped straight down on the step below and sat for a second.

Melinda grabbed her mouth and gasped, "Oh! Brady, are you ok?"

He shook his head like a cartoon and took to his feet again, dumping the bag at the bottom of the stairs. She shook her head and stepped around the debris to open the front door. Roger Johnson stood there laughing.

"We heard him hit clear out here," yelled Charlie Riffle from behind the idling truck at the curb.

Melinda waved to Charlie and welcomed Roger into the foyer, "Good morning. He didn't set the alarm." She walked into the kitchen to start the coffee and Johnson followed her in to survey the damage.

"Damn, Brady! You destroyed it," Johnson declared.

Brady had darted through the breezeway to the garage and was throwing the few boxes he'd packed into the bed of Riffle's truck. He came back in and raced past his friend and his wife in the kitchen to retrieve his bag and ran that out, too. Then he stood for a moment, looking at the house, and settled himself.

"It's all good, Brady," Charlie assured him. "Take a minute and tell her goodbye."

Brady smiled at his friend and went back in. Just inside, Johnson was coming toward the door waving a paper bag, Melinda trailing him with a thermos of hot coffee.

"Ham and cheese and Hot Fries for the road. You got the best one, Garlow. My wife sent me off with a half-hearted kiss and some ice-cold guilt!"

"I know it, man," Brady beamed as his friend passed by and headed for the truck.

He grabbed her in the middle, pulled her up into his arms, and stared at her face. He took in every lash, every fleck of color in her eyes, and she scanned his wiry brows and cowlick. She traced her finger over his lips, then pressed her mouth to them.

"I love you, husband," she said. He grinned. "It's really just that simple."

"Yep," he answered, "And I love you, wife." They kissed again, then he let her go, and they stood separated a foot or two, as if to try it out. They smiled and shrugged.

"I'll call you from the road."

"Just call me when you get there. Try to have some fun today. It's a road trip with your dumb friends. Enjoy it."

"You are the best one, Melinda!" he said, and darted out the door like a boy, toward his new adventure.

She walked to the open door and waved them out of sight. Melinda never felt closer to another human, but she was almost relieved to send Brady off for the coast. She made up her mind years ago that she was truly alone and that was hard to manage with a constant companion. For the first time in her life, she was actually alone... and strangely comforted by it.

‡

"The usual excuses, then Reynolds?" Miss M provoked, impatiently tapping her foot and looking at her watch.

"Sorry, Miss M, my old lady didn't wake me on time again."

Taking the keys she dangled in front of him, he raced past her to the garage beyond the side door where she'd been waiting only minutes. He threw open the doors and started the new white Cadillac. As always, he waited a moment to let the oil cycle, then slowly and carefully backed it out under the carport. Parking, he jumped to her side, took her by the elbow, and guided her down from the stoop and into the idling car.

"You are nearly 60 years old, you dimwit. Why on God's green earth would anyone have to wake a sixty-year-old man to get ready for work? You aren't working sixteen hour shifts at the glass factory. You just have to get an old woman where she's going on time. That's all you do. Don't you want to remain employed?"

"Yes ma'am. But Ike said since we were such close friends in school and all, that I'd always have a job working for the academy."

"Ike is an idiot for promising something to someone so hell bent on pissing off the owner of the academy."

"I thought he was the owner, ma'am."

"I am the owner of that school, Reynolds! As long as there is breath in my lungs, I run that school! And don't you forget that!" Mrs. Maxwell sat down hard in the back seat of the Cadillac and jerked her arm away from the withering Reynolds. "I swear to God! If this is the caliber of employee my son hires to drive me to work every day, I'd be better off wandering the streets of Cleveland alone and unarmed!"

"Yes ma'am," Reynolds agreed and wondered if that meant she was armed.

The rebuking continued through the handful of traffic lights connecting her stately home to the shoddier portion of town, ending at Merrifield Road. Urban blight had taken its toll on what once were picturesque neighborhoods and rows of small businesses. Now they passed more lawns overgrown than finely manicured, and barred windows where eye-catching displays and hanging flowers once welcomed customers to shop for everything under the sun. Mrs. Maxwell watched mournfully as they passed by the vacant barbershop across the street from the school. The fading red and white pole still stood just above the tattered canvas awning. A remnant of better days, the hollow storefront faced the avenue like the entrance to a forgotten tomb.

Reynolds pulled up to the front doors and parked to deliver his charge. He opened her door and offered his hand to help her navigate the curb. She batted him away with a growl and managed on her own.

"Go around to the big lot behind City Hall and find a spot," she instructed. "I don't trust it in the lot behind the school."

"But those spots are reserved for City Council, Miss M," Reynolds whined.

"Not a one of those crooked fools comes in on Fridays, Reynolds. Anyone who reads the papers knows that."

She left the scolded man to his task and entered the building. She made her way to the door on the side of the sentry booth where Jeannie sat reading a magazine. The knob barely turned before Mrs. Maxwell was part and parcel inside the tiny space, startling its lone occupant into a physical fit.

"Oh!" Jeannie squeaked. "Miss M! I didn't… um… I thought…"

"You had it right the first time, Jeannie. You didn't think." She watched as the woman scurried to gather herself and exit the room, then she slammed the door after her. "Run upstairs and tell them I'm here."

"Yes, Miss M."

Jeannie disappeared down the hall and around the corner to the elevators. Passing the next-to-the-last candidate for the new position, she charged into the fray and delivered her message.

"Miss M is here," she panted. "She's at her desk. She wanted me to let you know."

"Alright, Jeannie," Ike said, waving the frantic woman to sit. "So, one more applicant, then we can call mother and the others in? How about first thing after lunch?"

The group readily agreed since 'first thing after lunch' sometimes meant the school would spring for lunch. Once in a while, if they were patient and kept their heads down, and Deidre said they needed another receipt for a work expense, Ike would reward them with a spread from the Polish deli down the street or the Greek place around the corner. Fresh-baked breads and savory sausage sandwiches with homemade potato and macaroni salad to die for, or lamb gyros and salads loaded with black olives and feta. The kind of food that made your mouth water just smelling the take-out bags. Jeannie gathered all the applications and resumes and started the phone calls to the rest of the group.

By noon, the last applicant was gone, and the food had arrived just ahead of the board members. Sam, Manny, and Ike, of course, were present and accounted for, as well as Deidre, Jeannie, and Kitt. Then, one by one, the representatives of the Maxwell family appeared, fixed a plate, and took their place at the table.

Farmer was first, as usual. Isaak senior's only living sibling, Meyer 'Farmer' Maxwell, was dubbed so because he reportedly managed acres and acres of rye fields owned by the family just outside the city in the late 1920s. Rye that was rumored to have been sold across the lake to the Canadians to make whiskey during prohibition. At ninety-eight, Farmer now more resembled an apple head doll than a bootlegger. He was the oldest board member, but always the first one to come when they called. He was sweet and happy, knowing he'd been blessed with a much easier life than he could have had, were it not for his big brother.

Next to show, were Marta and Gus, Mrs. Maxwell's twins born in different years. As the story went, Marta was born at 11:51pm on December 31st, 1944, and not until fourteen minutes later did Gus arrive at 12:05am January 1st, 1945. The two made *The Sun Press* and were touted as a local anomaly in every New Year's Day issue since then. Marta graduated beauty school in her twenties and married a chauvinistic cop who wouldn't let her work in a salon. Her father bankrolled a renovation that converted her basement into a one chair setup and the only clients her husband allowed her to accept were other officers' wives. They had one son, Cliff, twenty-five, still living at home, and like his father, showed Marta little respect. Marta did her mother's hair once a week and charged her full price. Her mother never tipped. Gus married his high school sweetheart right after graduation, believing her to be stricken with the hereditary nervous condition that killed her mother young, only to find out that she had been misdiagnosed and instead suffered from debilitating hypochondria. He drove cab for Maxwell's Taxi service, another family financed business, and spent most nights sleeping around with everyone but his wife.

Finally arriving just ahead of her mother, Hildegarde entered the room. Hildy was a beauty in her day. Long legs, dark hair, and smiling blue eyes, she had been the prettiest of Mr. and Mrs. Maxwells' children. Her story included an engagement to and secret pregnancy by a young man who didn't return from Vietnam. Depending on which version you subscribed to, she either lost the baby or got an illegal abortion. The details, fuzzy even to her nearly forty years later, were cause for her daily drinking and the transformation of her fairness to the frazzled mess she had become. Hildy failed for years to hold a job and was listed on the payroll for the school as executive support staff. At meetings of the executive board, she made a valiant attempt to wait until after she exercised her duties before imbibing. She limited herself to an Irish coffee this morning. Just enough to keep her from shaking in front of her mother.

Just after Hildy was gently greeted by her Uncle Farmer and seated at the table with the plate of food she would leave undisturbed for the entirety of the proceedings, Mrs. Maxwell appeared in the doorway to the conference room.

"Is this everyone?"

"Yes, mother," Sam answered, pulling out her chair. "Can I get you something?"

"I'll eat after. Where are the applications?"

She sat at the near end of the long table while the others milled around the room, fixing their plates and taking their places. Manny placed the folder with the resumes on the table in front of her and she patted his hand. He glanced around the room to register her affection with his siblings.

They acted like they didn't see.

Jeannie sat on her right swallowing bites and readying her pen and pad to take notes once things began. Deidre and Kitt filed in on the other side of the old woman, leaving the rest of the table to the family. This was what was expected of the employees at the Cleveland Business Academy. Mrs. Maxwell hated having her children flanking her in these meetings competing for her favor and attention. She established long ago that business is business and if they were going to be a part of their father's business, there'd be none of that. She planted the women who actually taught closest to her to keep her efforts focused on the school and its operations and away from the distractions of her dysfunctional family. Once the entire group was seated, Ike began the meeting.

"To start this official meeting of the executive board of trustees for the Cleveland Business Academy, I'll ask Jeannie to record all in attendance and ask if there is any old business from the last meeting."

"No old business, sir," she answered, scribbling down everyone's name and position in her notes.

Ike continued, "Then on to the first item on today's agenda, the new hire for Beginning Accounting and Business Math. As you all know, these beginning classes can make or break a student's commitment to the program, so whomever we choose needs to know what they're doing and be ready to recruit and retain students."

"If they don't get the initial intro to basic accounting, they're lost by the time I get them in the advanced class," Deidre chimed in. "I don't want a repeat of what happened with the City Manager's grandson."

"No one does, Deidre," stated Ike. "Mother, there's one in particular we all thought would be a good fit."

Manny pointed toward the file, "It should be on top, Mother. Garlow."

"Melinda Garlow," she read from the resume. "What's so special about this one?"

"She is the great niece of Helen Harper," Ike answered.

"So?" she frowned. "Look around this room, son. What in God's name does being related to someone exceptional mean about an individual?"

"She was enrolled here herself, Miss M," offered Jeannie. "I looked up her transcripts. She got great marks." She handed a couple of loose pages to her boss.

"This was over a decade ago. What has she done since then?"

"That's exactly what I asked her," said Deidre.

"Part-time at the Cuyahoga County Public Library," added Sam. "The one in the mall."

"I still don't know why in hell they put a branch of the public library system in a god-forsaken shopping center!" Mrs. Maxwell was passionate about the sanctity of the public library systems.

"I said the same thing this morning, Miss M," Kitt agreed. "You want to know why? I'll tell you why…"

A collective groan rose from those who had endured her rant earlier in the day.

"Kitt, please, it really doesn't have any bearing on the task at hand, now does it?" Ike attempted to keep the group focused on their immediate chore. "Mother, we feel like she's the most qualified, and she comes from excellent stock. So, I think we should take a vote."

Farmer shook his head and smiled.

"What is it, Uncle Farmer?" Marta asked.

"I remember the day when your father would ruminate on his choices for a week or more before he'd even talk about it out loud. He'd call everyone in town to check out a new teacher for his school. Now we decide after meeting these people one time for ten minutes and 'poof' they're in!"

"The children will tell you that was a long time ago, Farmer. Nothing is the same as when my husband ran this school."

"Now Mother, don't say that," Marta whined.

Hildy's liquid breakfast was wearing off, and she piped up, "It doesn't matter anymore because people are disposable nowadays. If you're bad at your job or you flunk out of business school, they throw you away and get someone new to take your place." She snapped her fingers. "Just like that, and you were never here."

Everyone who knew, knew she wasn't just talking about teachers at the academy, but there was enough truth in what she said to pertain to the moment as well as her past.

"Yes. Well, with all due respect to these opinions, we simply don't have time to search the world over for the most devoted instructors," said Sam, attempting to bring logic to the conversation. "We are damn lucky to have Kitt, Deidre, and Jeannie. Manny and I couldn't do it without you ladies."

"Yes, Sam," Ike agreed. "We know that everyone here is doing their best. So, let's give this Garlow girl a chance to add to our ranks and see if she has the same stuff that her aunt did."

"Cuyahoga County Library in the mall…" Mrs. Maxwell lamented.

"I know." Kitt couldn't resist, and Jeannie shot her a look. The group let their matriarch continue to maul it over.

"Helen Harper was just about the finest we had at this school. The paper said she worked over fifty years at Higbee's. That's a career that she had because of what she learned under this roof."

Quiet hums of agreement worked their way around the table. Just another moment of silence to seal the deal and…

"Alright."

A collective sigh of relief blew out of everyone at once and they moved on to the next agenda item. Jeannie would make the call after the meeting concluded.

⸎

Her first day at the academy, Melinda chose a pair of navy dress pants and a silky printed shell to wear under her black blazer. She packed an apple and some trail mix in a brown paper bag and filled her thermos with black coffee. She found an empty spot in the lot behind the school and entered the building from the rear. Where the halls intersected at the elevator, she ran into Miss M coming from the front of the school.

"Good morning, Mrs. Maxwell," Melinda said as she summoned the elevator.

The aging women scowled at her, then down at the floor where she tapped her cane impatiently.

"Oh. I'm Melinda Garlow. I'm starting here today. I'm the new instructor."

Melinda jostled her lunch, purse, and the old attaché she kept from her Aunt Helen's things to shake Miss M's hand.

She slowly raised her head to look the girl in the eye.

"You–are Helen Harper's great niece?"

"Yes, ma'am." The elevator arrived, and Melinda retrieved her stranded hand and boarded after her boss.

"I remember your aunt."

"Yes ma'am. She was quite the virtuoso, I'm told."

"Helen Harper was all business!"

"You don't have to tell me that," Melinda agreed out the side of her mouth to humanize the moment. The old woman glared at her insolence. "I–I mean, she raised me and I never remember her being anything but all business."

"Mm-hm." Miss M turned away and waited for the doors to open. Melinda breathed in the stilted air between them, mentally flogging herself for her inaugural gaffe.

The doors released them onto the sixth floor and the elder led the blushing girl down to the conference room where her interview had taken place. The room was a buzzing hive again this morning, with the entire staff and even some of the board members of the academy in attendance. A buffet of breakfast food was assembled on a credenza that lined the far wall of the room. An urn of coffee, a giant foil pan of an egg casserole, bagels, biscuits, and fruit lined up after paper plates and plastic cutlery. The action in the place stopped when Miss M entered and everyone greeted her. She waved them on and took her place at the head of the table. Jeannie ran to the doorway to welcome the newcomer.

"Morning, Melinda," she chirped.

"Good morning, Jeannie. Where should I sit?"

"You can put your things next to me." Jeannie walked her to a seat on the other side of the table and pulled the chair free. "Here. Put your stuff down and fix a plate. Monday staff meetings are breakfast meetings!"

Melinda grinned at her enthusiasm and mouthed an exaggerated 'WOW!' She moved around the room, watching her new co-workers maneuver in and out of the line, observing what and how much they served themselves and to which seats they were assigned. Jeannie joined her at the buffet to walk her through, and she noticed no one was offering Miss M anything.

"Should I let Mrs. Maxwell go ahead?" she asked.

Jeannie shook her head and answered in whispered tones, "No. You go on."

"I'll eat after. Hurry it up, girls." Miss M commanded in an effort to establish her excellent hearing, as well as her authority.

Jeannie scurried away from the food and Melinda rushed to fix her plate and fill a cup with coffee. She slid into her seat and smiled around the table at the faces of the others. Everyone was well into their own routine. Uncle Farmer and Gus stayed near the food and ate standing up. Reynold's, Miss M's driver, joined them hurriedly, then the three men exited together, without a word. Sam was shoveling eggs in like a contestant at the fair. Kitt was debating with Manny about the quality of crème cheese and the difference between the toasted and untoasted bagel experience. Ike was looking at some report and poking at bits of pineapple with his fork.

Deidre was staring directly at Melinda's face, her head hanging in the steam of her coffee cup.

Melinda smiled as she swallowed a bit of egg and asked, "You don't go for breakfast, Deidre?"

"I have breakfast every morning, miss. Coffee and pills."

Melinda nodded and took in the woman's eyes with their dark purple circles and heavy lids.

Sam finished his race and began the meeting while the others continued eating.

"So, first things first this morning, we'd like to welcome our new instructor," he held his hand out to Melinda and then solicited a round of applause from the others. A quiet clap ensued.

"Thank you - ," she began.

"That's fine. What's next, Ike?" Miss M cut in and rolled right on past.

"We got the report back from the federal student loan people and so far, we're averaging a little higher at completion and post-graduate employment rates than the other tech schools in Ohio but not so great when we're up against the rest of the country. Our seniors are in their final days. Let's get those applications filled out and start placing these people."

"Ike's right. Without that federal student loan money, most people can't even consider applying here. Manny and Sam, get the lead out. You know what to do." Miss M returned her attention to her eldest son while a collective hangdog look bent his brothers at the neck. "What else?"

"You all have your budgets for supplies and what not for the incoming class. Please keep every receipt and turn them all in to Deidre A.S.A.P."

Deidre nodded. "Same rules as last term people. If they're two weeks past the next pay period, you will not be reimbursed."

"What supplies?" Melinda asked with a raised hand.

"Jeannie will get you a list of all the things you'll need," Sam answered. "Jeannie, she'll need all the stuff Madelyn used. Just let her in those drawers in the file room, and she can figure it out."

Jeannie winked in her direction. Melinda nodded back, even though her query was only semi-satisfied.

The meeting took up an hour all together, full of unfamiliar things to which Melinda only paid partial attention. If she couldn't 'figure it out' as Sam put it, she would ask someone about it. Once they concluded, everyone rose and started for their respective classrooms. Kitt leaned over the table in Melinda's direction.

"Your room is right across from mine," she gestured with a hitchhiker's thumb toward the door.

Melinda smiled and gathered her things to follow. "Do we cover the food?"

Kitt shook her head and turned down the hall, bypassing the elevator, toward the fire exit. Melinda caught up just before the closing metal door and trailed her down the stairs.

"Don't trust that elevator," Kitt began. "Hope you don't mind taking the stairs."

"No. Not at all."

"You and I are on the fourth floor. No numbers painted on the doors out here. You just have to keep count of how many landings."

The women descended the stairs, echoing through the space as their heels clicked on every step.

"Where is that file room I'm supposed to get to, Kitt?"

"Jeannie will come after you once she gets Miss M settled downstairs. Meanwhile, you can get a look at your classroom."

She arrived at the landing on the fourth floor and put her shoulder into the fire door. She held it open with her butt while Melinda caught up and went through. The hall was dark. Kitt switched on the overhead lights and the pale-yellow walls woke up. Heavy dark stained wainscotting met the dingy floor, only separating at the elevator, the doors to their classrooms and two others at the end of the hall.

"Bathrooms marked at the end there. My class is on the left and you're on the right."

Melinda stood facing her door and took a pause.

How weird to be back here. How weird to be teaching here. This was really happening. She grinned at her husband's promise that it was all just temporary.

"Go on," urged Kitt. "Get in there."

She whipped around to see Kitt disappear into her classroom. She turned the knob to her own and stepped inside. The room was big and dark. She flipped the lights on to discover three large windows with shades drawn. She crossed to the nearest one and raised the shade to find that they all faced the neighboring building. Nothing but bricks and the railing to a rickety fire escape covered in bird poop, readily in view. She strained to look down the gap in the buildings to the open space beyond. She could see the sun was shining in the alley behind the school, but little of its light was reaching her end of things.

Kitt walked in. "Yeah, there's no good light, but it's quieter than the front of the building."

"That's probably good, huh?"

"What do you think so far, Melinda?"

"It'll do. I can make this work."

"No. Not the room," Kitt corrected. "I mean, what do you think about the whole deal?"

"Oh! I'm glad to be here... I guess."

"You guess?"

"Everyone seems really nice. I'm glad to be coming to work here."

"I was too when I was new." Kitt looked around the empty classroom and smiled mysteriously. "Let me know if you need anything. I'm right across the hall."

Melinda smiled back and watched as she left and closed the door behind her.

She repeated her mantra aloud, "It's only temporary." Then took off her blazer and got to it.

Mid-morning Jeannie tapped on her door and entered to find her shoving chairs around the room.

"Oh my, Melinda! You're just jumping right in."

"Well," she answered, panting a little, "I thought I'd make it my own. You know, shake it up a little."

"You sure did. Madelyn never moved the furniture around."

"I wanted my desk in the far corner so I could get a glimpse of sunlight once in a while."

"Right… no view. But it's quieter than the front of the building."

"So I've heard."

There was an awkward pause while Melinda donned her blazer, then Jeannie snapped to it.

"If you're ready, we can go to the file room and get your materials."

"Let's do it!"

The women exited and took the elevator to the mezzanine overlooking the typing pool on the third floor.

"I remember being down in that pit," Melinda said as they walked past Sam at his desk and through to a back room with 'Employees Only' painted on the door.

"It drives me crazy to watch Sam's class for him," Jeannie confessed. "It's so loud!"

Safely behind the closed door, they could hear themselves again.

"Ugh! I don't know how he does it," Jeannie kept on. "He sits up above that racket at his desk, like he doesn't even hear it!"

"My guess is that you'd get used to it."

"It's worse when they're practicing for a competition. When he's trying to get them to better their times, it's like a factory down there." Jeannie lead Melinda to the back of a maze of shelves and cabinets and announced, "Here we are." She patted the tops of two chest-high metal filing cabinets. "These are Beginning Accounting and Business Math."

"Okey-doke."

Opening the top-drawer Jeannie began explaining, "The drawers are the latest teachers' files in front and older ones on back. Get it?"

"Sure."

"There are little tabs with their names on them."

Peering in Melinda noticed Madelyn's file was rather thin until she flipped past hers to the few after it, when she discovered it was about average. "How long was Madelyn here, Jeannie?"

"I think she made it a year."

Reading the tabs, Melinda inquired further, "And Melissa? And Janet C.? And Suzanne?"

"I remember Melissa was nine months because she got pregnant the day after she started here and then didn't come back after the baby… and… Janet C. was leaving when I got here two-ish years ago, so I don't know about anyone before that."

She was feeling relieved that she hadn't disclosed her plan for such brief employment as she made the observation to her co-worker, "A bit of attrition in Beginning Accounting and Business Math, huh?"

"Not just those. I don't think anyone except the family has been here longer than a few years."

"Not even Deidre?"

"Well, yes," Jeannie corrected herself. "Except for Deidre."

"What's her deal… Deidre's?" Melinda dared.

Jeannie shrugged. "I honestly don't know. Friend of the family, maybe." She pondered the question for just another beat, then dismissed it. "Oh well. Have fun. Copier is around the corner from Sam's desk in that open area. He should be around if you have any problems. When he's not teaching, he runs Ditto's Copies and Office Machines on the corner of Lee and Merrifield. He is kind of the resident expert."

"Good to know."

The young woman spun on her heel and left Melinda alone in the stuffy space. She looked around the room and spied a wheeled cart with an overhead projector on top that had obviously seen better days. Removing its dusty burden, she wheeled the vehicle over to her post. She spent the next hours thumbing through the material in the cabinets. She managed to extract workbooks, syllabi, and a teaching guide for both the math and accounting textbooks. When she thought she'd gathered enough to get the ball rolling, she closed the cabinets and pushed the heavy cart toward the door.

Sam was still seated at his desk when she backed out of the room and he jumped to hold the door for her.

"Thank you, sir," she said.

"You're welcome, Melinda. You can call me Sam."

"Thank you, Sam," she repeated.

"That's quite a haul there. Do you think you have enough for the first day?"

"I know you're joking, but I want to work ahead as much as I can before the first day."

He nodded, slightly impressed. "I see."

"What if I get a class that just blows past what I'm prepared for in the first week?"

He answered flatly, "You won't."

They smiled at each other, both thinking they probably knew something the other didn't. Being careful not to use up all her optimism on her first day, she marched on past him.

"Well, as they say, 'luck favors the prepared'."

"Then I wish you good luck!"

The last syllables of his wish would be drowned out by the clatter of the typing class, resuming their exercises as she headed back to the quiet of the elevator.

The rest of her first day at the academy would be spent planning and preparing. At its end, she followed most of the staff out the back entrance of the building toward her car in the parking lot behind it. She spied a long, white car idling behind hers, blocking her in.

Kitt passed it a pace ahead and turned back to inform her, "That's Reynolds. Don't even ask him to move before you-know-who comes out."

Melinda registered Kitt's hitchhiker thumb again and looked back to the building where Sam and Manny were flanking their mother on either side, slowly approaching the car. Watching for another moment until Mrs. Maxwell scowled in her direction, she made it quick to the safety of her front seat. She didn't even start her rusting Ford Probe before the new Caddy pulled away. She mocked the entire scene to the vacant lot as she pulled out.

"Who's the queen? She's the queen. She's the queen and still the queen!"

Melinda remembered the all-powerful presence of the woman when she attended the academy a dozen years ago. She smirked at the realization that the old girl still scared the shit out of everybody.

Once she got herself home and entered the empty house, Melinda stood for a moment, absorbing the solitude, not yet able to make up her mind if she hated it.

She made a light dinner and spread her books out on the kitchen table to dig into her lesson plans and by the time she finished what she'd wanted of both, night was fixed around her. Glancing at the clock, she wondered why she hadn't heard from Brady yet; sure he would call on her first day if he could. She let a work accident scenario scare her for a split second, shrugged it off and opted for his volunteering for overtime right off the bat. After tidying the table, she climbed the stairs. She paused for a moment under the damaged wooden trim Brady had bashed into in his mad dash to leave yesterday morning.

"Was that really just yesterday?" she asked herself aloud, shook the doubt from her tired head, and put herself to bed.

She drifted off to sleep, tallying time; yesterday Brady was in her bed, two weeks ago Aunt Helen was still alive, and twenty-nine years ago her mom and dad kissed her goodbye for the last time.

She needed to fix the trim over the stairs.

Brady got the overtime right from the start and apologized profusely by the end of their first week apart for not calling more often. They started late Friday night and talked into the early hours of the weekend. He told her about the factory, and the break-neck pace, and the overtime money, and Melinda entertained him with her character studies of all the staff and board members at the school.

"I remember when the old man died. I was in kindergarten and the family was all over the news," he said.

"When was that, sixty-nine?" she asked. "I was only two."

"Yep. It was a big deal. That's when all the business about the Merrifield Road Gang came out. It's all my dad could talk about that year."

"Yeah. I still don't know if I believe all that. How could they have stayed in business all this time if they were laundering money for the mob?"

"You don't believe it because you don't think like that, Melinda. That kind of anti-social behavior isn't even on your radar."

"You sound like you're accusing me of something."

"Just innocence and ignorance of the criminal underbelly of your hometown."

"Criminal underbelly! Listen to you!" she giggled. "Like you were some juvenile delinquent back then. What did you say you were, five?"

"When this happened, yes. But I'm just saying I was more aware of those kinds of people growing up."

"Ooh! I'm starting to think I don't really know my husband at all!"

"Ha-ha. Whatever," he conceded. "My dad was fascinated by that kind of thing. He read every book in the library on Al Capone and the crime families of the twenties and thirties. He memorized all the one-liners from any movie with Bogart, Cagney, or Edward G. Robinson in it."

"So, he was a mafiaphile?"

Brady laughed, "I guess you could call him that. The last movie we went to see together was The Untouchables and he couldn't stop talking about DeNiro's Capone. He loved it!"

"I loved that one!"

They each smiled into the phone and allowed an awkward pause to interrupt their conversation.

After a moment, Brady confessed, "I really miss you, honey."

Melinda clutched the phone a little tighter. "I know! It's only been a week. How are we going to make it all the way to the end of the year without seeing each other?"

"We won't have to make it all the way through the renovation. We will come home for a day or two in a couple of weeks. Roger's wife is insisting on it!"

"That's some consolation."

"I'd ask you to come out when you get a break, but I'd hate for you to drive that old Probe all the way here by yourself."

"I don't know if she would make it all the way to New Jersey!"

"Delaware, damn it!" he playfully scolded.

She laughed at getting a rise out of her husband. "I know. I know."

She yawned.

"Oh, you must be exhausted," he said. "Damn, Melinda, it's three o'clock in the morning!"

"I am a little tired. But I don't want you to go."

"I'm going to have to, honey. I asked for afternoon tomorrow, and I have to get some sleep."

"I know. I get it. When can you call me again?"

"I'm working doubles again next week, so it'll have to wait until the weekend. You'll have had your students for a whole week by then."

"I'm sure I'll have lots to tell you," she said without a trace of enthusiasm.

He hated disappointing his wife and apologized again, "I'm sorry, Melinda."

"Me too. But, I understand. I love you, husband."

"It's just that simple, huh?"

"You know it."

"I love you too, wife. G'night."

"Night, Brady."

That first weekend alone in the house was so weird. Melinda wandered around, washed the few dishes and clothes she dirtied, took a quick trip to the store for groceries, then ran out of things to do. She flipped through the TV stations looking for a movie to pass some time but found nothing to hold her interest. She walked around the neighborhood and washed the car. It wasn't just boredom or loneliness; she just really had nothing to do without Aunt Helen or Brady to take care of. She was only now realizing how much of her energy she spent caring for the other people in her life. What would she do with all this spare time? Volunteer? Take up a hobby? Maybe she'd drive by Clara's after work Monday and ask her.

❦

"Good morning everyone," Melinda opened. "I'm Melinda Garlow and I will teach you both Business Math, this term and Beginning Accounting, next." She moved out in front of her desk and handed the nearest student a stack of cards. "I'm passing out a little card with some questions about who you are and where you've come from to get here. I believe that to teach anything, you need to know your audience. So, while you're filling those out, and please, don't divulge anything you're not comfortable sharing, I'll let you know a little about me."

She moved along the aisles she created when she rearranged her room and began introducing herself.

"I'm a Cleveland native. I'm married. No kids… yet. I graduated from the two-year program here at the academy twelve years ago and then went to work part-time at the Richmond Town Square Branch of the Cuyahoga County Public Library. My great-aunt who raised me, also attended here. You might see her trophies in the case downstairs, in the main entrance. She won a ton of typing contests when she was a student and even took home the Isaac Lowell Maxwell Award for Excellence in Communication."

A hand raised.

"Yes, sir."

"You won this award?" the student asked, obviously not paying close enough attention.

"No." She was back up in front of the class again. "My great-aunt."

"And then you worked at the mall?"

"At the Cuyahoga County Public Library." He shrugged, and she conceded, "Yes. At the mall."

He narrowed his eyes and nodded like he caught her in a lie. First question of her teaching career and she's called out by some little-dick, wise guy who probably couldn't get into the university and has an uncanny capacity for pinpointing your insecurities and exposing them to everyone around you. 'It's a good thing this is temporary,' she thought.

"Yes. So, take a minute to thoughtfully fill out your cards and return them to me at the end of class."

She gestured to two students near the windows and asked, "Would you two mind handing out those textbooks stacked beside you?"

They obliged, and the class began examining the material.

"We are going to dive right into the beginning because there are some rudimentary practices that are important groundwork for the more complicated lessons we'll tackle later on in the term. But, after those few beginning chapters, we will skip around the text a little because I think some sections are easier to follow if they're paired with other lessons. You will need to bring this book to class every day. Your tuition covers one copy. If you lose or destroy your book, you must purchase its replacement at your own expense. You will also need a college-rule, spiral notebook and PENCILS! I'm sure that some of you are confident enough in your math skills to use ink pens but everyone makes mistakes, so to keep your assignments free from great scribbles of ink, blacking out your errors, we will only use pencil."

The non-verbals she was getting set her mind to ease. Everyone in the room was a little nervous and a little excited, including her. She read from the teacher's companion guide to the text to introduce the concepts they'd be tackling in the beginning chapters and asked a few general questions of the group, then ended the hour with a page of assigned problems to be reviewed in the morning.

As class concluded, the students exited, depositing their personal information cards in a sloppy stack on her desk. She waited until they cleared the room, neatly rotated the cards by their corners until she had a proper pile, then read.

She would repeat her debut performance once more before lunch and twice again after. The total freshman student body numbered eighty. After examining the cards from all the classes, she determined that nearly half of the students came in at eighteen, the minimum age requirement for adult education programs. She had twenty-nine twenty-two-year-olds. Those she guessed would have attempted college and couldn't get to the finish line for whatever reason. And she had twelve students in the forty-and-over group. The cards from these people said things like 'I've spent my whole life taking care of my family's finances and decided to learn how to do it and get paid.' and 'I was always good with numbers.' and the one that hit closest to home, 'My husband lost his job at the Ford plant and I need to get one that pays enough to keep my house.'

Melinda liked the idea of such a diverse group. Wrapping the cards in a rubber band, she stowed them in a bottom drawer of her desk. Keeping them close would ensure she could refer to them when interacting with her classes. Some of her favorite teachers took the time and effort to get to know her. She didn't care how temporary it was; she was going to do her best.

She found her way through town to the purple door again to visit with her psychic. Clara was sitting in her reception room with her watering can swinging between her knees when she heard Melinda trotting up the stairs. She stowed the can and dashed into the inner room. She reappeared just as Melinda closed the door to the stairway.

"My friend! Come. Come in. I've been expecting you."

Melinda followed Clara into the dark, panting from her ascent, and eager to get started. Clara repeated her familiar rituals while Melinda took a seat and settled her breath as she lit the candle in the center of the table and took Clara's hands before she had a chance to ask.

"Oh, my! We're really getting into it, huh, Melinda?" She set herself with a deep inhale, a slow exhale, and then closed her eyes. "We are open, spirits. We are here in heart and mind. What wisdom do you have for this one who seeks to know?"

Melinda waited patiently for the energy to change… for some shift in the air… nothing came.

"Open vessels, here to receive. Spirits, we are open to your wisdom." Clara took in another deep breath and held Melinda's hands a little tighter. "This one before you seeks to know."

Still nothing.

A defeated sigh escaped Melinda's parted lips.

"Don't be discouraged, my friend," Clara soothed. "They don't always have much to add. This could be a sign that your cares are minor at the moment. Tedium? Boredom?"

"Yes!" Melinda's eyes opened, and she started prattling on to Clara, whose eyes dilated in the candlelight. "Since Aunt Helen died and Brady left to work in Delaware, I've been bored out of my mind! I started teaching at the business school on Merrifield Road, today actually, so I'm sure I'll have more to do as my students turn things in to grade but all last week I wandered around the house with nothing to do..."

"Take a breath, Melinda! You're not tuning into the spirits if you're chittering like an auctioneer!"

"Sorry." Melinda shrunk with embarrassment. The two resumed their composure.

"So, Brady *is* off on a distant course?" Clara recapped smugly. "So that *was* revealed. And now you are wondering what you can do to pass the time while he's away. Right?"

"Yes."

"Spirits, is there any new direction Melinda could take to add to the emptiness of her days without her mate?"

Melinda frowned incredulously. She didn't exactly feel any emptier than usual. And she didn't like Brady referred to as her *mate*. It sounded like they were animals just together for a season to procreate. She chose this man to be her husband. That seemed more important than just mating.

"Melinda, you're not concentrating," Clara scolded, and released her client's hands.

"You're right. Forgive me, Clara."

"Don't you want help from your spirit guides?"

"Of course, I do, but you're right, this is just a teeny thing. They probably want me to figure it out on my own."

"Sometimes that is the message."

"That's probably it. Sorry to have wasted your time."

"Do you still want your numbers?"

"Sure, we can do that."

"Good!" Clara got the cards and her journal and began. "M-I-N-D-Y-J-O. I remembered. 4-1-5-1-1-7."

Melinda smiled.

"You know about the sign of the sun…"

Melinda nodded.

"So, even the term 'The Sun' computes to the Original Force Number 1. Powerful stuff. But people associated with this despite being talkative and appearing open can have great difficulty sharing deep emotional connections with others."

Melinda felt unmasked, and Clara read that loud and clear.

"That's you all over, Melinda. You're the iceberg in the water; a little peak up top and a whole other animal underneath. Am I right? Sound like you, my friend?"

"I don't go around telling everyone what I think and feel, if that's what you mean."

Clara sat back against the curt tone of her client. Melinda regrouped and answered again.

"I mean...yes. That sounds a little like me, Clara."

"And what do you stand to lose if you share your feelings?"

Melinda thought hard but came up empty.

"You've experienced so much loss in your life, my friend. Have you opened up to anyone about that?"

She hadn't. She couldn't.

"I just don't want to dwell on any of it. It's too painful."

"Yes. When more pain is on the line, we feel vulnerable to it. But great things can come from vulnerability. If you accept every aspect of the things you've come through, even the pain, then the universe with give you more and more."

"More pain? That's just what I'm afraid of!"

"No, sweet girl. More blessings.

Melinda nodded her head like a trained seal and thanked Clara for her insight, even though she didn't quite get the meaning of it all yet. She wrote her a check and headed for home.

Her first week of teaching, Melinda kept to herself. She saw the other instructors in the parking lot arriving in the morning and departing after school, but no one reached out to include her in any part of their day and she didn't invite herself. She got boxed in behind Miss M's driver every day; consistently enough to take it personally by Thursday. She ate in her room, brown bagging it with an apple and a sandwich from home, until Friday, when distracted because she might hear from Brady again that night, she went off and forgot her lunch on the counter. She only remembered after her first period class when she overheard a few students talking about where they were going to eat that day.

"Shit!" she muttered under her breath when the room was emptied.

She gathered some worksheets she needed copied and popped her head into Kitt's room.

"Hey, Kitt."

The woman raised her head from a task at her desk and smiled.

"Hey, Melinda. How's your first week shaping up?" She dropped her head and looked at the girl over her glasses. "You ready to quit yet?"

"Not yet, jeez!" Melinda felt comfortable enough to joke. "I'm tougher than I look."

"Good! I had my doubts about you," Kitt laughed.

"Very funny. Hey, listen, I was going to go get some copies made and thought I'd ask if you had anything that needed done."

"Thanks, but no. I'm good."

"Ok." Melinda turned to leave without asking what she'd really wanted, but then doubled back at the door and followed through. "Oh, and where's the quickest place to get lunch around here? I forgot mine today and I don't think I have time to run home."

"No! You'll never get in and out of midday traffic in time to get back to class. I'll come get you after second period and we'll just go out the back alley to Tiny's. Best hoagies in town."

"Tiny's? Ok."

Kitt led Melinda down their familiar emergency stairs to the hall that opened up to the rear exit of the building. They trekked out past the parking lot and down the dirty alley that ran perpendicular to Merrifield Road. They passed the back doors to all the little businesses that faced Randolph and Murphy Streets on either side, dry-cleaners, tailors, and the Holy Rosary Food Bank and Soup Kitchen. The line to the back door of the soup kitchen wrapped around the corner. Melinda felt ashamed for clutching her purse a little tighter while Kitt met the eyes of each soul in the queue with a smile of acceptance and encouragement. She even spoke to one lady in line, then confided in Melinda that she must be on the dope again because her mother throws her out if she does that shit in her house.

They came to a stop at a rusty metal door with no window and Kitt announced, "This is it!" and reached for the handle. Melinda entered a tight space with garbage cans lining the walls on both sides, just before the kitchen. Kitt closed in behind her and nudged her through to a swinging door that opened into a dimly lit, smoke-filled space where round tables cluttered the wooden floor and wooden booths accommodated rectangular ones along the walls. A full bar occupied the entire length of the front wall with a tiny ribbon of windows high above the shelves of liquor, allowing just enough light in so you could see your way around. Kitt passed Melinda up and headed for the bartender. She leaned over the counter and kissed him on the cheek.

"Tiny, this is Melinda. She just started teaching with me at the school this week. She forgot her lunch, and I told her you'd feed her today."

"Got that right, Miss Kitt." The giant man stretched his black hand across the bar to shake Melinda's. "I'm Tiny. What can I fix you ladies today?"

Kitt ordered for them, "We'll have a couple of steak hoagies." She checked with Melinda. "You eat red meat?" She got a nod in response and went on, "Mixed peppers, onions, and cheese, but no sauce."

Tiny winked.

"And do up a basket of pickles for us, Tiny."

"Yes ma'am," he obeyed. "You ladies find a seat and I'll bring you a sweet tea."

"Thank you, baby." Kitt smiled at the man and escorted her co-worker to a nearby table. "I've known that boy since he was in diapers. Me and his mom have been friends since second grade. He's her baby. Had four boys. Tiny grew up with my son, James."

"Are they all as big as Tiny?"

"Every damn one of them! But sweet as can be and they never give their mother any lip. I can vouch for that!"

Their drinks arrived and Melinda sipped at her tea, watching the action pick up as the lunch crowd hustled in. Kitt started a dozen stories or more, only to be interrupted by just as many passersby who all had some years-long connection with her or her family. Melinda felt like she was seeing the real Kitt for the first time since they met.

The food was quick to the table and arrived hot and fresh. Melinda tackled the oversized sandwich like a logger, biting sizeable chunks of the toasted bread and shaved steak, gooey with cheese. The mix of hot and mild peppers and caramelized onions gave the monster a sweet crunch that made it delectable. She dipped beer battered dill pickle slices in a house-made ketchup dressing and licked her fingers after every savory bite. Kitt grinned around the straw in her drink, enjoying the girl's first time at Tiny's.

They started back down the alley toward the school with full bellies and to-go bags of leftovers.

"Thanks, Kitt. That was amazing!"

"I told you, Melinda. Tiny knows how to take care of his friends."

"Well, how do I get to be one of Tiny's friends then?"

"You're already in, girl! All you had to do was show up with me. Now Tiny's going to have you down as one of mine. So, you're already in."

They walked back to struggle up the fire stairs together, reveling in their clout at Tiny's.

Melinda plopped down at her desk just minutes before her next class arrived, wondering if she'd ever bring lunch from home again.

That night, she told Brady all about her students, Tiny's hoagies, and her new connection with Kitt. He delighted in her telling it and hung on every word. She omitted her trip to Clara's this time. Truth be told, she was still mulling it over and the last thing she needed was Brady disapproving and shutting her down. She was afraid to risk a long-distance fight. If any more came of her predictions, she'd be sure to let him know Clara knew it all in advance.

☙

The new fall term at the Cleveland Business Academy began the same as it had for nearly seven decades for Miss M. She attended the program herself right out of high school and having met Isaak Maxwell when he frequented her father's barbershop across the street from the academy, found herself attracted to him almost instantly. In those days, he was quite a different man than their children ever knew. He was dark and bitter when they met. She had asked herself dozens of times what drew her to him in the beginning. She remembered now, even after all these years without him, that it was something in his eyes, a kindness, a gentleness, a genuinely tender heart.

This semester though, like all the others since his death, she rose in the mornings and completed her usual routine. She had one soft-boiled egg, dry toast, and coffee, washed her face and removed the toilet paper she wrapped her head in to sleep, poked her gray hairdo with the pointy end of a teasing comb, donned a smart petite size six ensemble, applied Rose Red No. 3 by Max Factor to her feathering lips, then waited for Reynolds. She sat alone in her spacious but sparse living room until 7:30, then moved to stand at the side door, the one that lead to the stoop alongside the drive. At 7:45, she locked the side door behind her and stood on the stoop, rain or shine. She'd been seen during blizzards and hail standing on that stoop, fine shoes tapping on the wet concrete and bricks, matching purse in hand, waiting for her driver. Her relationship with Reynolds had been an unusual one. She had fired him on multiple occasions, only to hire him back when his replacements proved even worse than him. He was a childhood friend of Ike's whom he owed for getting him out of some trouble her eldest son could never confess to her, so she took him back time after time. Reynolds arrived on the dot more often than not and kept the Cadillac serviced and spotless and took the old woman literally anywhere she asked to go. But in all the years he had worked for her, he never stepped foot in her house… practically no one did.

Miss M was picked up and chauffeured to the academy every weekday, then taken home directly after the last class was excused. Reynolds would pull up and park just in front of the garage door, help her out and up the steps to the stoop where she would wait until he put the car away, locked the garage, and returned the keys. She'd let herself in and close and lock the door behind her. He always waited in his car out front until he saw at least one light come on inside before dismissing himself to home. Ike must have done him a few favors in return to take the abuse she doled out, because despite her constant degradation, Reynolds couldn't help making sure the old lady was safe inside before he left her.

The staff endured Miss M's weekly reports to Ike regarding Reynolds' ineptitude during their Monday morning breakfast meetings for years, but lately they were more vicious. On the last Monday of September, it would nearly come to blows.

"Mother, I told you we could discuss this in private!" Ike shouted as he stood abruptly.

"Sit down!" Miss M demanded. "This man is an employee of the academy, and I will discuss his incompetence when the staff is reviewing current issues here. Believe me, Son, Reynolds is becoming an issue."

Manny interjected to diffuse the situation, "Mother, I think what Ike is saying is that we should review individual employee performance privately, away from other staff members."

Ike sat closed off, arms and legs crossed at his mother, nodding his agreement with his younger brother.

Manny continued, "It could make the other staff members uncomfortable."

He looked to his co-workers for support and each one nervously nodded, except for Melinda. She sat frozen in fear, her egg filled fork suspended just in front of her gaping mouth.

Miss M instantly honed in on the girl and recruited her as an ally.

"You get it don't you, Linda?" the old woman asked, pointing her out to the crowd. "Linda knows what I'm talking about, don't you?"

"It's Muh-linda, Miss M," Melinda squeaked, afraid to move.

"Linda, Melinda, whichever. You see my point. That if we have a problem with an employee at the school, we should be able to bring it up at these meetings."

"I guess so?"

"See, I told you she gets it. Excellent job, Linda," Miss M concluded triumphantly.

Melinda stuffed the eggs in her mouth and felt the blush of selling out that comes from siding with the bully on the playground. Sweat beaded in her hair and she could feel her heart thumping in her temples. She finished her breakfast without looking up. She waited until the meeting concluded, then bolted for the safety of the fire stairs.

She heard shouting erupt again when Kitt opened the heavy door and trailed her down the steps.

"Wait up, Linda!" Kitt cackled.

"Not funny, Kitt!" Melinda called back to her friend as she turned on the halfpace between floors to wait. "I just about pooped my pants!"

Kitt's laughter bounced around the stairwell, echoing in Melinda's head.

"I can't help it, girl. You *looked* like you were pooping your pants!"

"I've been here almost a month, and she hasn't even bothered to learn my name."

"Hey, that's not necessarily a bad thing. At least she noticed you today."

"Yeah and used me to pick a fight with her son over that poor man. Oh my God! Can you imagine being in a car with her every day?"

"No, ma'am!" Kitt had settled some. "They say she never used to be like this, but I find that hard to swallow. She's so good at it. Deidre says she got really bitter after her husband died. I can believe that. Loss can trigger some pretty rough changes in a woman."

"Well, I sure know that to be true, but she's brutal!"

"Deidre says she's getting worse."

"That's just sad."

"Now don't you go feeling sorry for that old broad, Melinda. She is getting whatever the good Lord feels she has coming to her," Kitt explained. "She'll have to answer for this bad behavior, same as any other jerk on the street. And I'm guessing sooner than later, she's almost ninety. No ma'am. You get what you give."

Kitt would have the last word as they entered the far end of the fourth-floor hall and split into their respective classrooms. Kitt's account left Melinda with less shame, but more to think about this crazy troupe she found herself a part of... temporarily.

After school that afternoon, Melinda watched in the rearview mirror as Sammy and Manny walked their mother to her waiting car, soothing her all the way there about how good she was to give Reynolds another chance. The driver sat stock still while they loaded her in and waited for her to wrap the back of his headrest with her cane to pull out from behind Melinda's spot. She watched the Caddy disappear out of the alley and shook her head. Backing out, she confided to her empty car.

"Well, if she's almost ninety, I guess Reynolds' plight is as temporary as my own. I bet he asks himself every day how long this is going to take."

October

By the middle of October, Melinda had found a rhythm. Her workdays were busy and after school, she graded papers and prepared new lessons. Brady had been home twice since he started, and even though they had a hard time getting out of bed on those weekends, they did a few little things around the house to get it ready for the renovations. They replaced the trim Brady decimated over the stairs, pulled a few dead and dying shrubs out, and listed some of the bigger pieces of furniture in the Ad Pad for sale.

The days grew shorter and colder and Melinda had to try harder to keep from dwelling on her loneliness. She splurged on a few pumpkins at the grocery store and carved them out to put on the porch.

At the academy, they always celebrated the holidays, much to the disdain of Miss M. Coming from Irish Catholic and Lutheran parents and marrying into a Jewish family, she maintained it wasn't always appropriate to celebrate occasions in which not everyone may participate… except for Halloween. Halloween was her favorite. In the early sixties when the Merrifield Road area was alive with commerce, Isaak Maxwell started a special merchant trick-or-treat night, on the night before Halloween proper, to treat all the kids living in the projects and apartments along the broad, bustling boulevard. Not as many businesses took part now, of course, with the economy the way it was, but the Cleveland Business Academy always had a blowout! The staff and students dressed in costume and decorated the downstairs halls with spider webs and jack-o'-lanterns, and everyone had buckets of candy to hand out. The children would come into the front of the building, move along the winding corridors, and pop out the back door with a hardy haul of sweet treats. After the trick-or-treaters trailed off, the music came on and the staff and students danced and played into the night.

Miss M got in on the action every year. She donned the one costume she spent good money on, an authentic rendition of the wicked queen from Snow White. Dressed in all black, she wore the widow's peak hooded cape and carried an oversized, glittery red apple which coordinated with her Rose Red No. 3. She loved carrying on the traditions that her husband had started at the school. This one in particular because it gave something back to the community that had supported the academy and all their other businesses for all these years. She even loved the self-deprecating costume she wore every season. It reminded her she still possessed a sense of humor, even if she only displayed it once a year.

This year, she was out of costume and seated quietly within the first few moments of the party starting, but she stayed and sipped at the 7&7s her adult children took turns mixing for her. A little before eleven o'clock, the night was winding down as students started exiting the party. When the crowd began thinning, it was apparent to those who remained Kitt, Deidre, Jeannie, and Melinda that the Maxwells had slipped out along with the rest and left Miss M behind. The four had come dressed as the cast of the Wizard of Oz and they stood staring at Miss M like the scene in the movie when Toto pulled back the curtain and exposed the wizard. She sat, slumped in a chair, dozing with her chin resting on her fist at the buffet table, completely unaware of her predicament. The four women whispered to one another to decide how to get her home.

"Maybe Reynolds is already out back," Jeannie a.k.a. Dorothy suggested. "I'll run and see."

She was out the back door and into the parking lot in a flash.

"She won't ride with me because my car smells like smoke," claimed Deidre, the Cowardly Lion. "So, I'm out." She found her coat and purse, shook a cigarette loose from a pack, gripped it between her lips, and saluted with a fur paw. "Let me know how it all works out."

Kitt the Tin Man, and Melinda the Scarecrow, stood looking blankly at the back of Deidre as Jeannie passed her on her way back in.

"He's not out there!" Jeannie panicked.

"Did you look behind my car?" Melinda asked. "He always blocks me in."

"The Cadillac is not in the lot. What are we going to do?"

"Go check out front, Jeannie," Kitt ordered. It was only a moment later that she came back in, shaking her head.

"Crap!" Melinda blurted out too loud.

"SHHHHHH!" hissed Kitt and Jeannie.

"What's that?" the groggy question slurred from Miss M. "What's the… where is everyone?"

Kitt and Jeannie pushed Melinda toward the waking woman.

"Uhm. Uh. Miss M, we can't find your car. I mean, your driver."

"What? What do you mean you can't find him?"

"Well, Jeannie looked out front and in the back lot… and… he's not there."

"Of all the… that stupid… incompetent…"

"Should we call Manny or Sam?" Jeannie offered.

"No!" she barked. "Lucinda can take me home."

The three women looked at each other for a split-second, wondering if the old woman was seeing someone who wasn't there. Then they realized she was talking about Melinda.

"You mean Melinda, Miss M," corrected Kitt as she nudged her friend closer to their boss.

Waving away the mistake, Miss M bobbed her head. "Yes, yes, that's what I said. The Scarecrow can take me home. Jeannie, go and get my coat."

"Melinda, you go pull your car around front so we don't have to navigate that back alley in the dark. Jeannie and I will bring her out to you."

Following Kitt's directive, Melinda grabbed her own coat and darted out the back to drive around the building. "What am I doing?" she asked herself as she neared the front entrance where her friends were just escorting their charge to the curb.

"That's a two-door," the old woman said flatly. "I can't ride in that back seat. I'll never be able to get out!"

Melinda got out of the car, took her arm, and loosed her from the other two. "You'll have to ride up front, Miss M," she stated with authority. "There's just no other way to get you home tonight. Come on."

Miss M looked into the face of this woman fifty-plus years her junior and marveled at her audacity. She allowed herself to be marched around the car and lowered into the front passenger's seat. Melinda reached in and around her and buckled her seatbelt, then closed the door and trotted to the other side, shooting her friends a threatening look just before getting in and driving away.

The two instructors stood dumbstruck on the curb, and Kitt admired their friend. "She may not have a brain, but that Scarecrow has the balls of a brass monkey!"

Melinda drove slower and more carefully than usual with her volatile cargo. Miss M sat silently, watching the lights along the way dictate their pace. She pointed left or right to direct the driver, but Melinda knew where she was going. Everyone in town knew the Maxwell home. It was the biggest, stateliest place on the block and it sat on nearly an acre of ground. One of the largest lots within the city limits. The quiet was growing uncomfortable, and Melinda attempted to ease it.

"I'm sorry you got stuck with me tonight, Miss M," she started.

Miss M held up her hand to signal the young woman to stop talking, and she did. They endured the rest of the ride without uttering another word. After what seemed an eternity, Melinda pulled into the driveway and parked. Miss M sat waiting until Melinda took the hint and jumped out to hurry to her door. She opened it and helped the woman struggle from the low base to her feet. She helped her up the steps to the stoop, then waited as she fumbled in her purse for her keys in the dim light of the porch lamp overhead.

Melinda couldn't figure out if she was tipsy from the 7&7s or if she was having a moment of confusion because of her age, but she decided in the next second to help.

"Here Miss M, let me help you." She took the purse from her and shook it to settle all the contents to the bottom and listen for the keys. They heard no jingle. Then it hit her. "Are your house keys and your car keys on the same ring?"

"Damn that sack of guts!" Miss M doubled up her fists and shook with rage. Melinda touched her arm.

"Let's not panic. I'm sure we can figure this out." She looked around the house. "I don't suppose you have a spare set of keys stashed somewhere, do you?"

"I do!" Miss M remembered. "But they're inside."

"Ok... let me think. Do you have a basement window around the back we could get into?"

"We?!"

"Me. Me could–I could get in to."

"Well, of course I have basement windows, but I don't see how on Earth you can…"

Melinda was off the stoop and back in her car for a flashlight and screwdriver she kept in the glove box. She looked back up to Miss M on the stoop and the old woman pointed around toward the back of the house. Melinda found her way to the first window well, between the rhododendrons bordering the foundation. She aimed the flashlight down into the leaf filled hollow and wondered to herself what slimy inhabitants it accommodated. Dismissing the thought, she leaned over it to the window frame and pried with the flat head of the screwdriver until it gave way.

"Yes! Thank you Jesus!" she exclaimed; her words, clouds of condensation puffing out into the crisp October night. She pushed the window in at its base as far as she could with her toe, then lowered the rest of her body down into the well, giggling nervously at the thought of getting stuck in this window dressed like a scarecrow. The young woman twisted onto her belly to drop down onto the basement floor, landing with a thud on the cement surface. Once she closed and latched the window tight, she paused and looked around the space. She took a minute to shine the light all over the room and discovered that except for the furnace, hot water tank, washer, and dryer, there was literally nothing down there. She puzzled over the vacancy for just another moment and went for the stairs. The door into the house was unlocked, and she gained access to the first floor.

Miss M saw the beam of the flashlight bouncing around the inside of her kitchen and knew the scarecrow had accomplished her mission. She flashed a rare smile just for an instant, then quickly returned to scowling and pounded on the door.

"I can see you in there. Let me in!"

Melinda rushed to the door to unlock it and grant the grand dame entry. Miss M pushed by her and turned on the light.

"Stay right there."

Melinda obeyed and wondered if she was going to get a reward for shimmying down into a basement in the middle of the night in her Halloween costume to let this old crane into her mansion.

Miss M came directly back into the kitchen and held out a set of keys.

"You keep these until we get my other set back from that asshat!"

Melinda took the keys and stared at the woman, bewildered.

"I'll be ready at 7:45 on Monday morning. Don't be late."

She turned on her heel and disappeared into the house, dismissing Melinda without question or debate.

"Is she going to pay you?" Brady asked his wife when he could get a word in edgewise.

"I don't know. Reynolds is on the payroll. We have to hear her rant about *that* at every Monday morning meeting, but she didn't even ask me if I wanted to do it. She just handed me the keys and said, 'Monday morning. Don't be late.'" Melinda was wound up. "I mean, what am I supposed to do, Brady?"

"I don't know, honey. It would save a little gas, I guess."

"It's on my way anyway. And I'd drive my car to get hers. I don't think it would save much gas."

"Do you want to do it?"

"Do I want to start every day of my workweek by getting verbally abused by my eighty-nine-year-old boss? No. I can't say that's something I want. No." She got quiet and Brady got defensive.

"To hell with her!"

"What?"

"No, Melinda. You are not one of her lackies to be pushed around like that. You are your Aunt Helen's legacy and a graduate of that institution. And you are my wife! You certainly don't deserve to be made to cart that old witch around at her beck and call."

She warmed at his heroic attempt… so Brady.

"Babe, I don't think it's as bad as all that."

"Well, I don't like it. I don't like that she didn't give you a chance to refuse. That's so arrogant."

"Brady, I don't even know if it will last. Wherever poor Reynolds escaped to tonight, he will probably be back on Monday to resume his position and this whole thing will blow over." She was feeling sorry she bothered him with it. She didn't think about how he must worry about her. "I'm going to show up on time next week and I'll bet she just dismisses me on to school."

"Alright. But I want to be on the record as *opposed*. You have enough to worry about without adding more stress from her."

"I promise I won't let it stress me," she vowed. "How about that?"

"Agreed."

"Now, husband, can we please change the subject?"

"Yes please, wife. The contractors."

"Good one," Melinda decided. "What? When? What do I need to know?"

"You got the money I wired this week?" he asked.

"Yes, and I already deposited it in checking."

"Good. Caldwell is coming by Saturday sometime to drop off some supplies and equipment and pick up the check. He'll let you know all the particulars. I told him his stuff would be safe in the garage."

"Ok."

"You can let him know how early is too early to come and how late is too late to stay, but remember, the more they work, the faster we get this done."

"I get it, Brady."

"I know you do, honey."

The couple talked into the wee hours again until they lost their battle with their heavy lids and tired brains. The contractor came as planned and agreed to arrive a full hour before Melinda needed to leave to be at Miss M's. He seemed kind and professional and thanked Melinda for her check and her business. She spent the rest of that Saturday and all day Sunday practicing for Monday morning.

Caldwell and two other men arrived on time and began carrying great spools of wire and bags of tools to the attic. Melinda left the coffee on for them and invited them to make more as they needed it. She checked the clock obsessively to make sure she had plenty of time to get to Miss M's. She left when she was confident she'd arrive a few minutes ahead of her 7:45 directive. Traffic was mild and every light she hit was green. She smiled at how charmed she felt in the moment. She arrived at her destination at precisely 7:39.

"Not bad, Melinda. Six minutes to spare," she congratulated herself. She grabbed her bags and used the key labeled 'GARAGE' to gain entry to the side door of the structure and discovered it was empty. "What the…"

"He totaled it," yapped Miss M from the stoop, startling Melinda into a spin.

"What? Who?"

"Reynolds. That boob got drunk and ran my Cadillac up a tree last Friday."

"Oh, my God! Is he alright?"

"He's fine," she signaled the girl to help her down the steps. "We'll have to take your car."

Melinda popped to her side, a little dazed, and walked her by the elbow to put her in the Probe. She opened the passenger side door, threw her things into the back, then helped Miss M in. She reached for the seatbelt again and the old woman stopped her.

"I can get it, Miranda."

"Oh," Melinda drew her hand back. "Sorry, Miss M but it's Melinda."

"What'd I say?"

"Muh… oh, never mind."

Melinda shut the car door and got around to get them where they needed to be. When the car started up again, the radio was still on from the first half of her commute and she lunged to turn it off.

"Sorry Miss M!" she squeaked. "I listen to music on my way to work in the morning."

"It's alright," she answered. "I don't mind it playing low. Maybe you won't feel so compelled to talk the whole way there if there's a little music on."

Melinda narrowed her stare and puckered her lips at the not-so-subtle hint her passenger threw out. She watched from the corner of her eye as she turned the dial to ON, then past it to a volume that produced an almost indiscernible wince from Miss M, then back down just a click.

Livin' la Vida Loca and *Genie in a Bottle*, two ads for businesses the Maxwells owned, and they were there. Melinda pulled up in front of the school, got her fare to the door, then got back behind the wheel and drove around to the rear lot to park. She took a deep breath and smiled. Even though she still didn't know what the actual deal was, if every morning went as smoothly as this one, she didn't need to worry about a thing. She entered the building and found her way to the breakfast meeting.

Miss M was already seated in her usual spot and the Maxwell boys were crowded around their mother when Melinda arrived in the conference room. The three men raised their heads in unison to eye the young woman and when she crossed to the food to fill a plate, she shot them a relaxed smile.

Jeannie and Kitt hurried to her side to get the skinny.

Kitt whispered, "We weren't sure we'd ever see you again. How was it?"

"You two kill me," Melinda whispered back. "It was fine. She's not as bad as everyone says."

"Hurry it up girls!" Miss M directed on cue. "The gossip can wait."

Jeannie's eyes got big as eggs, terrified that they'd been heard. She grabbed her mouth and scurried to her seat. Kitt followed and Melinda finished pouring her coffee, then did the same.

Sam began the meeting. "As most of you probably already heard, Mom's driver was in an accident Friday night."

"Wait," Miss M interrupted. "I can't complain about him at a breakfast meeting, but we're going to talk about him totaling my car this morning. Which is it, Sam?"

He looked to his big brothers for help. Ike rolled his eyes, but Manny jumped in again to keep the peace.

"We wanted to let people know about the accident in case they wanted to do anything to help."

"Help?" Melinda asked.

"Help Reynolds," Manny continued. "He was pretty badly hurt."

Melinda's head snapped toward Miss M.

The old broad looked down at her lap caught in a split second of shame then just as quickly shrugged it off. "Badly hurt. A few broken bones. He's lucky I didn't break his neck for what he did to my car."

"Mother!" Ike interjected. "The man has two broken arms and a fractured jaw!"

"Yes, Ike. Like I said, he's lucky."

Sam regained the room's attention to let the staff know they were sending a card and some food to the house if everyone could sign it and bring whatever they wanted to donate. The rest of the meeting went on with no more mention of Reynolds, or Miss M's car, or anything else pertaining to the subject. Melinda walked out at the end, more confused than before.

She and Kitt took their usual route to their classrooms that morning, and Kitt was full of questions Melinda couldn't answer.

"Are they paying you?"

"I don't know."

"Did you agree to do it?"

"No. She didn't ask. She just said, '7:45, don't be late.'"

"Well, get it square with them, Melinda," Kitt insisted. "Don't do anything for these people for free. They have the money."

"It's not the money, Kitt. I don't know if I want to have that kind of daily involvement with that woman." Melinda was reexamining the ride in. "I mean, it wasn't bad this morning, but did you see the way her sons looked at me when I came in? Am I doing something wrong that I don't know about?"

"Who knows with these people," Kitt admitted. "They're all nuts, if you ask me."

Again, Kitt's parting words would leave Melinda with more to think about during the length of her day. Her morning classes were uneventful, but midway through the first one after lunch, Sam knocked on her door. She excused herself and left the classroom. She closed the door behind her and discovered Manny had accompanied his brother on this mission.

"Hey guys," she tiptoed in. "What's up?"

"We just wanted to let you know we know you took Mom home Friday night after the party," Sam started.

"We felt awful about leaving her," Manny interrupted. "That never happens, just so you know."

"And we know you picked her up this morning and we really appreciate it," Sam kept on. "We tried to tell her we will find her a new car and a new driver, but she is insisting that the two of you already have… an arrangement?"

"What arrangement?" she asked.

"You don't?" asked Manny. Then he turned to his brother. "I told you. The poor thing has no idea."

"Sorry, Melinda. What my brother is trying to say is that our mother… has a way… of…" Sam was struggling. "She kind of rolls right over people without even considering their feelings."

"She's a tyrant!" Manny blurted, then clamped his fingers tight onto his lips.

"Ok… ok," Melinda soothed. "If she wants me to drive her to and from school in my car, that's fine. I can do that."

"You'll be compensated, of course," pledged Sam.

"It doesn't cost me a thing to stop and get her. She's on my way."

"You will be compensated for driving our mother," Manny insisted. "Don't be a martyr, Melinda. We all know what this woman is capable of. It may not cost you money to pick her up…"

"But it will take years off your life," Sam laughed knowingly.

Melinda lead the couple away from her door and asked if that was all they needed. They concluded their private conference and let the teacher get back to her students.

That afternoon, after school, Miss M met Melinda and Kitt coming from the stairwell, and the three women walked through the lot together. Miss M managed unassisted but for her cane, with Kitt and Melinda flanking her the way friends do when they're shopping downtown. Kitt left them at Melinda's car and for the first time since she had been an employee there, Miss M called to her, "Have a good night, Kitt."

Melinda settled the old girl in her seat, then smiled overtop the cars to her friend, who stood slack-jawed in shock and awe.

The two rode in silence until they reached Miss M's. Melinda pulled into the driveway and got out to assist her elder to the door. Miss M dug in her purse again for the set of keys she had returned to her by the sheriff when he reported the accident, and Melinda produced the set she was given.

"Here, Miss M. I guess I won't be needing these."

Finding the originals, she answered, "No. You keep those just in case. I don't want you catting around, breaking into my basement again if we lose mine."

She let herself in and turned back as she closed the door. "Thanks for the ride. See you tomorrow."

Melinda stood staring at the kitchen curtains, swinging back and forth with inertia from the closing door until she heard the lock latch and considered herself off the clock.

Back at the house, Caldwell's men were still at it, coming and going between the garage and the attic. She went to her room, changed into soft pants and a sweatshirt, and went to the kitchen to fix a bite. Settling for a sandwich and a cup of coleslaw left over from the fish she made the night before, she sat silently ruminating over the events of the day. She had a new job... or *another* new job. Was she really going to take money for carpooling with someone? Not just anyone. Mrs. Isaak Lowell Maxwell. She was giving an old lady a ride to work. What was that even worth? The coleslaw wasn't as good the second time, and she only felt like half the sandwich. She cleared the kitchen table and got her schoolwork out and began grading. The workmen concluded just after dark and thanked her for the coffee. She abandoned her student's assignments and walked Caldwell to the door. This would be her new routine... temporarily.

November

Little more effort was spent in Melinda's morning regimen to include the stop at Miss M's. Arriving five or six minutes early impressed the old girl, and she seemed easier to ride with following each pickup that first week. Ohio can be brutal in the early days of November and Melinda always came to the stoop with her umbrella ready to cover them when the freezing rain whipped up or the first wet and snowy signs of winter appeared.

When she dropped her off after school at the end of the first week they rode together, the two stood sheltering against the weather on the stoop until Miss M managed the lock and pushed inside. Melinda waved goodbye and turned to pop off when Miss M stopped her.

"Wait!"

Melinda hopped back up and leaned in to hear over the wind, "Yes, ma'am?"

"Come in out of that wind so I don't have to yell," Miss M said, aggravated.

Melinda closed her umbrella and left it leaning against the house, then stepped in and shook off the cold.

"Yes, Miss M. What is it?"

"I've got to pay you for the week." She reached in her purse, retrieved her wallet, and began counting out tens.

"Oh, no. You know, that's ok. I really don't mind it. I don't even go out of my way to get to you."

"Nonsense! You are doing me a service and I'm going to compensate you."

The woman folded a few bills over her thumb and jabbed it at Melinda.

"Miss M please, I don't mind driving you. As long as you don't mind being seen driving around in my old jalopy. We're good. Really."

"I don't know what your Aunt Helen taught you about this kind of thing, but if you don't value yourself, no one else will. Your time is worth something. I insist!" She jabbed again.

"Miss M do you appreciate me picking you up on the way to work?"

"Isn't that what I'm trying to say?" she asked, looking around the room. "Am I on Candid Camera here? That's precisely what I'm attempting to show you by paying you."

"I'd like to think that my Aunt Helen taught me to be the kind of person who helped others just to be helpful. I know you appreciate it, and that's enough for me."

Miss M raised her head and squinted at the woman. "I know what you're doing. You want me to owe you something." Melinda rolled her eyes. "That's it! Why settle for a couple extra dollars a week when you can call in some big fat favor later on? I'm on to you."

"You got me. Yes, Miss M that's me all over. I've been plotting to position myself to ask you for a big fat favor ever since I came to work for you. You figured me out," Melinda concluded with the glint of an angry tear in her eye.

Miss M was stunned. She hadn't meant to hurt the girl. She felt an uncomfortable pang of regret but had no way of recovering from it.

Shaking her head, Melinda helped her out and shut the whole thing down.

"Goodnight Miss M," she said and left the old broad planted in the pattern on the linoleum.

"I don't know, honey. I think I agree with Kitt, they are the kind of people who have the money, and we need the money!"

"Brady, I don't want to be a person who takes advantage of that. I would do this if she was just some poor old woman who needed a ride. It truly doesn't put me out in the least."

"But she'd be paying someone else if you didn't do it," Brady pointed out.

"You're missing my point. No one in that woman's life does anything for her just to be kind. Even her children only show up when it's payday!" Melinda was wrestling with deeper feelings than she recognized and she felt like she was struggling to make sense of them. "I don't know why I didn't take the money, Brady. But I didn't... and I won't!"

He sat quietly, defeated, until he heard her breathing relax.

"Sorry, honey. I'm not there. I've never even met these people."

"I know. Just let me do my thing and you do yours. Can we agree on that?"

"Agreed!"

She took a big deep breath and reset, "I miss your stupid face."

"I could have done without the 'stupid' but me too, Melinda."

"What is the plan for Thanksgiving?" she asked.

A noise escaped him she only heard him make when he didn't want to say what was next.

"What?" she probed.

"I can't come home for Thanksgiving, honey."

"No! Why not?" she whined. "Aren't Charlie and Roger coming home?"

"Charlie, yes. Roger, no."

"Oh Brady, that's going to suck so hard!"

"I know, I know, but we agreed Charlie would do Thanksgiving and Roger and I would get Christmas." He offered the consolation, "That's ok isn't it? Wouldn't you rather have me home at Christmas?"

"I guess," she conceded. "So, you won't be home until Christmas, Brady? That's seven more weeks!"

"I wish it was different, Melinda, but it's not. This overtime is everything we're going to need to finish the house and holiday pay is double. I'm thinking if I keep at it, by the end of the year we can list the house and you can get out of there and we can finally get settled over here somewhere."

Dread was all she felt for the long winter nights ahead of her. She did hate it. She hated being alone and wanted her old life back. No more teaching, no more Miss M. She wanted Brady back in her bed, and she wanted this whole thing behind her.

"Honey? You still there?" he asked.

She wasn't. She was years away, into the future or maybe the past, but not there by any stretch of the imagination.

She lied to her husband, "I'm here."

🌲

Melinda opened the door for Caldwell and his men in the dark of the early morning after the weekend off. They traded small talk about the worsening weather and their collective gratitude for inside work. Melinda was uneasy about returning to Miss M's after their last exchange. She wasn't even sure if the old bat would be there. And if she was, would she let Melinda keep taking her to school? She left on time, arrived the same, and sloshed through the light layer of snow to the door. Miss M was just inside donning her plastic rain bonnet to protect her newly styled hair. Melinda opened the screen door and Miss M the storm door in unison.

"Marta did my hair yesterday," she said matter-of-factly. "Don't want to risk losing my hairdo walking in this muck."

Melinda smiled and walked her to the car. She turned the radio back on and pulled away just as Miss M reached for the volume knob and turned it up just a skosh. Melinda took the hint. They would not talk about it. She was fine with that.

The instructors directed their students to change out the Halloween decor for Thanksgiving. Manny's Pitch and Presentation class dressed the display windows that faced Merrifield Road with golds and reds and ancient plastic food reused for decades pouring out of dusty horns of plenty. On the board in Jeannie's classroom, she started a running ticker of x-amount of days until Christmas. Sam's Typing and Keyboard class lined the top of the wall surrounding the typing pool with autumn leaf garland, and Kitt laid out an entire miniature turkey dinner across the front of her desk. Deidre even got into it a smidge. Her students cut out construction paper foods and wrote something they were thankful for on each one, then polluted the bulletin board in her room with the colorful pieces. Melinda thought it was stupid. These were grownups, not children in grammar school. Jeannie brought her a posterboard turkey in a top hat and Melinda reluctantly asked one of her students to find a place for him. He ended up on the door to her classroom. Miss M resisted every effort to decorate the sentry booth, stating she couldn't stand the clutter. That warmed Melinda to her core.

On the walk to the car after school that day, Melinda told Kitt about Brady not coming home for Thanksgiving, and her friend was visibly moved.

"Oh! Melinda, I'm so sorry," she said. "You're welcome to join us. My house is always full of stragglers during the holidays. We'd love to have you."

"Thanks, Kitt. That's awfully sweet. I'll consider it."

Kitt left the ladies at their ride and bid them goodnight. Melinda waited for the wipers and heater to do their things while Miss M found what she wanted to hear on the radio.

"Shame about your husband, Melissa," Miss M started. "I hate all the pressure on people to visit over the holidays."

Melinda ignored the misnomer, sat on her hands to warm them, and agreed, "I know exactly how you feel, Miss M. Aunt Helen never made any fuss over the holidays. She didn't see the merit in it. If you took care of each other on all the ordinary days of the year, why did you need to do something special for the holidays?"

The old woman nodded. "My sentiments exactly."

"I mean, what about the other Thursdays? When we're old and thinking back on all the days we've lived, will we only remember the Thanksgivings, or will we think about all the other Thursdays that were just… Thursdays?"

As she backed the car out of the space, kindred energy sparked between the women and produced a telling smile on them both, though neither of them noticed the other's.

Monday, the twenty-second, the breakfast meeting began as scheduled and proceeded smoothly until the calendar was brought up.

"Everyone remember to bring a covered dish for lunch Wednesday," Sam reminded them. "And of course, we're off that afternoon and the rest of the week for the holiday."

"Wait!" Miss M interrupted. "Wednesday afternoon *and* Friday?"

"Mother, you know that's the tradition," reminded Sam.

"Why in hell do they need Friday off?"

"It's just what they do," explained Ike. "Mother, it's only been that way for decades. Have you forgotten?"

"Forgotten!" Miss M slammed her hand on the table. "My mind is as sharp as it's ever been, Ike! Don't you ever accuse me of forgetting."

The room was still waiting for the rest of what they'd become accustomed to witnessing. But nothing else came. Miss M straightened her herringbone jacket over her matching dress and glanced at Melinda.

"Any excuse to get out of work," she said to Melinda alone.

Melinda shook her head, ashamed of whomever Miss M was referring to, staff, students, her children. The rest of the room shared bewildered stares.

"Alright. Go on," prompted the matriarch.

"Manny, what about the food?" Ike proceeded cautiously.

"We're doing the turkey, of course, and Jeannie's got the sign-up sheet for all the rest."

When the meeting concluded, it was Manny who caught up to Melinda on her way to the fire exit with Kitt.

"Wait up, Melinda!" he called, trotting to her side in the open doorway. "Kitt, go on. I just need her for a minute."

He hooked her arm in his and walked her back half the length of the hall, waited for it to empty, and started in barely above a whisper, "Melinda…"

"Yes," she answered, matching his hushed tone.

"You've been spending a lot of time with Mother lately."

"Have I? Just driving her to and from school, really. I don't know that I'd call that a lot of time, Manny."

"Mm. Well, that's more than most of us are getting with her," he confessed. "More consistently any way. You know what I mean?"

"I guess so, yes."

"We just wanted to know if she needed anything, or if you think she's doing alright, or just you know, what's up with her?"

Miss M's cane could be heard tapping from the conference room into the hall toward the secret confab and she called out to her son, whose voice she obviously picked up on despite his efforts to go undetected.

"If you want to know if anything is *up*, Manfred, why don't you just ask me?"

He laughed nervously, then looked beyond his mother's silhouette to his brothers looming behind her.

"I was just telling Melinda that we're close to finding a new car for you, Mother," Manny lied.

"No you weren't, Son. You were attempting to enlist Glenda here to spy on me."

"Now Mother," Ike defended from behind her. "You know that's not what he's doing."

"You're wasting your time, aren't they, Glenda?" Miss M winked at Melinda. "They think you know something they don't." She giggled. "You won't get this one to turn. She's got no skin in the game. Come on, Glenda. I'll give you a ride to the fourth floor."

The old woman pushed past her family and waited at the elevator with Melinda while her sons stood thwarted in the hall. She brandished her cane at them and they retreated to the conference room. The doors split open and the two women climbed in.

"Can you believe that? There's just no accounting for some people's children."

"Miss M I don't think he was…,"

"Nope. Don't defend them," Miss M warned. "They're always snooping around my business. They're terrified I'm going to spend their inheritance on someone *else* before I die and leave them all penniless."

"Penniless?" Melinda asked. "I thought they all had their own businesses."

"They're all tied into this school. No one gets a thing if there's no money left in this school. And all the money in this school is mine!"

The doors opened on the fourth floor and Miss M held her cane out for Melinda to exit. Puzzled, she turned around to ask, "Miss M, did you tell them I wouldn't accept any money for driving you?"

"Yes I did."

"And what did they say?"

"They said they didn't trust it."

"Miss M…"

"I know your name, Melinda." She pulled her cane out and as the doors closed, she added, "But I've got to give them something to stew over."

Melinda wandered back to her classroom in a fog. She was beginning to get the old broad. And not just to *get* her, but she was developing a genuine fondness for her. She loved the way she pushed those men around, and the way she made everyone look over their shoulder when she was within earshot. She didn't love the meanness, but honestly, Melinda thought she noticed that Miss M didn't seem so mean since she'd been riding with her.

"That's probably what has her family suspicious… she's nicer!" she said to herself, entering her room and switching on the light. "She's nicer, and they don't know how to deal

127

with that. And she intends to treat it like a sport!" She shook her head and grinned. "Those poor people."

When the students had been dismissed after the Wednesday luncheon, the staff made a beeline for the doors. Miss M asked Melinda if she minded waiting a minute or two until the parking lot emptied, knowing she wasn't hurrying home to anyone, anyway. Melinda didn't mind.

The catering staff hired to bring the Maxwell's portion of the dinner carefully wrapped each foil pan of leftover turkey, dressing, gravy, and mash then stacked them neatly on the end of one of the folding conference tables they'd assembled for the meal. Miss M spoke to the man in charge then watched as he gathered his crew and directed each of them to take a pan. Melinda eyed them as they walked out the back of the school and Miss M beckoned her to join in, exiting behind them.

The two women walked to Melinda's car as usual, but the catering staff walked past through the lot and kept on down the alley. She didn't ask, but Melinda took the right out of the lot instead of her usual left toward Merrifield Road and trailed down the alley to see the young men in their white coats entering the back of the Holy Rosary Food Bank and Soup Kitchen.

Melinda grinned like a Cheshire Cat at the discovery that Miss M waited until no one would know that she didn't throw all that leftover food away but instead donated it to the church to feed those less fortunate. She thought about it for another moment. There's no way she is as hard and mean as she lets on. This woman could be a secret saint.

"Well?" Miss M asked, waiting.

"I didn't see a thing."

"That's what I thought."

"So, are you going to Ike's tomorrow or do Sam or Manny do a big dinner for the family?"

"Manny?" the old woman laughed. "Manny doesn't have any family and Sam's wife is dumb as a tree. They all drive out to Ike's. He has the whole big spread of food and all those simpletons get drunk and argue. It's always such a giant mess!"

"That's too bad, Miss M," Melinda sympathized. "Will one of them come into town to get you?"

"I suppose."

"Well, if it's turns out to be a thing, I could always take you. I don't have anything going on."

"Are you fishing for an invitation?"

"Oh! No ma'am! I would never impose on your family dinner like that. No thank you."

Miss M sat quietly for a moment and Melinda squirmed. She hoped she hadn't crossed a line. There's no way she wanted to subject herself to this family's private time. She saw what they were like with strangers in the room. God only knows what happened behind closed doors. Lost in her internal argument, she didn't see Miss M's furrowed brow and unconscious smile.

"Hmmm," hummed the old woman.

"Hmmm," Melinda mimicked. "Hmmm, what? Miss M what are you plotting?"

"I *do* need a ride tomorrow, Melinda," she said. "I want you to come dressed for dinner at 4:30 tomorrow afternoon."

"Miss M you can't use me to get at your children. I won't let you start something that puts me in the middle of things."

"Really, Melinda!" she scoffed, admonishing the girl. "I'm surprised at you! I am inviting an employee who has nowhere to eat Thanksgiving dinner."

Melinda cut her eyes.

"What? You know how charitable I am. You just caught me giving food to the poor, for God's sake."

"Miss M."

"Why are you even trying to argue with me? Plus, if you take me, I can leave whenever I want instead of waiting for someone to sober up enough to get me home. One year I called a cab!"

They arrived in front of her home and she formally proposed.

"Melinda, will you please accompany me to Thanksgiving dinner tomorrow?"

Melinda puffed out a sigh and got out of the car without answering. When she got around to help Miss M out, the old woman sat with arms folded, set in the seat.

"Oh my goodness!" Melinda rolled her eyes and relented, "Ok!"

Miss M beamed and patted her hands together in a tiny ovation.

⚜

Melinda stood in front of the mirror behind the door in her bedroom, judging this, the fifth thing she'd tried on. Brown pleated slacks and her rust-colored oxfords, a beige collared blouse, and her brown tweed blazer. She looked smart, and the outfit was comfortable. She donned the small gold hoops Brady gave her for her birthday last summer and found Aunt Helen's old gold hat pin to dress up her jacket.

"Too much?" She examined the pin. "I don't need all this." She removed the pin and placed it back in her jewelry box. She returned to her reflection and decided. "This is fine."

Even though she wasn't the least bit late, Miss M was already on the stoop when Melinda drove up. She didn't even wait until her driver stopped the car to step down to the drive and, to Melinda's dismay, she opened her own door and let herself down into the seat.

"Well, good afternoon, Miss M," she said. "Aren't you Johnny-on-the-spot today?"

"I just want to get there and get back. Come on, let's go."

Melinda backed onto the street and proceeded to their destination. It was at the far end of town, away from the blight of the Rust Belt that Ike and his wife resided, past a couple of new developments on a very large parcel of land with curated lawns and pristine white fences surrounding the house. The sweeping circle drive was jammed with nicer cars than hers and Melinda flushed with a little shame when she pulled up in the lane they'd left for her to deliver their matriarch.

"Let's get you out and then I'll move the car."

"Don't you dare move this car!"

"Miss M, I can't park right in front of the house."

"Says who?" Miss M waited for Melinda to turn off the engine. "Melinda, put this car in park and take the keys out of the ignition this instant. You are parking right here."

Melinda did as she was told, yanked her e-brake with an attitude, and got out.

"This is going to be a shit show," she whispered to herself as she walked around the car to get Miss M.

"One you'll never forget," the old woman answered her. "You need to watch talking to yourself, Melinda. People can hear you, you know. It makes you look crazy."

Dumbfounded, the young woman escorted her boss to the door of the grand house. She knocked.

"Watch, they'll have hired some poor old thing to act as footman or valet or whatever to greet their guests."

Melinda leaned in and whispered, "I think you mean butler."

The door opened and there stood a stranger in white gloves to grant them entry.

"Ha! I told you."

Miss M passed by the man and waited while Melinda helped her off with her coat. The girl surrendered it to the man, and the two proceeded through a doorway on their left into a yawning room full of people.

"Mother!" Manny called from his perch on the hearth of a massive fireplace. He started toward her with his arms open, a lime-garnished tumbler of gin in one hand. "And Melinda!"

He reached the women and threw his arms around their necks. They craned around his curly hair to see each other.

"What'd I tell you?" Miss M said in hushed tones. "And this is before dinner!"

In one great clump, the family members and their guests greeted Miss M and Melinda with what seemed like sincere warmth; but it could have been the warmth of their cocktails. She met Sam's dumb wife and Ike's snobby one, who excused their missing daughters away at boarding school. They introduced her to Marta's son and husband. Even Farmer brought a date, a lady from his work with Bikur Cholim of Cleveland. Gus's wife didn't feel well enough to attend, as per her usual, and even though Hildy didn't either, she was there, if only in body. Hildy's disfunction wasn't as readily visible when the entire clan was high.

They moved through to the dining room like a slow, clumsy stampede and took their places around a beautifully appointed table. Ike stood at the head and raised his glass to toast his guests.

"Everyone! Could I have your attention? Please, family!"

The group simmered down.

"I want to thank you all for coming out today to celebrate our bountiful life together. I know we've spent our lifetimes arguing whether we were copying the Gentiles," he gestured to Farmer, "But, I have always loved gathering at this time of year to share my gratitude for each and every one of you." He raised his glass higher. "To the Maxwells!"

"To the Maxwell's!" the group chimed.

"L'Chaim! Let's eat!" toasted Farmer.

The food was passed, and the plates began piling high with deliciousness. Melinda tried to take in the entire room at once, her eyes darting from one person to another to watch them interact. She saw everyone sipping at their pre-dinner drinks and raising empty glasses to the help when they needed refilled. The food was delectable, nothing like she'd ever eaten. Textures and tastes that could only be afforded by families like this one. The crunch of chestnuts in the stuffing, whipped potatoes made with heavy cream and dotted with fresh chives, gravy so smooth it poured like tan paint. She savored bite after bite, admitting to herself this sure beat the hell out of a turkey sub and a bag of chips from the deli.

Miss M filled a plate but only took a couple bites of everything, then moved the rest around with her fork. Melinda was so enthralled with the rest of the table that she hadn't noticed her date had stopped imbibing. When she finally did, she leaned in and asked, "Are you ok, Miss M?"

The woman nodded and with a flick of her hand, dismissed the girl back to filling her guts and watching the show. Melinda tilted her head toward Miss M and said, "This isn't as bad as you said it would be."

Miss M smiled knowingly and replied, "Just wait a minute."

Within that minute, it began. Marta's husband fumbled a blob of mashed potatoes onto his silky black shirt and kicked away from the table as if a tarantula had dropped into his lap.

"Goddamnit!" he coughed, his mouth still full of the last bite he actually managed to get in.

Marta flung herself onto his lap, swatting at the bolus as if he were on fire.

"Jesus Joe! It's just mashed potatoes," Manny slurred. "Why do you have to scream like that?"

"Shut up, Manny! This is a silk shirt. I paid good money for this shirt!"

"Oh, he knows all about the silky shirts," interjected Marta's grown son, Cliff, with a snide smile.

"Leave him alone, Cliff!" Sam jumped in. "Mind your own business."

Marta defended her boy, "Don't talk to my son like that, Sam, you little punk!"

Now Gus was up. "Marta, you and Joe do this every time we sit down to eat. One of you starts something, then you get the whole damn family irate over it!"

"Ah siddown!" Hildy tried. "You're all being so loud!"

Miss M shot a privy look at Melinda, who was sitting motionless, mouth agape, watching the action unfold.

Ike attempted twice to restore calm to the table, but the group was too far gone to reel them back in. Farmer put his head in his hands and his date rubbed his back and kept on eating. Miss M tapped Melinda on the leg and shook her head, signaling she'd had enough. Melinda wiped her mouth and slipped out from the table, helped the old woman to her feet, and the two snuck out undetected as the mayhem ensued. The same stranger who had greeted them now helped them into their coats and assisted them to their car.

As he reached for her door to shut her inside, he said softly, "Goodnight, ladies."

"You'll have to excuse that lot," Miss M said sincerely. "They were raised better than that."

She wouldn't speak again until they were nearer her neighborhood, and she was sure the conversation wouldn't be a long one.

"I'm sorry I put you through that, Melinda."

"What? I'm fine. The food was unbelievable, and the entertainment was rare and unique."

"You have to work with those people. I don't want you to lose respect for my children."

They drove a little way longer in silence, then Miss M said, "I suppose they aren't as bad as some. And they are all I have. I just wish you could have known us when their father was alive. We were all so very different."

"Really? How?"

"Oh… in lots of ways, I guess."

They pulled into her drive.

"That's for another night. I think you've had enough of the Maxwells for one day."

"I'd love to hear about it sometime. I have so few stories about my family. Yours *have* to be more interesting than mine."

Miss M let Melinda walk her to the stoop, then got herself into the house and thanked her for being such a good sport. Melinda drove home confused about how she felt about the whole experience. She felt a little sorry for the Maxwells. It was as if they were completely oblivious to the significance of having each other. She entered the house feeling more alone than she could ever remember. Even with all the fighting and drinking and dysfunction, those people had people, and she knew what that was worth.

December

After Thanksgiving, the rides to and from work required less of the distraction the radio had provided for the women, and Melinda and Miss M really began to communicate. It was small talk at first, Miss M having provided a new cast of characters for Melinda to ask after, but then it grew to deeper subjects. One morning in early December, the topic turned briefly to religion.

"Isaak followed all the Jewish traditions with his first wife," explained Miss M.

"First wife? I don't know that I ever heard he was married before," Melinda confessed.

"Yes. Beryl. I only saw her once or twice from the window of my father's barbershop across from the school." She took a minute with the memory. "She was stunning."

Melinda smiled at her friend's nostalgia. "What happened?"

"She died giving birth to their son, Jacob. And after that I guess you young people would say, he broke up with God." She thought for a moment and drew a familial comparison. "Come to think of it, my dad did the same thing. They both just lost their faith."

"That's heart-breaking," said Melinda. "What happened to baby Jacob? Is that sad too?"

"Don't be such a sap, Melinda. Babies die!"

The words struck Melinda's spine like an electric shock, and her energy turned on a dime. Miss M felt the shift and knew she'd trod onto something she shouldn't have. She flipped nervously through lines in her head to excuse herself or redirect the conversation, but only sat in the awkward silence created by the quiet swelling between them.

She couldn't look at the girl, but she sensed heat emanating from the driver's seat. She wasn't sure if she'd hurt her feelings or pissed her off until they pulled into the back lot behind the school and Melinda turned off the car and unbuckled, then looked at her and said, "Here we are."

The young woman's eyes were glossed with restrained tears and her cheeks and neck blotchy red. The elder concluded it was probably a mixture of hurt *and* mad.

"I didn't mean…" Miss M tried.

Melinda cut her off, "No, ma'am. I know."

Melinda shook it off during the course of the day as she had any time someone unknowingly struck that particularly sensitive nerve in the past. She was used to it. How could you tell by looking at her she had endured six miscarriages, two in the last year, and the two before that as late as the second and third trimesters? The scars of loss aren't always visible. She didn't quit on life like Hildy or cheat on her spouse like Gus or chain smoke like Deidre. She left no outward clue how deeply her grief flowed beneath her everyday life. Miss M had no idea the thing she said could hurt her friend so deeply.

Miss M struggled with the misstep all day. She stewed over it through lunch with Marta and continued punishing herself clear up until she joined Melinda in the car to go for home that night.

The young woman plopped down in the warming car after clearing the windshields of their winter load and Miss M grabbed her arm when she reached to engage the gears.

"Wait!" she sounded much sharper than she meant to. "Sorry, Melinda. But could you wait a moment until we start for home? I'd like to ask you something. Well, I'd like to tell you something first," she fumbled, confusing them both.

"Miss M, what's going on? Are you ok?"

"No. I'm trying to tell you I'm sorry. I'm sorry for what I said this morning." She hung her head, shaking it. "I could tell that I upset you and I wouldn't have done that for the world. You just have to forgive me for what I said."

Melinda had turned to look out her window for fear of tearing up again and realized the sincerity in the old girl's voice warranted more respect than that. She turned back to face her and was met with the most human version of this woman yet. Now Miss M was wet-eyed and red in the face. She was truly contrite.

"Miss M," Melinda began, grabbing her friend's hands in hers. "It's alright. You didn't know. You didn't mean anything by it. I know you didn't. Please don't beat yourself up about that. I forgot all about it."

"No. Now, Melinda, it's true I didn't know why it upset you. How could I know?"

"I know. It's ok, really."

"No. You don't understand. I *want* to know. I want to know about your baby."

Melinda's energy changed again, but in a wholly different way. She softened. She warmed. Someone was asking about her baby... not her failed pregnancy... her *baby*. She smiled a curious smile. It wasn't joy she felt, or even relief to share the pain with someone. She felt both a sense of vulnerability and validation at the same time.

She felt seen.

They sat in the car while the parking lot emptied and the early darkness of winter in Ohio nestled in around them. No radio. Just friends talking with one another.

"We didn't start trying right away. Brady wanted to get a little money in the bank. He's very responsible like that."

"I think I like him. Go on."

"We were married for two years when we got pregnant the first time. It was spring of '89. We were so excited."

"I bet."

"He started clearing his weights out of the tiny second bedroom at the apartment. I signed us up for Lamaze classes. They teach them at the Y."

"Marta and Joe went to those when they had Cliff," added Miss M. "Marta loved that kind of thing."

"Well, we didn't get to go. I lost that first one just inside the second month."

"That's awful. How did your husband react?"

"He cried."

Miss M nodded, "Men. They take things so hard."

"He cried for weeks. He didn't think I knew, but I could hear him in the shower, in the garage, when he took the trash out at night. It broke his heart."

"Of course, it did, Melinda. But honey, what about you?"

"I was in shock. I had just started to think that I would have a real family, you know? And then, just like that, it was gone."

"What did Helen say about it?"

Melinda smiled, "You knew my Aunt Helen. She was very matter of fact. She told me not to waste my time wondering why, just do what comes next."

"That sounds like Helen."

"The doctor said I was fine to try again as soon as we were ready. Needless to say, we waited a little."

"So, they couldn't tell you why you couldn't carry the baby?"

"No. We got the 'these things happen'… 'you're perfectly healthy'… 'there's no reason to think you can't get pregnant again and have a perfectly healthy baby'."

"So, you tried again. When?"

"We tried again at the end of that same year and lost that one in the following February. On Valentine's Day!"

"Oh no! That must have been awful. Were you celebrating?" Miss M asked, teasing.

"No, thank God! Miss M, you surprise me!"

"What, an old woman can't think about sex? Isn't all this because of sex?"

"Dear Lord!" Melinda looked up to the dotted headliner in the car. "If we'd have lost a baby after having sex, Brady might have killed himself."

"Oh no. Poor Brady."

"So that was early 1990. We didn't try again that year."

"No one could blame you for that."

"We actually wouldn't go again until the end of the summer of '92. I waited to tell Brady until I was two months along, and we waited to tell anyone else until close to the end of the second trimester. I remember we told Aunt Helen on Thanksgiving."

"You mean *Thursday*?" They giggled at their private joke.

"Right. We told Aunt Helen on a Thursday and Brady called her from the emergency room a couple of weeks later. I was so far along, I had to have a D&C after that one."

"What's a D&C again?"

"I forget what it stands for. Aunt Helen called it my dusting and cleaning."

"Ha!" the sharp loud sound escaped Miss M before she could catch it. "Sorry, Melinda. I know this isn't funny."

"You're good. Aunt Helen *was* funny. She just wouldn't let me get depressed about it, you know?" Melinda thought about her aunt for a quiet moment and confessed, "I never thought of her as particularly nurturing but in her own weird way, she really was taking the best care of me. She didn't want to see me crack up over something I couldn't control."

Miss M nodded knowingly. "That's taking care of your people alright. I wish I could have done that with Hildy. That was an awful mess she found herself in."

Melinda waited for what she thought would be more of the story, but Miss M dismissed it and returned her attention to the babies.

"Sorry. So, you had the D&C and did they discover anything wrong then?"

"Nope. Still told me it would happen. Just no real reason it hadn't." She calculated the time in her head for a moment, then continued, "We decided to quit trying for a bit. I went to work at the library. I thought maybe if I was too busy to

146

dwell on it, I might relax and get it done. Then in '94, we were positive again. I carried her until the end of the first week of my third trimester."

"Her?"

"We had the ultrasound and found out it was a girl." Melinda's head dropped, and she pulled at the tips of her gloves. "She was the only one I carried long enough to know. That one was really hard. It's different when you can see them on that x-ray."

"I can only imagine," offered Miss M. "Of course, they didn't have any of that fancy-schmancy technology when I was having children. Things are so crazy these days." She saw the young woman was having trouble going on from where she'd left off. "What was her name?"

Melinda spoke without looking away from her gloves, "Annie."

Miss M reached for her hands. "Sweet baby, Annie."

Melinda clamped her hand down on top of Miss M's and looked into her face, with tears streaming down her own. "I was so in love with the thought of being her mom."

The tears poured from them both and Miss M scrambled in her purse for a hankie while Melinda tried to go on, sobbing and croaking out the details.

"I talked to her every day and told her all about her sweet dad and her crazy Aunt Helen. I read to her…"

Miss M recovered some loose Kleenex and shared them with the crying girl.

"I thought for sure this was going to be the one I got to keep." She wiped her eyes and her breathing stuttered back to normal. "I even wrote a poem about her."

"Really? I didn't know you wrote poetry?" Miss M said, refolding her tissue to blot the last of her tears off her own flushing cheeks.

"I don't. I felt her disconnecting from me. It was awful and meant to be, I guess. But I just got up in the middle of the night one night after I lost her and started writing. It's dumb. I've never told anyone about that. Brady doesn't even know I did it. I've never shown it to him. It would break his heart all over again."

"Brady sounds like the best people, Melinda."

Their tears had subsided, and they were glowing in the swirling love and loss of Melinda's story.

"He is the finest man I know, Miss M. It's just that simple," she grinned. "That's what we say. We say, 'I love you, it's just that simple.'."

"I like that. That's what love should be."

Melinda's head bobbed in agreement. She inhaled deeply and resolved to finish her account.

"So, after Annie, we didn't try again until December, a year ago. Is that right?" she questioned herself, then confirmed. "Yes. Because we found out right before Aunt Helen had her fall in January of this year. We didn't tell her right away to keep from worrying her and by the time we got her home, we lost that one too."

"Stress probably," guessed Miss M.

"Probably. That was a stressful time. Aunt Helen didn't do well after she was laid up. She didn't know how to *not* do anything."

"That was Helen Harper!" Miss M remembered. "Man! That girl was a doer!"

"Yes, she was. But what a bear to try and take care of when she couldn't do any more. It like to have killed us all."

"Did she recover in one of those nursing-rehab joints?"

"That lasted exactly four days from the time she was discharged from the hospital. She checked herself out and demanded we come take her home. She said she could do the exercises at home and didn't have to stomach that terrible food."

"Hospital food *is* the worst."

"No, my Aunt Helen's food was the worst. She ate more fried bologna than any other meat!"

"Did she grow up poor?"

"I don't know much about how she grew up, but she certainly made enough money to buy a chicken breast or a pork chop now and again."

They laughed again at Aunt Helen's expense and Melinda kept on to the end of her story.

"We took a three-day weekend trip to Virginia Beach at Easter this past year. Aunt Helen was on her feet using her walker and she contended she was ok on her own. I guess I was pretty exhausted from everything because I remember Brady and Aunt Helen *both* insisting that he get me out of town. The winter wears on me anyway, but this was a rough winter, to be sure."

"Last winter?"

"Yes, this past winter. So, we drove down Good Friday and drove back on Easter Sunday. It was nice. It was gray but much warmer and I got to put my toes in the sand. That was a treat."

"Never been much of a beach person. Sand is just dirt. Like walking in a giant ashtray."

"It was nice," Melinda insisted. "We weren't trying that time, but a couple of weeks later, I peed on another stick and there were those two pink lines again."

"Did you tell Helen about *that* one?"

"No. We still don't know what went on when we went down south, but when we came back, something had changed. She really went downhill fast after that."

"Physically?"

"Physically, mentally. I think she fell again and hit her head. Brady asked her and she emphatically denied it. But she was different. She just wasn't as sharp and she quit eating. It was awful. I didn't have the energy to cry over losing that baby. I was too worried about what was happening with her."

"Was that your last one?"

"Yes. That was it."

"How long did Helen last after that?"

"That was April and we buried her right before I started at the academy, so... four months."

Miss M shook her head, sorry for the end Helen Harper met. With every one of her peers who went on ahead of her, she felt her own mortality. She was older than Helen by twenty years, but their circles overlapped some in their adult lives and that has a way of evening out the discrepancies of age and class. She'd have never guessed about the bologna.

Melinda felt as if she had been exorcised. Staring out at the snow, crossing into the beams of her headlights cutting through the dark parking lot, she could breathe. She hadn't felt that relaxed in as long as she could remember. She smiled at her passenger. "Thank you, Miss M."

The old lady smiled back.

"I can't tell you what it means to me that you took the time to ask me about the babies. You just don't know what it means."

"I know what loss is, sweet girl. Everybody does. Now what do you say we get home before we freeze to death in this wretched parking lot and the bums eat us like TV dinners?"

They laughed at that one all the way home.

Caldwell called Melinda at school one blustery Friday in the middle of December to let her know she wouldn't have heat that night when she returned from work. A part they needed to update the furnace wouldn't be in until Monday, so she'd need to find somewhere else to stay to be safe. It worried her to leave the house unattended and cold in the middle of winter, but he assured her he wrapped all the pipes and it would be safe until he could get back to it. She sat in the conference room at lunch, calling around for hotel rooms. She hated to spend the money, but she didn't have anywhere else to go.

Kitt found her halfway through her chore and started in. "There you are! I looked for you to go to Tiny's again today. He asked after you."

"I wish I could have gone with you, Kitt. Next time."

"What are you doing up here?"

"My contractor called and said I can't go home tonight. The furnace won't be functioning until Monday."

"Ooh. It's supposed to get down to freezing this weekend. Where are you going to stay?"

"I've been calling all over Cleveland to get a room, and they're all booked."

"Yeah. Cavs have a home game tonight. My boys are all coming home to watch with their dad."

"That figures."

"Hey! Why don't you come to my place?" Kitt offered. "We always do up a big pot of barbeque and the kids bring their girlfriends. It'll be fun."

"That's so sweet of you," Melinda admitted. "But it sounds like you'll have a houseful. Would there even be room?"

"You might be right," Kitt agreed with a laugh. "There's barely enough room for me in my own kitchen when those kids come home. Still, we'd make a hole for you, even if you had to sleep in the bathtub!"

"I'll keep it in mind, but if it's all the same to you, I'm going to keep looking for a room somewhere."

"Suit yourself," she said. "Offer still stands."

Melinda smiled at what a good friend she'd made in Kitt. For a split second she imagined herself surrounded by mammoth men like Tiny, shouting at the TV while the basketball game went on into the night. That *would* make for a raucous weekend. It was good to have a last resort that wasn't the all-night laundry mat, but she'd keep trying for something else.

At the end of class, Melinda quizzed her students on affordable hotels in their areas, explaining her plight. A few had suggestions she hadn't tried, and she noted them on a scrap of paper to call when she went home to pack.

When Kitt walked with Melinda and Miss M to the parking lot after school, she checked in on her friend's progress.

"Did you find any rooms for the weekend, Melinda?"

"No, but a few of my students gave me names I hadn't tried at lunch. I'll find something."

"Offer still stands to hole up at my place. Nobody has more fun than us!"

"I'm sure of it." Melinda got Miss M settled in the front seat of the car and called back to Kitt, "Thanks again for the offer. I'll call you if I need you!"

Kitt waved behind her head and disappeared into the exiting traffic.

While the car warmed, Miss M questioned her driver, "What was all that about a room?"

"My contractor dismantled my furnace and can't get a part it needs to put it back together until Monday. He called to tell me it wouldn't be safe to stay in the house this weekend."

"What was Kitt saying about it?"

"She offered to put me up but her kids are coming in to watch the basketball game and it doesn't sound like she'll have enough -..."

"You can stay with me," Miss M interrupted.

Melinda's head snapped to look at her passenger.

"Why wouldn't you?" she asked. "I'm all alone in that big house and I have plenty of room... and heat."

"Miss M, I couldn't impose on you like that. I will find a room."

"Maybe. Or maybe you'll have to sleep in Kitt's bathtub."

"She said that! She said they'd make room even if I had to sleep in the bathtub."

"Yeah. It's settled. You're staying with me."

"Ok," Melinda agreed. "But only if you let me cook you dinner."

"Oh Lord! That isn't necessary. We could order in or run through and get sandwiches somewhere."

"No, ma'am, I insist!" Melinda was emphatic. "I was taught to return a kindness of this magnitude. I'll drop you off, then go get my things and swing by the supermarket and get back. You *have* to let me do this."

"Ok," Miss M relented. "Whatever you need to do."

"I'm glad that's settled… and thank you."

The house was already cold when she got around to pack the things she'd need for her brief stay away. She changed the message on the machine so Brady wouldn't worry when he called for their weekly Friday night wrap up. She shivered as she locked up and started toward Shulman's for the supplies she needed for dinner. Melinda's cooking was good enough for Brady and Aunt Helen, but she realized while she shopped, she hadn't cooked for anyone else… ever. She found a nice round steak and some beautiful green peppers, rare at this time of year in the Midwest, and thought she could put a nice braciole together. She also grabbed stuff for breakfast and some sandwich fixings so she wouldn't have to go back out. That ought to be enough for a couple of days. She checked out and allowed the bagger to help her load everything in her car.

Miss M left the side door unlocked and called to her to come on in when she knocked, her hands full of brown bags. Melinda finagled her way into the kitchen and returned to the car a couple more times until all her parcels were dispatched. Miss M wandered into the room after the chore was complete and asked what she could do.

"Not a thing, Miss M. You go about your usual Friday night routine and I'll have dinner on the table in about an hour-forty."

"Alright. Let me know if you need any help."

"Yes ma'am," Melinda agreed, shuffling her out of the way.

She unpacked the bags, folding and stowing them in a space already stuffed with some in the tiny boot room she passed through from the side door into the kitchen proper. Turning the oven on, she located a pan in the drawer below it. She opened cabinet doors and drawers to find a mallet and string for the meat and retrieved the knives she needed for cutting the vegetables with which to stuff it. Melinda was impressed with the logical way Miss M laid out her kitchen. She only had to look once or twice to find the things she needed. The waxed paper and foil were naturally in the bottom drawer nearest the stove, the big spoons and spatulas were in a deep drawer on the opposite side, and the spices were just above in the cabinet to the right. She felt quite at home.

Melinda toiled away at the meal while Miss M changed out of her street clothes into lounging pajamas and fuzzy slippers. She took a book from her nightstand and made her way back to the living room to get comfortable in her chair near the fireplace.

Once Melinda had the dish in the oven, she washed up, took her bag, and found her host to ask where she could put her things.

"At the top of the stairs, first door on your left."

"Great, thanks," Melinda chirped. She stopped and turned around before she was out of the room to thank her friend again, properly. "Seriously, Miss M I can't thank you enough for doing this. I really appreciate it."

"I know, I know. I just hope this dinner is worth waiting for."

"It will be, I promise!" she grinned and crossed her fingers. "I hope!"

She bounded up the wooden stairs, running her hand along the railing to the newel posts marking the landings, then slowed to enter the long hall at the top. Taking inventory of all the closed doors she reached for the knob to the first one on her left. She felt for a switch inside the doorframe and flipped it on to illuminate a sizeable space with tall windows and heavy woodwork that matched the simple but well-made designs in the rest of the house. A queen-size bed sat centered between the frames and a floral rug took up most of the hardwood floor, save a strip about six inches wide, all around the room. One dresser faced the bed from behind the door to the left and closet doors stood centered on the wall to the right. An easy chair shared a table with the bedside and filled the outside corner of the closet wall. She walked in, sat on the bed, bounced once or twice to get a feel for the mattress, then popped off to examine the closet. It was gaping and empty as a tomb. Not so much as a hatbox or old suitcase on the shelf above the rod. A cluster of metal hangers clumped together in the center of the vacant space reminded Melinda that she needed to hang her work clothes up before they wrinkled to the point of needing an iron. God forbid! She stowed the rest of her things in the empty dresser and noted the room once again. Nothing on the walls. No family photos or art of any kind or doilies on the dresser or bedside table. No throw pillows accenting the bed. The walls were covered in a white on white wallpaper pattern, barely discernable in the dim light of the fixture overhead. It was curious to Melinda that the family home of this pillar in the community wouldn't have shelves of priceless figurines, or antique framed art, or some decoration of sorts.

She shrugged it off to individual taste. Miss M was such a no-nonsense person out in the world, it only stood to reason that personal style would be reflected in her home.

She grabbed her cosmetic bag and, looking for the bathroom, wandered around the upper floor. The hall was only illuminated by two tiny candelabra-style sconces, barely enough to see much. She went to the room next to hers and found another simply appointed bedroom. She kept on to the next, at the end of the hall, and there it was. Depositing her bag on the vanity, she checked her face in the mirror. She only really looked at herself once a day when she applied her modest makeup in the morning. She was never really that concerned with her looks. Melinda was basically pretty, in the way that gets spoiled when too much attention is paid to it. She darkened her reddish lashes with a little mascara and covered her lips with a bit of color. Occasionally she brushed on a little eye shadow if she was feeling particularly fresh, but more often than not ended up wiping it off, feeling too conspicuous for comfort. But tonight, in the light of a strange bathroom, she studied her face for a moment. She leaned into the mirror and saw the creases under her eyes and around her mouth. Moving her hand across her cheek and up, she folded her hair behind her ear. She wasn't a girl anymore. That had been her truth for years, but every time she was reminded of it lately, she could hear the milling of the sand rapidly trickling through her hourglass.

She shook herself free and left it to the mirror to work it out. She joined Miss M in the living room, interrupting her reading.

"Should I start a fire?" she asked, taking a seat on the sofa opposite Miss M.

"If you like. It's gas." Miss M peered over her readers and admitted, "I haven't lit that thing since the dark ages. I'm not sure I know how."

"I'll figure it out," Melinda offered and kneeled down to the hearth to open the doors. "Here's the valve. Now all I need is a match. Where's the junk drawer?"

"What?"

"The junk drawer. You know where you keep your gum bands and paperclips."

Miss M looked confused.

"The place you throw old batteries and wheels that come off stuff. Your junk drawer."

"Why in God's name would anyone devote an entire drawer to junk? I do not have a junk drawer. I do not have junk."

Now Melinda was confused and feeling a little judged.

"Let's try this again. Miss M, where are your matches?"

"There are some in the toolbox in the boot room."

Melinda ducked back through the kitchen to the tiny space between it and the side door and spied sparse shelves with only one or two items each. She yanked on the pull-string to activate the overhead light to see better, located a red metal box on a low perch, opened it, and found a matchbox.

"Gottem!" she called back to her friend.

Melinda promptly returned to ignite the fireplace. She opened the flue and the match caught the gas and sent orange and blue flames surging up the chimney. She smiled triumphantly.

"Nice," said Miss M. "We can eat by firelight."

Melinda resumed her spot on the sofa and tapped her fingers together as Miss M went back to reading. Not wishing to interrupt her further, Melinda returned to the kitchen to check on dinner.

"About an hour to braciole, Miss M!" she called to no response.

She hiked her butt onto a stool she found neatly tucked under an empty countertop next to the refrigerator. She had paid little attention while she was cooking, but now she let her eyes wander the room and was reminded again at how little the woman had adorned her home. No clock. No trivets. Not even a pattern on the kitchen curtains. Plain white cabinets with mustard-yellow Formica countertops. There was a green-on-green pattern in the avocado linoleum, and one plain gold tea towel folded in a square on the counter by the sink.

This room was just as stark as the ones upstairs. She tried to remember what the walls in the living room looked like and left the stool to tiptoe toward the doorway through to where Miss M still read. She stopped just out of sight to spy around the room. Just as before, nothing but the essentials.

"What are you lurking around for?" barked Miss M. "Don't just skulk in the doorway, come in and sit down."

"I was trying not to disturb your reading."

"Anymore, you mean?"

"Sorry," Melinda said, and crossed to the sofa. "I know I told you to go about your usual business, but I thought maybe you'd want to talk."

Marking her book, Miss M put it on a table at her right elbow, took her glasses off and folded them in her lap.

"What shall we talk about?"

"Oh!" Melinda adjusted in her seat. "I was just admiring your home. It's beautiful."

"But you're wondering why I don't have all the trappings of wealth like that gaudy show in Ike's house?"

"Gaudy? I don't know if I'd call his style gaudy."

"Expensive, ornate, overdone. That is what I'd call it," said Miss M. "And gaudy!"

"Well, your place has such grand design and beautiful woodwork, I just assumed you'd have… you know… things about."

"Things?" asked Miss M.

"Décor. Like art or vases or accents."

"Junk."

"Some would call it stylish, Miss M."

"I would call it unnecessary. So, the answer to this question is the same as the one for why I don't have a junk drawer. I don't keep junk."

"You don't have any extra stuff anywhere?" Melinda asked.

"I raised six children in this house, Melinda," Miss M explained. "We had six beds, six dressers, six bicycles, doll houses, tree houses, bats, balls, go carts, roller skates. You name it, we had it… six times over! When each of my children grew up and out of the house, I told them to take whatever they wanted with them, but I wouldn't be keeping anything that didn't belong to me."

"And they did?"

"Ike left first, and he didn't believe me. I guess he thought I would stuff my attic full of his childhood things to feed the mice. I told him the night he moved out that whatever he didn't take with him would be on the curb by noon the next day."

"Miss M, you didn't!"

"No, *I* didn't. I made the other children carry it all down. Manny couldn't quit crying and stole away to phone him and rat me out, and he came back around sundown that night to gather it up. Sam and Manny helped him. Manny was scared he'd never come back home, but Sam kept saying 'She told you to take what you wanted'."

Melinda's face took on a sympathetic shape, and Miss M jumped her. "Don't look like that, Melinda! You do not know what it's like to have that much stuff under your feet all the time."

"I'll bet you didn't have any trouble with the others when they left, did you?"

"That's precisely why I enlisted them to do the heavy lifting. They never forgot it. And no, I didn't have a smidge of trouble from any of them after that."

"Well, it does seem to have been effective," the girl agreed. "So, you're telling me that your attic is as barren as your basement?"

"My basement! When have *you* seen my basement?"

"Halloween, when I shimmied down through the window… remember?"

"Yes, yes, yes," Miss M agreed. "And again, yes, my attic is clean, my basement is clean, my garage is clean, and I don't have a junk drawer. There are you satisfied?"

Melinda shook her head in disbelief.

"The less I leave behind, the less those ungrateful children of mine will have to fight over."

Melinda's face returned to its sympathetic shape but this time she felt sorry for Miss M. She thought it must be pure torture to love your family and feel like they're only devotion to you is attached to what you'll be leaving them when you die.

"Well, (A) I think you'll be the last man standing and (B) if you *do* go before any of them, what makes you think they wouldn't want some little thing to remember you by?" Melinda wanted that for them and hoped, "I think you're selling them short."

"If they want something, they can have the pictures," Miss M conceded.

"What pictures?" Melinda looked around the room. "I haven't seen any pictures."

"They used to be in the room off my bedroom downstairs, but I had my bathroom redone when I got my step-in tub and had them moved to the bedroom at the top of the stairs."

Melinda retraced her steps in the upstairs hall and remembered she tried every door on the left side of the hall, but that left two more on the right. One of *those* was the picture room. The timer buzzed on the oven and she dropped the subject, determined to get back to it after dinner.

When she plated the meal, Miss M sent her back to the boot room for two TV trays stowed neatly in a space between the shelves and the wall. They sat by the fire and enjoyed the meal, talking small about recipes and produce, like girlfriends.

When they finished, Miss M was full and sleepy.

"Oh! My Lord, Melinda," she said. "That was the best meal I've had in years."

"Thank you," Melinda swelled with pride as she gathered their dishes and disappeared back into the kitchen. "I'm so glad it turned out. Sometimes my cooking is hit or miss."

Miss M stood and folded her tray up and handed it off to Melinda upon her return.

"Sorry to eat and run, but I'm beat. You stay by the fire as long as you like, but I've got to get to bed."

Melinda took the tray from her and excused her. "Of course. Goodnight Miss M."

"Night Melinda."

Melinda washed and dried the dishes, determined to leave the kitchen as pristine as she found it, then reclined by the fire. She laid her head back on the arm of the couch and watched the flames. The gas fire was nice, but it lacked the smell of burning wood and the flicker and pop that a 'real' fireplace provides. Still, she found herself warmed and relaxed by it. Her mind doubled back to the pictures Miss

M spoke of and imagined a few thin albums stacked neatly on a shelf in one of the remaining bedrooms. She inventoried the things she kept after her mom and dad died, their bowling balls, all three birthday cards they gave her, his American flag lapel pin, her pearl clip-on earrings. She had a tiny trove of forget-me-nots that fit in her jewelry box, except the bowling balls. Surely Miss M would grant her children some little piece of their lives with her. She stayed put for only another moment, then her curiosity got the best of her. She jumped to extinguish the fire and headed up the stairs.

Miss M was just drifting off when she heard the door squeak and knew her houseguest was snooping. She grinned to herself.

"I guess we'll have to talk all about *that* in the morning."

✹

Morning could not have come any faster for Melinda. After her discovery the night before, she was dying to talk more about the pictures. She was up by first light, dressed, and down the stairs in a hot minute.

Miss M was already up and in the kitchen, pouring her third cup of coffee.

"Good morning. Get yourself a cup," she said nonchalantly as she tucked the freshly delivered copy of *The Sun Press* under one arm and headed for the dining room. "I always have my coffee at the table while I read the headlines."

Melinda rolled her eyes and plucked a mug out of the cabinet to pour her share. She waited all night to ask her and now had to wait until she was done reading the paper. She cringed under the weight of her impatience and reset herself to join Miss M in the dining room.

She took a seat across from the old girl and sipped at her coffee, drumming her fingers on the side of the cup while she waited. Miss M sipped slowly and read slowly, never looking up at her eager guest. She folded the pages of the paper back and forth and perused at her leisure, sure she was tormenting Melinda beyond the edge of fair play.

When she finished a section of the paper, she offered it up. "Do you want to read any?"

"No, ma'am. I'm fine," Melinda answered, jittering from the caffeine and anticipation.

When she'd had her fun, Miss M reassembled the daily and clasped her hands over its folded pages and smiled, "So you want to know about the pictures?"

"YES!"

"It's going to cost you another cup of coffee."

Melinda grabbed her friend's cup, racing back to the kitchen, then returned in a minute with a top-off and bated breath.

"Those are all my pictures."

"Miss M, there have to be forty or fifty boxes. Are you telling me that every one of those boxes is full of photo albums?"

"No, of course not. They're not in albums," the old woman confessed. "They're just loose in all those boxes. Those are my picture boxes."

"You don't have them in albums?" asked Melinda.

"No. I had a handful of photographs from my childhood and my early days with Isaak. You know, my wedding picture and things like that, and I kept them in a small wooden box on my desk," she explained. "Then when the children were born, we just took more and more pictures and I needed more and more boxes."

Melinda's mouth hung open.

"So, those are my picture boxes."

"Miss M, your children will want those pictures!"

"Nah!" she dismissed the thought. "They won't even bother going through those. They wouldn't take the time."

She felt a little like she was intruding and a lot like she was badgering this old woman, but Melinda couldn't quit pressing.

"Miss M, if you were to take the time to organize those photographs, marking them with dates and the places they were taken, I guarantee your children would appreciate it. Those pictures have to mean something to you or you would have gotten rid of them a long time ago. I'm sure they'll mean something to *them* too. They will be a reminder of the best times between you."

Miss M was flabbergasted. How this tiny, waif of a thing could come into her life, into her home, and make such accurate assumptions about her and her family was beyond her understanding.

She felt exposed, but safe at the same time. She trusted Melinda.

"Miss M?"

She snapped back to respond.

"I suppose I could try and go through them."

"I could help you!" Melinda offered insistently. "I can go to the camera store on Euclid. They have the nicest albums and they have little tags and things you can use to label everything."

"I don't want anything fancy. "

"No ma'am, I know. I was going to look for plain black or navy blue."

"Something like that would be fine," agreed Miss M. "Go get my pocketbook and I'll send you with a blank check."

Melinda ran for the purse, grabbed her coat and gloves and headed off, passionate about her mission.

Miss M stewed a moment after she left, then dressed and readied for the day.

Melinda hurried through the cold Cleveland air to accomplish her errand and beat it back to begin. She couldn't remember being this excited about anything in her recent past. She handed over the check at the counter for an even dozen photo albums and the bits with which to label them.

Back at the house, Miss M picked her hair into shape and studied herself in the mirror. She saw the accentuated signs of aging that signaled the end of her eighty-ninth year. There were more and more with every decade. The lines on her forehead started around fifty-five. The peach fuzz and coarse chin hair showed up sometime in her sixties. Seventy brought the lip lines and fading eye color. And the turkey neck got more leathery when she turned the corner to eighty. The image of her own mortality stared at her from the reflection. It would do her good to remember the beauty of her youth. She hadn't looked at those pictures for years. The old girl smiled at the prospect of visiting her former self and traced her smile with Red Rose #3.

Melinda rushed the side door, bounding through the kitchen past Miss M at the coffeepot and into the dining room. She thrust the bags onto the table and began her report.

"I got twelve albums and everything we need to label the pictures. I thought that would be a good starting point."

Miss M walked calmly into the room to watch Melinda wildly releasing her arms from her coat and dumping the contents of the bags.

"Do you want to do it here, or should we go upstairs?"

"There's barely enough room to turn around in that room. If you think you can carry the boxes down, we can set it up here."

"Of course, I can!" Melinda squealed and dashed past her host to the stairs. She grabbed the first box closest to the door and made it back in no time, then went for a second before Miss M could object.

Once she delivered that one, Miss M slowed her down.

"Ok. That's enough for now. I brewed a fresh pot of coffee. Go fix us a cup and we can get started."

Melinda beamed. When she returned with the hot cups, Miss M opened a box.

"How are we going to do this?"

Melinda placed the coffee out of the way at the far end of the table and tipped the box to deliver a slurry of black and white and faded color photographs in front of her friend.

Then she laid out her idea for the project and moved around until they were side-by-side.

"You sit down right there, Miss M, and go through every picture. We'll make separate albums for you and each of the children. As you tell me which ones go where, I'll place them in the albums and label them. How about that?"

The old woman sat, then shrugged and said, "I guess that's as good a plan as any."

She took her cheaters from her pocket and began.

The project was off to a benign start as the first few pictures were just records of the typical life of a family like theirs. The hole in Sam's smile where he lost his first tooth. Hildy, a toddler with a messy piece of birthday cake on the tray of her highchair. A shot of the twins in full feathered headdresses in a grade school Thanksgiving pageant. Miss M impressed her helper with the dates and details she recalled about each memory. After a few dozen photos, she came across one of her and her parents and she paused. Melinda watched her face while she took it in.

"This is me with Mother and Dad boarding the boat to come to America."

The photo was stiffer and more yellowed than the others. The image, grainy and haunting, transported Miss M to another life.

"When was this taken?" Melinda gently asked.

"I was four when we left Germany, so 1914, just before The Great War broke out." She smiled. "Look at how beautiful they were." She handed the photo off to Melinda and leaned toward her to elaborate. "My dad was so dapper. I remember they wore the same hats and coats they wore when they were married to celebrate the voyage. It was a big deal."

"I've barely been out of Cleveland. I can't fathom what it was like to leave your home country."

"Mother didn't want to go." She took the photo back to keep telling the story. "I remember her crying for weeks before we sailed and Dad said she was just excited, but I think I knew even then that there was more to it than that." She watched the people in the photo as if they were speaking to her. "I remember hearing him trying to calm her. He'd say, 'Tensa, don't cry. We're going to be fine; you'll see.'."

"Tensa?"

"Her name was Hortense, but he called her Tensa," she remembered fondly.

"Was she worried about starting over in a strange land, or was it leaving her family?"

"She had no one left. Her parents were long gone. I only knew them as portraits on the mantel. And she had twin sisters that died when she was in her teens. That's who I'm named for."

"That's so sweet."

"Yes. I'm Emalina after Emma and Lina. They were four or five when they contracted influenza and died within hours of one another. Her parents never got over it. They both died within a year of burying the girls and Mother was alone in the world… until she met Dad."

"Your father was so handsome. But wasn't he worried about leaving Germany too?"

"He was Irish. Leonidas 'Laddie' Malloy. He had already left his home country to find work. He knocked around Europe for a while, then took an apprenticeship with a barber in Berlin."

"No wonder he looks so smart. He made other men look good for a living."

Miss M giggled at the memory of all the men she watched come in and out of her dad's chair.

"Man, you aren't kidding. Laddie Malloy could take a lump of coal and shave a diamond out of it."

The two women laughed.

"He was something. Always happy and smiling, very Irish. Never a cross word. I never heard him raise his voice or argue. He was just the salt of the earth, you know?"

"And what was your mother like?"

"She was something *else*. Very German. She was stoic and reserved. She wasn't big on hugging or kissing like Dad. But she did let me sit on her lap when she read to me."

"Aww."

"They were both big readers. They taught me to read by the time I was two. Dad especially. He wanted me to read everything I could get my hands on. That was what inspired him to move us."

"Reading?"

"The public libraries." She handed over the picture and took up her coffee cup. She sipped for a moment to wet her memory and then told it. "He grew up in a tiny town called Kilculliheen across the River Suir from Waterford. Andrew Carnegie was building libraries all over the English-speaking world at the time and pledged to build one in Waterford. He visited to lay the keystone and my dad borrowed his father's tugboat to get across to see him do it. Dad took a beating when he brought back the boat, but he said it was worth it. He was fascinated by the man and his philosophies. Carnegie thought that the only way for man to grow and evolve was to seek more and more knowledge and he thought that a populous that could read would be one that could solve its problems more intelligently, more peacefully. He was a staunch advocate for an end to all wars. He crusaded for peace."

"Is this the Carnegie Hall guy?" Melinda asked.

"One in the same, child. He was no less than a hero to my father. He wanted to raise me in Pittsburgh, Pennsylvania, where he read Carnegie lived."

"So, you lived in Pennsylvania?"

"We aimed for Pittsburgh and stayed there for several years. I started school there."

"When did you move to Cleveland?"

"I was… eleven when my mother became ill."

"Oh no. What was it?"

"No one could tell us. She became listless and depressed. She complained of stomach and head pain, and nothing seemed to help her. Then, after nearly a year, she was so weak she couldn't even do for herself and my father had had it with the local doctors."

"Oh my God! How terrifying."

"The Cleveland Clinic had just opened, and it was touting the finest doctors and treatments available in the country. So, my dad packed us up, and we headed west."

"I don't think I knew The Cleveland Clinic had been around that long. Did they help your mom?"

"They tried. They put her on a regimen of vitamins and medication to boost her appetite and encourage weight gain. She spent hours every day in the sunny solarium for fresh air and sun. They tested her and put her through all kinds of trials, but nothing seemed to help."

Melinda sat riveted by Miss M's story telling.

"I remember the last day we spent together. I visited after school and they had her in the solarium sipping ginger tea, all wrapped up in blankets because it was the middle of October… in Cleveland. She asked me to read to her. She knew I would have stopped by the library on the way to see her. That day I checked out Yeats' *The Wild Swans at Coole*. Yeats was my favorite. I think Dad liked it that my favorite was a fellow Irishman. I sat there forever, lost in the verse. She never said a word, just listened. I read every poem in the collection and when I was done, the nurse came to take her back to her room. She held my hand as I walked alongside the wheelchair until they went inside. I stood at the door for a long time, staring. Maybe I knew. I must have sensed it."

She stared ahead like she had when she was a girl. Then she breathed deep and leaned back toward the photo for one last look.

"I heard Dad answer the door to the barbershop downstairs that night. It was a messenger from the hospital… she was gone. He cried all night long. In the morning we went to church, lit a candle, and he told me. He said, 'It's only her body that's gone, darlin'. The rest we keep in our hearts and minds for all eternity.' That was the last time we were in the Catholic Church, or *any* church for that matter. She was cremated. He kept her ashes in his room and made me promise to mix them with his when he went on so they could be together forever."

Miss M thought about the loss and remembered something more.

"One night, not long after she passed away, there was a lunar eclipse. We had learned about it in school and my dad was insistent that we stay up to watch it. He set everything up on the roof of the barbershop before dark. We stayed up reading and listening to the radio until programming ended. Then we put our coats on over our pajamas and climbed the fire escape to the roof. We laid out our sleeping bags, blankets, and pillows. He brought a bag of chocolate-covered peanuts and a thermos of hot chocolate. We sat and talked about Mother by the light of a kerosene lantern."

"Your dad sounds like a doll baby!" said Melinda.

"He was so smart. He knew that losing my mother, as young as I was, might make me feel like I wasn't real or connected in the same way. So as we watched that eclipse, he explained how sometimes it's easy to question our importance when things can come and go in this life, important things like our mothers. Then we watched the shadow of the earth move in front of the moon and he said, 'See, there's the proof. We are here. We are still here.'"

Melinda felt her eyes well, and she put her hand on Miss M's and squeezed. "No matter how long they're gone, you miss them a little every day."

"That is something I wish you didn't know," Miss M said.

The young woman shrugged, "Life. Am I right?"

Miss M clapped her hand on top of Melinda's, "Right you are, my dear." She took in another deep breath and huffed it out. "What's next?"

Melinda worked diligently, recording every point of reference Miss M could conjure with each photo. She watched the old woman's face soften and change with every memory. Some took her back to her life before Isaak, others after the children were born, and still more of friends, now long dead, she made growing up in the apartment above the barbershop. The barber shop sitting directly across the street from the academy. The one left tattered and torn with neglect that Miss M passed every day to go into the school.

Miss M was finally telling her story and endearing her young friend with every turn.

The furnace part was delivered and installed first thing Monday morning. It ran all day, and the house was toasty by the time Melinda came home after school. Caldwell apologized for running her out and hoped it wasn't too much of an inconvenience. She assured him she wasn't put out in the least, that indeed she had a great weekend staying with friends. After the crew left, she fixed a bowl of oatmeal and looked over her students' work for a moment. Her mind wandered, and it wasn't any time at all before she was completely distracted.

"Where's your head, girl?" she asked herself aloud. She finished her cereal and rose to wash out her bowl. She looked out the kitchen window into the cold dark. "I wonder if she looked through any more of them?"

The words barely had time to leave her lips when the phone rang.

"Hello."

"Melinda, are you busy?"

"Miss M? Is that you?"

"Yes. It's me. Are you busy?"

"No ma'am. I just finished dinner. Is everything ok?"

"Of course, it is. I was just wondering if you don't have plans tonight, if you'd care to come back over and work on the pictures again."

"I'd love to! Do you need anything while I'm out?"

"No. Not a thing. I'll put some fresh coffee on."

"I'll be there in a few minutes."

"Be careful."

"Yes ma'am."

The side door was open and Melinda came in and hung her snowy coat and hat on a hook in the boot room and helped herself to coffee.

"I'm in the dining room!" Miss M called out. Melinda made it around the corner to see two fresh boxes sitting by the China cabinet.

"Miss M! What did you do?" Melinda was wild-eyed at the risk the old woman took to get those boxes down the steps.

"Relax. I drug them down one step at a time. I'm not completely helpless, you know."

"I know but, I said I was coming right over. You couldn't have waited?"

"I brought them down before I called you. I thought I could do some more myself, but it's so much easier when you do the labels and put them in the books."

"Ok. So, if we're doing this together, then you shouldn't need to bring any more boxes down by yourself. You'll wait for me next time, right?"

"Oh, Melinda! Don't talk to me like I'm a child. Do you want to help me or not?"

The young woman narrowed her eyes and took her place next to her friend. She blew on her hot cup and then nodded for her to proceed.

Miss M settled down into her chair and reached into the pile for more remembrances.

"This is me and Dad at my graduation from the academy. If you look closely, there in the background, that's Isaak looking at us. I didn't see this when we got the pictures developed. Do you know when I saw it?"

"When?"

"Right after Isaak died."

"Wow. That must have given you chills."

"It was strangely comforting."

"Were you two an item while you were a student?"

"No. He was adamant about not pursuing me until after I got my certificate. He told my father he would honor his wishes to see me educated."

"So, he asked for your hand? That's so romantic."

"Something like that," teased the old girl.

"Oh no, no, no. You can't do that. Something like *what*?"

Miss M squirmed in her seat, sipped at her coffee, then turned to face Melinda.

"I told you about Beryl and baby Jacob."

"The wife and son he lost? Yes, so sad."

"So, my dad's shop was a kind of gathering place for... shall we say, of a lot of Irish businessmen along Merrifield Road. A lot of businessmen that Isaak was in business *with*."

"Okay."

"When I was in high school, I can remember countless times that these men would talk shop in the barber chair. I could hear their conversations from the landing on the stairs. And every time the subject turned to money, Isaak Maxwell's name came up. Everyone in town knew him. He was a successful accountant with his own firm and ran the school; prominent in the community."

Melinda listened, rapt.

"One day, when the Merrifield Road businessmen were discussing some endeavor that was about to ensue, I heard an unfamiliar voice in the mix."

"Isaak!"

"Yes. I made up some excuse to go downstairs and interrupt so I could get a look at him. Needless to say, the conversation stopped dead when I popped in and Dad was furious. He obviously didn't want me around that element, but those people didn't scare me."

"Miss M are you talking about the Irish mob?" asked Melinda, fascinated.

"The Merrifield Road Gang. You've heard of them, I'm sure."

"My father-in-law followed their every move, according to Brady."

"They were not to be trifled with, and in hindsight, Isaak and I both should have taken them more seriously." Her face lost its shine, and she hardened against the ghosts in her head. "I saw Isaak up close that day for the first time and he was so handsome. Jet black wavey hair, a powerful jaw, and the most beautiful blue eyes you could ever imagine."

"He sounds gorgeous."

"He was." She looked at the blurry image in the shadows behind her and her father and ran her fingertip over it. "He and Beryl were newly married then, and I could enjoy my secret crush, knowing I was safe from ever having to act on it. But then he lost them both, and he was just… broken. I would see him coming and going from the academy and he looked like the soul had drained out of him. My dad mourned my mother, but this was different. He was like the walking dead."

"That's so awful. I don't know how anyone recovers from that depth of grief."

Miss M looked at Melinda with surprise. "Yes you do, honey."

Melinda acknowledged the credit and smiled.

"One night, after running around with my friends in the pouring rain, they dropped me off in front of the shop. I was under the awning searching for my key when I noticed someone banging around at the front door of the school. My first instinct was to go in and get Dad up, but then I heard his voice. It was Isaak. He was drunk and crying in the rain. It broke my heart to see him like that and in the next moment, I was running across the street to his side. I helped him to his feet and slung his arm over my shoulder to get him back across Merrifield Road to the barbershop. He was a mess. He kept saying that he was sorry, that he couldn't save them, that it hurt so bad. I got him into the shop and he slumped into the barber chair and wept." She shook her head. "I didn't know what to do with him. I reclined the chair to keep him from sliding out onto the floor, then went to the back room and brought the coffeepot up front and plugged it in to try and sober him up. While it percolated, I pulled and tugged at him until I got some of his wet things off. I managed his coat, his shoes, and his socks. I toweled him off the best I could and hung his wet things over the radiator to dry. He must have realized he was in the barbershop because he kept saying, 'Laddie, what can I do?' I was afraid he'd wake my dad, and I knew he didn't want anyone else to see him like this, so I warmed a towel and wrapped his face in it. He was so drunk I think he thought he had come in for a haircut. I went in the back to get us some cups and when I came back, he was out like a light."

She stopped telling it for a moment and smiled like a schoolgirl.

"I tiptoed around that chair and took that towel off his wonderful sad face and just stared at him. The depth of his grief was coming from the depth of the love he had for that poor girl. His face was ravaged by both. I felt so helpless in the moment. Then I did the only thing I could think of to comfort him. I gave him a straight razor shave."

"How romantic is that!" Melinda swooned.

"It kind of was. We were all alone in that dark barber shop with the rain drumming on the awning out front. As I smoothed the shaving cream on his cheeks, he opened his eyes a little and smiled, then went right on sleeping. I took my time and was as careful as could be. I gave him a good shave. Close and clean. When I was done, I wrote a little note and put it by the coffeepot, *Help yourself, Emalina.*

"What then?"

"I went to bed and when I woke up the next day, the shop was empty, and he had taken the note. He told me on our wedding night that with that one act of kindness and the two little words on that note *Help yourself,* everything changed. He felt like living again. And he did. *We* did. We were meant for each other. I may not know much about how or why things happen, but that I know for sure."

"This one is going in your personal album Miss M," Melinda said as she carefully placed the photograph in the book.

"Me and Dad and Isaak, academy graduation, Spring of 1930. Write that on the label."

They went back to the pile for the next round and found vacations, more birthdays, bar mitzvahs, and holidays with menorahs and decorated trees. Melinda imagined their family traditions blending and budding into a uniqueness all their own.

"So, you raised the children across both religions?" asked Melinda.

"I guess you could say that," answered Miss M. "His family didn't like it much that he married outside his faith but by then he was only celebrating the high holy days for his mother's sake anyway. And none of the kosher stuff, his favorite food was a BLT."

"Is it shiksa?" Melinda asked carefully, making her friend laugh.

"Yes, Melinda. I am what they'd call a shiksa."

"But they warmed up to you?"

"His father died soon after we were married. And his mother, who had been so hard to win over in the beginning, told me right before she passed away that she was grateful to me for bringing her son back to her. So, I think it all evened out in the end."

"In-laws are a lot, I guess. Brady's people died right after we got together. They were old when they had him, so he never imagined them being around when he was grown. I only met them a couple of times."

"It's sad he lost his people so young, but I'm glad you didn't have to put up with any foolishness from somebody else's parents."

"Yes, me too."

"What about *your* parents, Melinda?" Miss M asked innocently.

Melinda went silent.

She found herself in another moment, like the one in the car. Only this time she didn't feel grateful for the question. She felt ambushed. She was so deep into Miss M's family story that she disconnected all together from her own. As safely as they had unpacked her friend's past, Melinda just didn't feel the same level of security in revealing all of hers. She portioned out just enough to satisfy the question.

"I don't remember much. I was only three when they died."

Her flat tone put an abrupt end to any more queries on the matter. Miss M read her loud and clear and wasn't about to put her foot in her mouth a second time with this sensitive girl. The subject changed back to the next adventure displayed in black and white, and that little bump in the road was long forgotten by the end of the night.

Melinda and Miss M would gather again twice more before the Wednesday, before Christmas Eve, and the weekend that marked the beginning of their holiday break from school. And while they were only about halfway through the pictures, Miss M was growing more and more excited about turning them over to her children. They would have liked to have had them done in time for holiday gifts, but the sheer volume of the project would take longer. Melinda assured her friend that as soon as they came back from break, they would think of an impressive way to surprise the family with the albums. She saw the old woman safely into her home, then sprinted for the car.

Brady was coming home!

The house was dark save the dwindling candlelight from the tapers all but melted on the dining room table. Melinda was folded over at her place at the table, set with Aunt Helen's China, sound asleep when Brady tiptoed in. The smell of pot roast wafted from the slow cooker and permeated the whole place. He drew in the scents of home and knelt down next to his wife.

"Honey," he whispered. "I'm home."

She rolled off her arm and ran her hands through her hair in a stretch. He grabbed her ribs and kissed her open neck. She wrapped her arms around him and took in *his* scent.

"I made a roast, baby," she said in his ear. "Are you hungry?"

"Not for roast."

He barely got out all the words before he devoured her mouth with a passionate kiss, lifting her into his arms and carrying her up the stairs to their bedroom.

"Watch your head!" she warned just before he ducked under the new trim.

They locked lips again and heated with the longing of their separation. He took her in the comfort of their old room. His desire was pressing, but his touch was as gentle as always, and she matched his lust with her own appetite. It had been so long since she felt the weight of him or the stroke of his hand; she trembled at the contact. His skin prickled with electricity when he held her naked body tight against his. Making love had always been about more than sex to them both, but tonight they let their bodies go for what they needed with abandon. They peaked and dove in again and again to exhaust all their cravings, then lay spent and panting to catch their breath.

Neither of them said a word. They stayed tangled together and fell into deep and peaceful sleep.

With the first light of day, Brady opened his eyes to his wife, staring into his at close range. He took her in; her auburn hair tousled over their pillows, her fresh face, and hazel eyes rested and happy. He drew his finger across her forehead to clear a wisp of hair away from those happy eyes.

"Good morning, Mrs. Garlow," he started. "How did you sleep?"

"Better than I have in four months, Mr. Garlow. You?"

"Same." He stretched, and she bowed back off his chest to give him room. He quickly retrieved her and pulled her close again. "No, no, no, you don't. Last night was just round one."

She smiled, and he kissed her teeth.

"When does round two start?" she asked.

"Ding! Ding! Ding!"

He rolled onto her tiny frame and parted her legs again with his knees, entering her and folding his arms under her back as she arched from the flat of the bed. They romped and played and fucked, hard and soft, until they'd finished rounds two and three before Brady called a timeout.

"Whew! Melinda Garlow, *you* are a machine!"

"You done?" she teased. "C'mon, Brady! Round four? Ding! Ding! Ding!"

He held her in a bear hug so she couldn't reach for him and declared an intermission.

"I gotta get some food in me."

She gasped, "The roast!"

She jumped from the bed and into her robe, then lit down the stairs to the kitchen and the crock-pot. Steam rolled out to cloud her view of the stew as she opened the lid. She poked a fork into a potato that disintegrated on contact.

Brady appeared behind her, barefoot in his jeans, pulling his tee shirt over his head as he looked over her shoulder.

"Can it be salvaged?"

"The vegetables are pure mush, but the meat ought to be fork tender." She skewered a chunk of the roast and it shredded into the broth. "We won't even have to chew it."

They laughed, and he squeezed her, kissing her ears and neck.

"Let me take you out for breakfast, honey."

"I'd love that. After all, it *is* a Thursday. Let's celebrate!"

"Go throw something on."

She darted out of the kitchen and yelled back as she bounded up the stairs, "I know the best place!"

Tiny's opened early and stayed open late from the Friday after Thanksgiving all the way to Christmas Eve. With Cleveland's downtown attempting to compete with the malls, he thought it would be smart to offer shoppers a place to stop in for breakfast, lunch, and dinner. Kitt let Melinda in on the secret weeks ago. She was so excited to introduce her husband to that part of her new temporary life.

They parked in the empty school lot and walked down the blustery alley. She led her husband through the back door and Tiny welcomed her with what had become her customary hug. She presented Brady and the two big men shared a hardy handshake and talked small about the Browns and the Cavs for a second, before Tiny told them the specials. They settled on their choices and took a seat.

"He seems nice."

"He's a gem. Kitt and I come in here a couple times a week. They make the best hoagies."

"Maybe I can get one to go next week when I head back."

Melinda's posture collapsed, and she whined, "No! You just got home; we can't talk about you leaving already!"

He laughed, "Sorry, honey." He reached for her. "I'm so sorry. Not another word, I promise." He locked his lips.

"Ok." She sighed and scooted her chair closer to his, then hooked her arm in the crook of his elbow. "I missed the holy shit out of you, you know that?"

He kissed her head. "You couldn't have missed me more than I missed you. I am so glad to be home."

Tiny delivered their dishes and before he could ask for it, produced a bottle of hot sauce from his apron for Brady.

"What? How did you know I was gonna ask for that?"

"You look like a guy that can bring the heat," Tiny answered, winked, and left them to eat.

Their love making had left them famished, though neither one knew just how much. They broke out in laughter when they each realized the other hadn't spoken since they dug in.

"It's so good!" Brady exclaimed.

"Agreed!"

"Do you think he'd do us up some hoagies to go for tonight?"

"Tiny will do up anything I want," she bragged. "I'm inside the circle, man. I got you."

She rose and kissed him hard on the mouth. "Wow!" She fanned her face. "I think I got a little hot sauce on that one."

She leaned over the bar and made her requests, and Tiny high-fived her with delight. She returned to the table just in time for their waitress to warm her coffee.

"Thanks, Bebe," she said familiarly.

"You got it Melinda. Merry Christmas!" the girl answered.

"Merry Christmas!" said Brady and Melinda in unison.

"You *do* know your way around in here. You weren't kidding."

"Tiny's people are the sweetest. And Kitt. I wish you could meet Kitt. She's the one that got me in here. She's turned out to be a real friend."

"So how did it go at Miss M's last weekend?"

"Oh my God, Brady! I have so much to tell you!" she was wild-eyed with excitement. "So, you know I went to Ike's for Thanksgiving."

"Right. The fancy-schmancy place with the servants."

"Yes. So, Miss M's place is completely the opposite. She has zero décor."

"What does that even mean?"

"Nothing on the walls, no do-dads, no knick-knacks, not even accents!"

"In that huge place where they've lived all those years?"

"Yep. Completely devoid of anything extra. Except… one whole room full of photographs."

He squinted with confusion. "You mean pictures all over the walls?"

"No. I mean cardboard boxes stacked to the ceiling full of loose pictures from her whole life and the life of her family."

"Loose in boxes?"

"Yes. Can you believe that?"

"I guess so. I mean, it's a little eccentric, but what do you expect from this family?"

"Well, she and I have been putting every one of her pictures into separate photo albums for her to give to her children."

"Really? That sounds like a huge undertaking."

"We worked for hours last weekend! I've been going over after dinner most nights to help her in the evenings too."

"Melinda, that's too much. She can't work you like that."

"Brady, it's not work!" she cautioned. "I love it. She has a memory like a steel trap and she has these amazing stories about every picture. I'm loving it. She really is kind of fascinating."

"That sounds like a truly intimate thing to do with someone. Driving her to work and back is one thing, but this is personal. I don't want to see you get so attached to this old bat that you end up staying in Cleveland to take care of her, *too*!"

Melinda felt judged.

"How could you think that I'd stay in Cleveland when you're making a new life for us in Delaware?"

"Delaware!"

"I said 'Delaware' that time, Brady."

"Oh. Sorry, honey," he apologized. "I just really want this part of our lives to be over."

"So do I."

He shook his head and started over.

"Ok... so... she's a fascinating storyteller... and..."

"That's just it," she continued. "She has lived all this life and has a detailed story to go with every photo."

"Have you found out any dirt on the family yet?"

"I'm glad you asked." She looked both ways over her shoulders then leaned in close to whisper, "Isaak *was* the accountant for the Merrifield Road Gang!" He beamed and she went on, "They met in her dad's barbershop to talk shop all the time when she was growing up."

"I knew it!" Brady slapped his hands together. "Do you know what happened to the money?"

"She hasn't told me anything about any money, Brady." Melinda frowned. "Why is everything about money with you?"

Now Brady felt judged.

"Seriously? I moved out of state, seven hours away from my wife, to earn enough to bail us out of the mess you inherited from your Aunt Helen, and you want to know why money means so much to me?"

"Brady…"

He reddened and shook his head, his eyes wet and staring in disbelief.

"Brady, babe. I'm sorry."

He shrugged out of his anger, and, in an instant, regretted the overreaction.

"Oh Jesus, Melinda, honey. *I'm* the one who should be sorry." He grabbed her hands up in his and kissed them. "I didn't even know that was there. I guess I'm just really ready for all this to be behind us."

"No, no, babe. I know. Me too," his wife soothed. "You're entitled to every bit of this frustration. I can't even think about where I'd be without you right now. Thank you, Brady. Thank you so much for everything you're doing for our family. I love you, baby."

"I love you, Melinda."

He kissed her hands again and Tiny appeared with brown paper bags dotted with grease, bearing their dinner for later. Brady thanked him for both meals with another sturdy handshake, followed him to the bar to settle their bill, and escorted his wife out the way they came.

They raved about the breakfast and their mouths watered at the smell of the sandwiches escaping their foil cocoons inside the brown paper bags.

"I'm so full, we're going to have to wait at least thirty minutes before round four can commence."

"Just like we're going back in the lake after lunch."

He laughed. "Yeah. Hey, what's the update on the house? Has Caldwell said anything about when they'll be done?"

She shook her head.

"Has Mary called back to say when she could list it?"

"She's waiting for him to finish."

"I think I'll call him while I'm in and see where we stand. We're going to have to know when he wants the rest of that money."

"Agreed."

Once home, Brady made the call and Melinda went upstairs to soak in the tub. He found her covered in bubbles and sat down on the toilet to report what he learned.

"Caldwell says he should be done by the end of next month. So, we've got all of January to get the money together."

"That should be enough time, right?" Melinda asked.

"Plenty. Nothing to worry about."

"I'll call Mary next week and let her know that's what he's shooting for."

"And let her know this…"

He batted the bubbles from atop the bath water.

"Oh!"

"Let her know I'm coming in to ravage my wife again!"

He kicked his shoes off, peeled off his shirt, and dropped his jeans to the floor while she giggled and squirmed in the water. He lowered himself into the bath overflowing the sides and fondled his slippery wife until they were deep into it again.

"Ding! Ding! Ding!" she whispered as he took her over.

When night fell, she lay asleep in their bed and he warmed the hoagies downstairs. He put a tray together to deliver the food and a couple of cold beers to his slumbering partner.

"Honey, wake up," he whispered into her hair.

She stirred and groaned. "Aww. I was already dreaming, baby."

"I heated up the hoagies. We have to eat supper."

"Yum," she hummed. "I didn't know you were cooking. Did you do them in the oven?"

"Yes, ma'am. I know it's better for the bread."

"Yes, better for the bread," she said, nodding her approval and sitting up in bed. "This is nice. But I think I could have slept the clock around."

"It's too early." He flipped on the T.V. "If we go to bed now, we'll be up in the middle of the night." He settled on an old black-and-white movie, then tore into his sandwich.

"No. I'm going to need some sleep tonight. You're wearing me out!"

He grinned at her, tackling her hoagie, and said, "You look like you could handle a few more rounds."

She swatted at him and moaned with delight over the bite, then offered a garbled, "Agreed!" with her chops full.

They satisfied their hunger and propped up against each other to finish their beers, then promptly fell asleep before the movie ended.

Christmas morning found them spooning under the covers, their empty cans and dishes undisturbed at the foot of the bed.

Melinda kissed the arm he had resting over her shoulder and he moved it to under her arms, pulling her body back to his.

"Morning, honey. Merry Christmas," he breathed onto her neck.

"G'morning, Santa," she teased, turning around to face him. "I got you something."

He kissed her and blinked his eyes awake. "What do you have for me, little girl?"

She fished around under the covers and found him already hard. "I have a little something for your elf down here."

He wriggled onto his back, and a smile spread out across his face. Then he scooped her up to fix her on top of him. "That's funny. He wants to give you something, too."

They ignored the limitations of their holiday and stayed lost in one another with no regard to time. They fed each other, body and soul, and pretended they wouldn't be separated when the sun rose again. Even though it wasn't in their history to make a lot out of the traditions of Christmas, they each bought the other a simple gift to mark the occasion.

With a small package hidden behind his back, Brady went first.

"I know we agreed no spending money we didn't have, but I did do just one little thing."

"Oh good. Me too!" she said and jumped up from the bed to retrieve hers.

When she returned, he presented her with the gift.

"Merry Christmas, Melinda," he said and kissed her.

She took the box and tore into the wrapping like a wild animal while he giggled at her. Her efforts revealed a deep wooden frame with glass and a patterned background.

"It's a shadow box. You can put your trinkets in it."

"Dad's American flag pin."

"And your mom's pearl earrings and that hideous gold hat pin of Aunt Helen's."

She batted at him for judging the dead woman's taste, then held the frame close to her chest.

"I love it, babe." She held it out to imagine her cherished things in place and reached a hand out to her husband's face. "I really love it."

They kissed again, and he knew he had nailed it.

"Now me!"

She straightened and presented her offering. He slowly and carefully pulled at the tape, driving her crazy with anticipation.

"The is how you show gratitude for a gift. You respect the time and attention that went into wrapping it," he teased.

She squirmed and harrumphed. When he finally got to it and realized what he was looking at, he erupted from the floor and cheered.

"YES! How in the world did you get this?"

She watched him ogling it and explained, "One of Kitt's sons lives in Pittsburgh and was going to the game, so I asked her to see if he'd save the ticket for me. She told him about you being away and how I wanted to surprise you for Christmas."

"Oh my God! Melinda!"

"But I didn't ask for the program and autograph. He just took it upon himself to get it. And he wouldn't even take any money for it."

"No!"

"No. He said he wanted to do it for his mom's friend. And none of us expected the game to turn out like that."

"No way! Little free-agent Phillie Dawson, kicking a forty yard field goal with two seconds left on the clock to beat the mighty Steelers on their own field in game ten!"

He shook his head in disbelief.

"Man, wait'll Charlie and Roger get a load of this!"

"I can't wait to tell Kitt your reaction," she squealed. "She's going to be so pleased."

"Oh my God, honey! Please, please thank them for me. This is awesome! Ha-HA!"

They reveled in their gifts and giving, cooked dinner, did laundry, and made plans. Morning came too soon and Melinda put herself back to bed after her husband loaded up in Johnson's truck again and disappeared down the block. She knew 'temporary' was coming closer and closer to an end but letting him go was getting more and more difficult. She allowed herself a good cry and got squared up.

Staff reported the week between Christmas and New Year's, even though classes were not held. The federal student loan numbers were compiled at year-end and the administrators enlisted the instructors in compiling the data. The schedule was a relaxed version of their normal as the employees were permitted to dress down and only clocked in for half a day. They met the Monday after the long weekend, as usual, in the conference room for breakfast.

Melinda drove Miss M, and they exchanged details about their holiday. She bragged about Brady's reaction to her gift, and Miss M teased her about how rosy her complexion seemed after his visit. Of course, Melinda spared her aging friend the intimate details, but her blushing cheeks confirmed the suspicion that more had been exchanged than Christmas gifts.

Miss M wore the new coat her children bought for her, and the ones around the conference table seemed surprised and delighted to see it.

Melinda fixed her plate and another for Miss M and the others stared in disbelief at their familiarity.

Manny and Sam exchanged curious looks.

"Thank you, Melinda," Miss M said with a pat of her hand. "Let's begin."

Ike took the lead.

"Yes, well...this week, as we explained, will be all about student loan data. Deidre will lead the charge, so get with her after breakfast, and she'll give you your assignments."

He nodded to Deidre, and she stared into her coffee. "Also, because of all the controversy surrounding the banks and the Y2K business, we're paying you in advance for the next two weeks."

A cheerful hum emanated from the group.

"We just don't want anyone going hungry in the middle of winter because of some stupid computer thing," Miss M offered.

Everyone stopped in their tracks.

Who *was* this woman?

She was kind, compassionate… different.

"Thank you, Miss M," said Kitt. "I really appreciate that. Who knows what's going to happen?"

"Nothing is going to happen, Kitt. I can assure you of that. But if it makes my people feel safer to get their paychecks ahead of the new year, then we'll do it. Right, boys?"

The matriarch went on enjoying her breakfast, and her sons turned to one another with gaping mouths and puzzled faces.

"Ok…," Sam waded in cautiously. "And that brings up the New Year's Eve function we have every year. We thought it best to just skip it altogether this year and celebrate at home."

Another murmur of agreement from the group.

"But!" Manny jumped in. "We are planning a party in January. Our own Miss M is turning ninety on the 31st of next month and we're going to have a blowout to celebrate!"

The room hung still, waiting for Miss M to violently object, but she didn't.

"Manny, you make too much of it. It's just another day."

"No Mother. You're becoming a nonagenarian. That's something to celebrate."

Miss M looked around the table at the faces she often saw but barely knew and smiled.

"I think a big party would be fun." She turned to Melinda and asked, "Don't you think a big party would be fun?"

Melinda nodded, then registered Miss M's hard intent behind the question.

"Yes! Yes! A big party. That would be the perfect thing."

No one else was privy to the plot. They proceeded with the meeting's agenda and into the day's work.

Deidre set up an assembly line of sorts to compile the information needed to file the data with the state and federal agencies in charge of issuing the aid checks to the school. Melinda was at a table by herself, adding past repayment statistics to the current numbers to plot on a graph.

After setting the whole machine in motion, Deidre topped off her coffee and pulled a chair up next to Melinda, hard at work.

"This is interesting, Deidre," she said. "I didn't know these figures helped designate how much aid the school was eligible for."

"People don't know how hard it is to keep track of all this crap, either. It's a full-time job on its own. Let alone teaching others how to do it."

"Which do you prefer? Teaching or accounting?"

The woman puffed out a sigh and responded, "I'm so tired of both right now, I couldn't answer that."

Melinda grinned. "Maybe with the year-end stuff done, you can get a break."

"Then the taxes will need to be filed and *that* nightmare, I wouldn't wish on my worst enemy!"

Melinda met her tired eyes with an empathetic look, and Deidre sensed a confidential connection that she never felt with another staff member before.

"Let's go get a cigarette."

"I don't smoke," Melinda responded naively.

"Let's go get a cigarette, anyway."

Deidre didn't wait for her to catch on but hurried out of the room and down the back stairs to the rear exit. Melinda looked around at the others in the room, hard at work, and followed her out.

The building shielded the women from the cutting winter wind coming off Lake Erie, but they still folded in on themselves to brace against the cold.

"How can you stand out here all winter long like this, Deidre?"

"I'm addicted. It's as simple as that." She drew in a long drag to heat her lungs. "Besides, if I didn't have a reason to walk out of here every couple of hours, I'd go stark-raving mad."

"I'm only starting to see how much is involved with the school's finances. But is it really that much more doing the family's taxes?"

"UUUUGGGGGHHH!" Deidre moaned, "Are you kidding me? They are the worst! Always angling to move this account out of the red and that one into the black, but not too much or that'll raise an eyebrow with the IRS! It's exhausting!"

"Why do you do it?" Melinda asked, but instantly felt like she'd overstepped. "Forget I asked that. Don't answer that. I didn't mean to pry."

"No. It's all good. I owe them." Deidre took a deep drag and told it. "My folks owned a bar in the flats, Sixth City Inn?" She waited for some recognition from the woman and when all Melinda returned was an empty shrug, she went on, "Doesn't matter. Anyway, Dad found himself behind the eight ball with a certain organization of businessmen that Mr. Maxwell was affiliated with…"

"The Merrifield Road Gang?" Melinda whispered. Deidre's eyebrows raised to affirm. "Really? A Jewish accountant for the Irish Mob? Isn't that a little cliché, not to mention a smidge antisemitic? I mean not every Jewish guy is good with money."

"No." Deidre instinctively looked over her shoulder and wagged a smokey hand in front of Melinda to hush her, "But just about every crime family had a Jewish guy to keep their books. You know, The Combination? Look it up. Anyway…Isaak, Sr. wasn't *that* Jewish, but he was *that* good with money." She took another drag. "These businessmen were threatening to burn our place down and Isaak, Sr. intervened."

"How?"

"He paid the debt and enrolled me in school 'on scholarship' in exchange for my coming to work for him. He never asked for repayment, but he never paid for a drink or a meal in our place the rest of his life. My mother cried and hugged him every time he came in." Deidre's hard, dark eyes smiled at the memory. "And of course, I get paid more. I charge them what they'd have to pay a professional to do it."

"Then why don't they take their taxes to a professional?"

"Because a professional wouldn't play all these hide and seek games with their money. I could get in a lot of trouble for doing what I do for them. No professional is going to risk their license for that."

"What about your license?"

"I don't have one." Deidre lit a second cigarette from the ember of the first, snuffed out the old butt in the snow, and turned to the young woman. "I never took the test. But Isaak hired me right out of school and taught me how he wanted things done."

"Wow! You have been here longer than anyone."

"I just turned twenty when he was killed."

"Killed? I thought he died in a car wreck."

"He was run over by a car. It was the Merrifield Road Gang."

"A hit?"

"Yep. He and Miss M were out driving around the lake in their new car and they got a flat in this sketchy part of town. Isaak remembered a service station a couple blocks back and started walking back when they ran him down in the street."

"Oh my God!" Melinda looked horrified and held her hands to her mouth.

"Miss M heard it and jumped out of the car to see them speeding away. She ran to his side, and he died in her arms." She shook her head, "Tragic."

Melinda felt a chill that wasn't anything to do with the snow she was standing in, and she shivered. "Poor Miss M. I didn't know she was there."

"Yeah. The cops pressed her for an I.D. of the car, but she was in shock. She couldn't remember a thing." Deidre watched the smoke from her nose mix with the vapor of their warm breath in the cold air and continued to trust her co-worker. "It was just after that all the money started moving around."

"What do you mean, moving around?"

"The mob was under investigation by the IRS. You know the way they caught Capone?" Melinda nodded even though she only barely remembered something about that. "So, Isaak… camouflaged, shall we say, a truckload of their liquid assets to keep the feds from tying it to jobs. Extortion, gambling, prostitution rings. He hid it in the trades.

"The trades?" asked Melinda.

"The copy shop, cab company, beauty parlor, etc. Then they ended up paying someone off at the IRS and the agency dropped everything. Only Isaak didn't want to reintroduce the dough back out into circulation yet. He argued it was safer where it was."

"So, they killed him for it?"

"They ran him down like a dog." Deidre shook her head again at the thought. "THEN, they put their made man from the IRS onto Miss M!"

"No!"

"But that old girl was the savviest of the bunch. She must have known they'd come for it so she hid it good." Deidre puffed away and laughed a little. "Even *I* don't know where all of it is!"

"I had no idea it got so violent." Melinda thought of her friend and how much she loved her late husband. "No wonder she's bitter."

Deidre nodded in agreement and smashed her cigarette under her boot, exhaled the menthol, and invited Melinda to reenter the building. The two women stood just inside for a moment and rubbed their arms to warm back up.

"Not everyone knows all this stuff about the money, Melinda," Deidre warned.

"Oh, I won't say a word. I wouldn't want any harm to come to anyone here, especially Miss M. She's been through enough."

"Good girl. The last of the gang died in prison years ago, but you never know," Deidre said, and led the way back up to the sixth floor.

Melinda was quiet on the ride home that night. Hearing Deidre lay out all the details of Isaak's death made her heart hurt, and she was trying not to let it show. Miss M may not have noticed anyway, but she was distracted by the scenario her birthday party presented and didn't pick up on Melinda's discomfort right away.

"This party will be the best place to give the children the pictures, Melinda," she beamed. "We couldn't have planned that any better ourselves."

"No ma'am. You're right about that."

"Are you coming around again after supper?"

"Sure."

They were in the drive when Miss M suggested, "Why don't you just stay and we'll eat together? I know you don't want to go back to that big empty house without your man at home."

"Right again, Miss M!"

"Good," she settled it. "Park the car and let's get in out of the cold."

Miss M heated some potato soup and Melinda buttered and broiled a split loaf of French bread for dipping. They ate in the dining room at the end of the table, not already occupied by their ongoing project.

Face-to-face over the hot bowls, Miss M deciphered something *was* bothering Melinda, and she asked after it, "What's the matter with you tonight, Melinda? You're uncharacteristically quiet. You and Brady have a fight before he left?"

She smiled and lied to keep from talking about what was really bothering her. "A little one. It's ok. Just makes it hard when I can't see him or talk to him."

"I know how that feels."

A rush of regret washed over the young woman and she fumbled to steer the conversation in a new direction.

"Of course, you do… how stupid of me! How about all this snow? I really want to start walking around my neighborhood for fitness. I'm getting so fat! The weather's not likely to cooperate with those plans any time soon."

Miss M was flustered for a moment by the abrupt change-of-course and suspected something might truly be amiss.

"What's that nonsense? Tell me the truth, young lady!"

Melinda collapsed in tears, her mouth full of French bread. "I'm sorry… Miss M… I… Deidre told me…" she garbled and snorted until the bread was swallowed.

"Easy, girl. You'll choke to death!"

She sobbed to a stop and confessed, "I know how your husband died!"

Miss M reached for her hand. "Melinda, is that what's got you so upset?"

Melinda blew her nose on her napkin and bobbed her head.

"Who did this to you?"

Melinda refused to answer with more than a shake of her head.

"Deidre. You said Deidre told you." Miss M narrowed her eyes and looked off at an imaginary foe. "Damn that old wretch. Now why in hell would she go and do a thing like that?"

"She wasn't gossiping, she was just venting about the end-of-year and tax season and it sort of came out. But… oh, Miss M… how awful for you!"

"Not this! No pity!" she commanded. "I will not tolerate your sympathy, Melinda, and neither would Isaak. Now dry up. There's no use crying over something that happened thirty years ago."

Melinda was mildly shocked that the old woman was so emotionless over the entire thing, but she did as she was told and straightened up.

"You done with your soup?" Miss M asked.

"Yes, ma'am. Thank you."

Miss M rose from the table, hooked her cane over her arm and stacked the empty bowls into the bread basket, then made off with them to the kitchen. Melinda cleared her throat and dried her eyes once and for all and moved around the table to get started. Miss M came back with fresh coffee for them both.

"This will get us through a couple of books, anyway."

"That's just what we need." Melinda sipped at the hot cup, then confessed again, "I lied earlier about fighting with Brady. Sorry."

"I thought as much. You're forgiven. You two don't fight at all, do you?"

"Not *never*, but not often."

Miss M picked up a clump of photographs and turned their corners until they made a neat square in her hand and began thumbing through.

"This is a great picture!" she started. "This was taken a few weeks after we were married, at the Club Hugo. He would take me around to all the joints when he went to balance their books and while he was in the back rooms, I would sit at the bar and just watch."

"Watch what?"

"Everything!" Her eyes twinkled with delight. "I knew all the bartenders on a first name basis, but they called me Mrs. Maxwell. They knew not to disrespect the accountant's wife. They were so sweet. But I would sit and watch all the ins and outs of the daytime activities that went on in these dives."

"What in the world would that look like?" Melinda asked.

Miss M looked out over the spread of pictures beyond her and fished through for some examples.

"Here… this is a good one." She looked through the bottom of her bifocals and pointed to two men at a table playing cards with a third. "These two are the card sharks, Burt and Leonard. They drove a beautiful 1932 two-toned, red and white Ford roadster in from Indianapolis or Chicago or somewhere around Lake Michigan."

"And they were professional poker players?"

"No, they were professional poker winners! They would play a few hands with the owner and if he couldn't see how they were cheating, they could come back when the place opened and he would let them in the game for a cut of what they won."

"Really?" Melinda was enthralled.

"Yes! And they were good."

"Do you know how they did it?"

"Flynn at the bar told me they had multiple decks. They had a cold deck they kept on the radiator and a scratch deck they marked by taking a pin and scratching a tiny detail of the design off the back of the cards. You know the Bee playing cards?" The girl nodded. "You know how busy that pattern is? No one could see it. But they knew where every card was marked."

"Where you ever around them when they played?"

"Oh no. We never went to those places when they were open to the public. They'd go upstairs and tick out until after the place got good and busy, then come down and wait to be asked into a game."

"What's 'tick out'?"

"Sleep. There were usually a couple of rooms above the bar where a man could sleep or take a girl for the night. Just a bare mattress made of ticking on a metal bedframe and a washbasin. Pretty crude. But Burt and Leonard never complained."

"Who else?"

Miss M fished around some more and found another one.

"This guy in the back by the pool table… that's the Dice Mechanic."

Melinda's eyes were wide with curiosity.

"I saw him first at the Harvest Moon, but he made his rounds around the entire local circuit, eventually."

"What was his game?"

"Craps, of course, but he didn't look like your average dice shooter. He came in wearing the finest suits and his shoes were always shined to a high gloss and his hat band and pocket square always matched. That man was debonair!" She closed her eyes to conjure the image of him. "And he smelled like musk and lilacs."

Melinda watched as the young woman within her aging friend swooned.

"Miss M! Did you have a crush on the Dice Mechanic?"

"Of course, I did, Melinda! I had a crush on all of them!"

They giggled.

"This man brought an attaché case fitted with a velvet lined form inside with every kind of trick die you could imagine. Totally undetectable to the naked eye, they even felt the same as the others. But they were weighted and shaped to roll consistently in favor of the shooter."

"Wouldn't the other players pick him out with his shiny shoes and fancy clothes?"

"He played the part of the traveling salesman. The trick to these cons was to let the locals spot *them* as marks and invite them in because they looked like they wouldn't know the score. They would have a few watered down drinks and appear to be a little tipsy, then get themselves invited to play and hustle the whole bar."

"You loved this life, didn't you?" Melinda accused.

"You know something? I did. All that time growing up spying on those men in my dad's barber chair and they couldn't have been any nicer to us. I never got the idea for one minute that my dad was mixed up with them. But I also knew he didn't fear them. I mean, I know he didn't want me to end up with any of those hoods, but he seemed almost relieved that Isaak and I found each other. I know he thought Isaak was just a step or two above all the vice and could give me a good life." She paused for a moment to remember the two men that meant the most to her in her youth. "And he did."

"But they *were* dangerous, in the end," Melinda dared.

"Yes. Isaak underestimated them in the end, but that was just as much his own fault as theirs, Melinda. You would never understand this, but even after what happened to Isaak, they eventually left me and the children alone... and I think that was because I wasn't just Mrs. Maxwell. I was also Laddie Malloy's little girl."

Miss M's personal album was filling with recollections of the loves of her life, but the project was supposed to be for the children. They still had much work to do.

The week continued with the first half of every day at school and the last half and well into the night at Miss M's. They had all but exhausted the oldest boxes and discovered the chronicle of her children's lives in the ones remaining, the true purpose of their project.

Melinda had devised a system where she could identify the child in the picture and they began making great piles attributed to each person. Miss M would go into each one and the labeling would begin. She went in birth order.

"Alright," Melinda grunted as she circled her arms around the sloppy stack of photographs and scooted them toward her boss. "These are all Ike."

"Ok." Miss M straightened in her chair and rolled up her sleeves. She waited for Melinda to position herself with her pen at the ready and began. "Here he is in the high school band. Tuba!"

"That's a lot."

"You don't even know!"

"Do we need the date?"

"Just put sophomore year. He only played one year."

"Oh?"

"Here's one from grade school." She held it closer to see, "Yes. That's that damned Reynolds in the background. They moved in the summer of his third-grade year."

"So, third grade?"

"That'll do."

"Here he is at his college graduation. Oh! He looked so much like his father."

"College?" Melinda asked. "Didn't he go to the academy?"

"Isaak insisted on sending him for a four-year degree. He went to the University of Cincinnati."

"Hmm."

"He wanted him to take a step away, learn more than just the basics."

"And he did well?"

"He hated it." Miss M giggled, "He called twice a week asking to talk to his father because he wanted to quit. But I wouldn't let him."

"Why not?"

"Because Isaak would have allowed it. He was always too soft on these children. He spoiled them stupid and then left them to *me* to discipline."

"That hardly seems fair," Melinda said. "But don't you think it was because of Beryl and Jacob?"

"I never said I didn't understand *why* he did it. But that didn't make it any easier on me." Miss M studied the young man's face in the photograph and spoke to that version of her son. "I knew you'd regret it for the rest of your life if I let you come home. You had to make it somewhere you weren't Isaak Lowell Maxwell's son."

Melinda sat still as to not intrude on the moment between them.

"I wish they knew." Miss M gave the picture up and looked for the next.

"You wish they knew what, Miss M?"

The old girl shook her head and forged on. "It doesn't matter."

Melinda delighted in the lore behind each image, but the things Miss M wasn't disclosing presented a clearer picture than the ones in the albums. This woman had done nothing the way she wanted to her entire life. She did what her father dictated, then what Isaak wanted, and since his death, she had been at the mercy of what her children saw fit. Her image was in these pictures, but the real Emalina Malloy Maxwell was nowhere to be found.

"I'm tired of Ike. Where's Hildegard's pile?"

Melinda moved the piles around with one swift shuffle and opened Hildy's album.

"I wish you could have known my daughter before all that business with her fiancé," Miss M began. "Look at her here in her prom gown."

Melinda leaned in for a look. "Wow! She's gorgeous!"

"She stood so tall and was so beautiful."

"She's stunning. What year?"

"That's her senior prom, so '60."

"And was she engaged yet?"

"He asked her father before he left for bootcamp and Isaak said no."

"Oh no!"

"Then the two of them came to me and told me about the baby and I said yes."

"But I thought Isaak was the softhearted one."

"It wasn't about romance, Melinda. Things were different back then. You didn't want to be the single girl with a baby in 1960 Cleveland. I told them they could announce their engagement on the night he left. He was scheduled to be home in three months before he shipped out and they were to be married then."

"So, they were married before he died?"

"No. His unit was sent straight from camp overseas. He was killed when they tried to land over there. He never made it off the helicopter."

"That's just awful."

"Hildy almost lost her mind." Miss M stared at the beautiful girl in the photo, untouched by the future pain she would endure just months after it was taken. "I had that gown made for her. Matching gloves." She pointed to the detail.

"It's lovely."

Miss M surrendered the picture and dictated, "Senior prom, 1960."

Melinda left the baby question in the air between them. She had heard it both ways, either an illegal abortion or miscarriage. Either way, it was a loss too close to home to explore. Until that story, she felt a safe distance removed from her own grief. Coming this close served as a sobering reminder that pain of that depth doesn't fade quickly or easily, and for some, not at all. Poor Hildy.

"I don't know if I'm ready to do Hildy just yet," her mother confessed.

"How about the twins?" offered Melinda.

Miss M agreed, answering with a nod and they carried on and found some shots of the two as toddlers. Gus was spindly and frail compared to his hefty sister. Miss M said that Gustav caught every bug that the others brought home, but Marta was never sick a day in her life.

"Here they are, home with the chicken pox. Look! Gus has them on his lips and on his eyelids. He was a mess. And there's roly-poly Marta, with her one chicken pock right in the dimple of her double chin."

"One pock?" Melinda asked in disbelief. "You swear to God?"

"I swear on a stack of Gideons! I checked that chubby little thing from top knot to tail feathers and she didn't have another one." She took off her glasses and held it closer to prove it to herself again. "See for yourself. Look at her grin."

"Aww, Gus looks miserable."

"Oh, my goodness. He ran a fever, he couldn't eat. He had the worst case of all the children. And there was his sister with that one tiny bump somewhere you'd never see the scar. He *hated* her!"

"Really? They didn't get along. I thought twins were like their own little unit in a family."

"Not Gus and Marta. Everything came so easy for her. She barely even tried and little Gustav struggled with everything… his whole life." Miss M pulled a few more pictures out of the two. "Constantly competing. Look at his face in this one. She caught a bigger fish."

"Aww."

"Of course, it didn't help that his brothers razzed him at every turn. It made him so bitter. She still thinks she's better than he is. And the truth is, neither of them did anything worth a damn. Her dad put her through beauty school and paid to put that shop in her basement and that overbearing ass of a husband won't let her work on anyone but his friend's wives. And we financed the cab company so Gus could have something of his own and he uses it to pick up women when he should be picking up fares."

"But they're doing alright, aren't they?"

"Not without subsidies!"

"Oh. Well, I know what that's like. Aunt Helen helped us out dozens of times."

"Your Aunt knew what she was doing. She probably left you plenty to invest for yourself."

"She left us plenty. That's for sure."

"You know, when we're done with my family's chronicle, we'll have to start an album for you."

Melinda didn't want to invite any more attention to that subject and reached for an exit line.

"That wouldn't take nearly as long as all this. Let's say ten more pictures, then we'll call it a night."

"Ten it is. But I don't want to know who I'm going to get."

Miss M stood, closed her eyes, and moved her outstretched palms over the stacks of photos on the other side of the table to draw the final entries. Melinda grinned and imagined Miss M as a carnival fortune teller.

"Clara!" she said under her breath.

"What?" Miss M asked, peeking one eye open in her direction. "Who's Clara?"

"Oh! She's just a friend I hadn't thought of in a while."

"And she just popped into your head?" she went back to the blind selection.

"Yes. Isn't that funny?" Melinda accepted the sign. "I guess I should call her."

"It's often been my experience that when you think of someone out of the blue like that, you must have business with them."

"I'll check in with her tomorrow. Have you got your ten?"

"Yes." She sat back down and looked at her haul. "Aww! I was hoping to find this one." The old woman held out a shot of a stunningly beautiful female figure.

"Is that Hildy?"

"Nope."

"Marta?"

"Wrong again."

Melinda looked stumped.

"This is my son Manfred Paul Maxwell. Isn't he gorgeous!"

"Holy crap! That's Manny?"

"He went to Chicago on a theatre scholarship. This was the follies his junior year. He… was… magnificent."

Melinda smiled at the pride beaming from her friend. "He *was* magnificent," she agreed. "Did his father know about *that*?"

Miss M looked over the top of her cheaters at the inquiring girl. "What do *you* think?"

"I think he could have made a living as a drag queen. Why didn't he stay in theatre?"

"Why do any of us change course, Melinda? He fell in love."

"That old chestnut?"

"Story as old as the hills, only with a little twist." She sipped her coffee and went on. "They met in a cabaret and were inseparable from the start. But he wanted Manny to move to California because Chicago was a battleground for their kind at the time. They had a couple of friends attacked at the places they went to meet up. Manny used to call me crying, wanting to bring him home to the safety of Ohio."

"But you wouldn't let him."

"Don't judge me, missy. Again, it was a different time. I was certain Isaak knew about Manny, and I was pretty sure the other children knew as well. But knowing and accepting were two different things. If he stayed away, if he found a life and a group outside his family, maybe we could all go on just pretending everything was ok."

"Denial goes a long way."

Miss M inhaled, "Yes."

"So, they moved to California then."

"They did." She reexamined the photo. "He seemed so happy. They were together for twenty-one years." She dropped her head. "He died of A.I.D.S. in '82."

Melinda's heart was suddenly so heavy. All these lives. All this grief. And Miss M was holding it all. They had no clue. These children, these ungrateful children, only saw their mother as this embittered, hard case when she had been carrying all their pain on top of hers their whole lives. Melinda was bearing witness to it. With every memory, every picture, Miss M brought back the time and the emotion attached to it. Their mother knew every tear, every sleepless night, every loss, and every triumph. She knew it; felt it; lived it *for* them. And they had no clue. Why do families do this to one another? Making up their minds they know everything there is to know but never ask. Why didn't Aunt Helen tell her she was broke? What secrets would her parents have kept from her if they would have lived?

"Ok. Nine to go." Miss M broke into Melinda's head.

She felt a rush of heat. Shame? Anger? She couldn't name it, but she couldn't shake it either. She reddened and began to sweat. "Miss M, I hate to, but I think I need to call it a night." She rose and bussed her cup to the kitchen.

"But we have nine to go. You said ten more."

She poked her head back into the dining room as she donned her coat. "We'll get back to it after school tomorrow. I want to get home before it gets too late. G'night!"

"Good…" The door slapped shut before she could get the rest out. Miss M looked around the empty room and concluded, "Must have struck a nerve."

The night air cooled Melinda's skin so quickly as she sprinted for the car, that the tears streaming down her face burned like alcohol. She wasn't even fully aware that she was crying. But the salt in the back of her throat and the sting on her cheeks convinced her she was. She looked at her watch before the dome light faded off and realized it wasn't too late to run to Clara's.

She made a beeline across town.

When she pulled to a stop at the curb in front of the place, she waited as a dark figure walked out the purple door. Then she headed in and up. Clara met her at the top of the stairs, locking the door to her place.

"Clara, wait!" she called to her breathlessly.

"Melinda? Is that you?"

"Please, can you spare just one more minute?" she begged. "I'll pay extra."

Clara reached a gloved hand out to the women's tear-streaked face and touched her tenderly. "Girl, what's got you so jammed up? Extra!" She turned around and unlocked the door. "Like I would charge you extra. Please! Get in here, you crazy person."

Melinda trailed her inside and followed behind as Clara turned the lights back on and lead her into the back room. She plopped down at the table, scooted in, planted her elbows and rested her forehead on the heels of her hands.

"Goodness, child," Clara declared as she relit the candles and incense around the room and stowed her coat and bag. "We have some work to do, huh?"

"I'm sorry, but I don't know why I'm here. You popped into my head earlier, then I got upset..." her words stuck in her dry mouth. "I don't know what happened."

"Shh. It's ok, Melinda," Clara soothed and handed her the matches from the amber bowl.

Melinda lit the candle. Clara waited for the flame to stabilize, then closed her eyes and took her client's hands.

"We are open, spirits. We are here in heart and mind. What wisdom do you have for this one who seeks to know?"

The room was quiet for a moment, then the candle spurted and sputtered. Both women opened their eyes and stared as the flame weaved from side to side, then... went out!

"Oh!" Melinda jumped and pulled her hands back.

"Not to worry, friend," Clara started. "Just a surge of spiritual activity."

Melinda watched by the dimmer light of the other candles as Clara bade her back to join hands again.

"It seems someone else is with us today, Melinda."

"Not Aunt Helen again, I hope."

"No... but a female."

"My mother?"

"Umm, no. It isn't clear who has made themselves present, but I feel her energy just the same."

Melinda waited a second, then asked, "What is she telling you?"

Clara tilted her head and furrowed her brow, to try to discern a sound from the quiet. She shook her head and breathed deeply. "No message. She's not telling me anything. She's waiting."

"Waiting for what?"

"Watching and waiting."

"Watching for what?"

Clara concentrated, squeezing Melinda's hands tighter. "She's watching *you*... and... waiting."

"Waiting for me to do what?"

"Nope. Not for you to do anything. Just watching and waiting... *for* you."

Melinda puzzled over it for a moment more.

"And you're sure you can't make out who it is?"

"She doesn't know who she is to you yet."

"Doesn't know... who... what?"

"Doesn't know who *she* is to *you*. She has a connection to you, but it's unclear how she relates."

"Is it someone I used to know? Someone I used to be related to?"

"Melinda, she can't or she won't reveal herself. You must respect her wishes."

"Respect her…?"

Clara cut her off. "She is clearly a benevolent energy and on your side. She just doesn't know where she fits yet. I have every indication that she is someone of great importance to you."

"But it's nobody dead?" Melinda was growing anxious.

"Her energy is not of the departed. I can be sure of that."

Melinda slumped in her chair and sobbed.

Clara released her hands and reached behind her own chair to turn on the floor lamp.

"Melinda, what has you so upset? What are you looking for?"

"I don't know!" she burst. "I've just had it! I've been working so hard to see that everything is getting done. The house… Brady… school! Who else am I letting down? Who else is watching and waiting to take something from me?"

"Melinda."

"WHO?!" she screeched. "I have nothing else to give, Clara."

Clara reached for her hands to comfort her this time and Melinda drew them back, afraid of reconnecting with this new energy watching her.

"No, no. No more tonight. Take a deep breath."

The two women inhaled together.

"Now let it out."

They exhaled slow and long.

"Now then," she reached out to her again. "Just let me hold on to you for a minute."

Melinda surrendered her hands.

"You've been at it all your life, Melinda Garlow. Seeing to everyone and everything your whole life. You're tired. You're exhausted, mind, body, and soul."

Melinda took another deep breath in, exhaled, and nodded.

"I am."

"So, what does this new energy need from you?"

Melinda searched the seer's face for the truth.

"I think she needs you to take care of yourself, to heal, to put the heaviest things in your heart to rest."

Clara stroked her hands and calmed her friend with a touch of the pressure points on her wrists. When Melinda's breathing settled and her heartrate slowed, the seer released her hands and sat back against her chair.

Melinda wiped her face and returned her folded hands to the table.

"Should we do the cards tonight?"

"Not tonight. We don't need to."

"Why is that?" she sniffed.

"No need. We got what we wanted. You got what you came here for."

She nodded in agreement and reached for her purse.

"No charge for this session, Melinda," Clara said.

"But I…"

"No charge."

The psychic rose from the table and stretched her arm around to scoop Melinda out of her chair and held her by the shoulder until she saw her all the way down and through the purple door.

"You heed what you've learned here tonight, Melinda," she said. "Healing… self-care… rest. Clear out your heart, lay your burden down, and rest."

Melinda nodded obediently, then turned and hugged the woman. "Thank you, Clara."

"Your welcome, sweet girl."

Clara squeezed her, then patted her free and watched her drive into the winter night.

Melinda went straight home and dug out the family Bible again. She wiggled free from her coat and lugged the heavy book up the stairs. She kicked her shoes off and climbed on the bed, opening the great volume to free all the slips and clippings hidden away in its pages.

She gripped the covers in both hands and shook the thin pages to make sure she rattled out all the ghosts. She laid it down and fanned through them like she was shuffling a giant deck of cards so as not to miss a single secret hidden in its sheets. When she was satisfied, she set the book aside and gathered all the pieces up to study each one.

The first she retrieved were obituaries held together by a rusted paperclip. She gently took them apart and recognized each as her Great-grandmother and Great-grandfather Harper's. She read they died the summer of '47 within a month of each other. Peggy first, 'after a long illness' and then Pete, in his sleep. "Probably heart. I think Aunt Helen said they had weak hearts on his side." She read in each one how Helen and her sister Polly were the only family left behind.

She clipped them back together and reached in for another.

There were two more clippings folded into one another. She separated them with great care.

The first was a front-page article from *The Sun* dated September 6, 1948, about a man who had been found dead in the county jail where he was being held without bond for multiple assault and robbery charges. She didn't recognize the man's name, nor anyone else's name in the article. He had been a transient worker at the rail yard and matched the description of a man reported to have molested several young women in the area. When police searched his belongings, they discovered wallets and change purses, along with jewelry reported stolen in the attacks. She read it a second time all the way through but gleaned no more insight.

She picked up the one folded into the first and read it aloud.

"Polly Sue Harper, 16 of Cleveland died at her home on Friday, May 13, 1949." She recognized the name as her maternal grandmother's. "Miss Harper, born July 11, 1933, was the daughter of Pete and Margaret 'Peggy' Morley-Harper, formerly of Chillicothe. She was a senior at Cleveland Heights High School. Miss Harper leaves behind her infant daughter, Lucille and her sister F. Helen Harper. She was preceded in death by her parents. A private service for her family has been arranged by Cummings and Davis Funeral Home. Messages of condolence for the Harpers may be mailed in c/o Cummings and Davis, 13201 Euclid Avenue, Cleveland, Ohio 44112."

She took a second. "Ok. No surprises here. I knew she killed herself just after Mom was born."

She looked the obituary over again. "Wait… she was still in high school?"

She returned her attention to the news article. It began to add up.

"Jesus! My grandfather was a criminal."

She read them both again and sat, shocked, staring up at the ceiling.

"Oh, Aunt Helen, what you must have gone through?"

She checked the dates and fished through the slips remaining on the bed for Aunt Helen's obit.

"How old was Aunt Helen when she buried her parents... and her sister?" she asked herself, searching for her dead aunt's birthdate from the paper. "Born February 5, 1929." She scanned Polly's and the parents' again for the dates of death. "Died May 13, 1949... and... summer of '47." Calculating the math in her head, she winced, "Eighteen and two years later at twenty years old? Oh my God! The summer you graduate from high school, you bury your parents within a month of each other, then the next summer... it had to be... August, September, October, November, December, January, February, March, April," she counted the nine months on her fingers, "your sister is raped and impregnated by a man who is murdered awaiting trial! Then once she has the baby, in the spring of her senior year in high school, she hangs herself in her closet for you to come home and discover!"

She fell back against the headboard, flabbergasted by the weight of it all. She almost couldn't believe all her family had endured. *All* her family, hell! All her Aunt Helen *alone* had endured! No wonder she was so distant and cold. Her heart was broken again and again before she was even grown.

"Why didn't you tell me?" she asked the empty house. "I would have seen you so differently if I'd have known all this."

She thought about all the maneuvering Miss M had done to keep her family from suffering over one another's losses and imagined that must have been behind Aunt Helen keeping all *this* tucked away. She felt a surge of emotion wash over her.

Love.

She felt deeply and unconditionally loved. The feeling wasn't in her head. It warmed her guts, and she reached for her middle. She felt it spread to her hands and arms and down her legs. And when it rose to the top of her head and washed over her face, she felt tears again. This time, she knew what they were. She was crying tears of joy because she realized she was loved by her aunt since the day she was born. She could have given Lucille away, she could have gone on with no one to call family after Polly's death. But she didn't: she raised her sister's little girl and then *her* daughter after that.

That sequence snapped her out of her head and back to the clippings on the bed.

There was one more to read.

This one she knew by heart and the story that Aunt Helen told with it every time they read it together.

Her father, Robert "Red" Tennant, got his first bonus check as a junior sales executive at the Ford dealership and decided to take her mother on a trip to St Maarten. Lucille had tried to convince him to put the money away to start their savings, but Red was so proud of himself and wanted to spoil his wife. There would be plenty more bonuses to sock away. They were spending this one! They were on ALM Flight 980 when it ditched into the Caribbean. She traced the print of *The Sun* article about the crash with her index finger until she found their names and read them aloud. "Among the dead were Cleveland couple Red and Lucille Tennant. They leave behind their three-year-old daughter, Melinda."

How many times had she read that clipping? Too many to count. So often during her middle school years that Aunt

Helen had hidden it in her underpants drawer until after Melinda and Brady were married.

All her aunt did for her was done out of love. Even the indifference she showed each time Melinda miscarried was her way of helping her deal with the grief. Her niece sat alone in her homeplace, reliving memories of the only mother she'd ever really had and soothing her soul with the moments she recalled, one after the other.

She sank into the warmth of the big bed, and restful sleep finally overtook her tired heart.

✿

Friday night's call went on into the wee hours of Saturday morning as per their usual, but this one was very lopsided; Melinda couldn't stop talking.

"I can't explain it, Brady, but I feel like I'm supposed to be helping Miss M get to this new place with her kids before I leave town. It's become my mission."

"Melinda, we talked about you getting sucked into this woman's story and here you are on a mission. I don't know if I like where you're going with this."

"Brady, don't you see? This is a family that's fractured itself into all these tiny pieces that Miss M has been trying to keep together her entire life. These pictures aren't just a record of their lives together, it's proof that she's always been there for them, routing for them, hurting for them, *their* entire lives."

"Keywords here, honey, are *her* and *them*. This isn't your family, Melinda."

She sat with the truth of her husband's caveat for a moment, then risked the rest of her revelation.

"Clara said there was a benevolent energy…"

"Oh, not this," he interrupted.

"A benevolent female energy," she overruled. "That is watching and waiting to see who she is to me."

"And?"

"And I believe it's Miss M."

"And who do you think she is to you, Melinda? Your matriarch? The mother you wish you had?"

"Brady, you haven't been listening!"

"She's your boss, Melinda! That's all. You work for her. There… mystery solved."

She felt the sting of his judgement and instantly shifted into defense mode.

"I can't believe that's all you see… after everything I've told you."

The silence between them was deafening but short-lived.

"Can you honestly say that you don't have any notion what she means to me? My time with her has made this entire thing tolerable. Do you have any idea how hard this would have been on me if we hadn't gotten so close?"

Now Brady sat hushed and judged.

"She's my friend, Brady."

"Of course, she is, honey. I didn't mean anything by—"

"She's my friend and I love her."

He felt awful, but he was so tired. It was nearly dawn, and his wife hadn't stopped talking about these people for hours. He never really trusted the Maxwells and now Melinda seemed so engrained in the family that it scared him just a little. Still, he tried to be patient when she droned on about them. At this juncture, though, his patience was wearing thin.

"Melinda, we're almost there," he tried. "In a couple of weeks, the house will be done, Mary will list it, and you can come join me on the coast."

She listened.

"We're in the home stretch. You knew this situation was temporary, but now it seems like you're digging in. I'm getting worried you might not want to go when it's all over. Honey, we had a plan."

So, there it was.

He wasn't leery of the Maxwells. He was afraid Melinda wouldn't leave Cleveland. Clarity swelled between them.

"Brady Garlow! Are you nuts?"

He wondered.

"I have no intention of ruining our plan. I want out of here worse than ever now. We're moving to Delaware. We're starting our new life together far away from this place and all the shit we've endured here. You don't need to worry one minute over that, you crazy man!"

He rubbed his tired face and conceded to the insanity of it.

"I'm doing it again, aren't I?" He shook his head. "I just want it all to be over and to start our new life together. It's all I think about. We've waited so long."

"And we *are* almost there. I get it. This stuff with Miss M won't hold me back, babe. It's just been the best thing for me right now. I feel like befriending her and helping her, has helped me too. I'm just really hopeful that the albums do what she wants them to. That all this work will pay off for her. That's all. I'm just excited for my friend."

"Of course, you are. And again, I'm so sorry I was sitting on all that fear; I'm just seriously over living with Riffle and Johnson! Please come and rescue me soon… PLEASE!"

They laughed now, relieved of the weight of the moment, and reconnected in their common goal.

"I feel bad for keeping you up all night, Brady."

"I *am* pooped," he admitted. "And you know I hate to, but I'm going to need to get off here and get some sleep."

"I know, baby. You go to bed and I'll talk to you next week."

"Ok."

"I love you, husband."

"I love you, wife."

"You know when you get down to it…"

"Yeah, it's just that simple."

"Bye Melinda."

"Night Brady."

She settled back into bed and ran over the conversation in her head. Brady was right about some of what worried him. It would be hard for her to leave Miss M since they'd become so close. It would be another grief; so would leaving the house and their hometown. But it could also be a way of breaking the cycle of pain and loss, especially if she could get her friend to a place of new beginnings with her family. Their time together might be temporary, but the gifts it yielded would last for a lifetime.

January

Melinda kept their plan in the back of her mind and focused on the end of her first semester as an instructor. The end of January would see her student's final grades recorded, Miss M's birthday party, and the culmination of the photo project.

She checked in with Caldwell before leaving the morning she returned to classes, and he surprised her with some good news.

"Since that basement box was already there, we've been able to cut about two weeks off the end of the job all together."

"Seriously?" she asked, wide-eyed.

"Yep. We look to have everything up and ready by the fifteenth."

She let loose with a squeal and leapt into the contractor's arms for a brief celebration, then caught herself and quickly released him and backed off.

"Oh my goodness! I'm so sorry," she said, pressing her clothes down to reset herself.

"It's ok. I don't get that reaction often because we're rarely done early. I guess that means you're happy with the progress."

Shaking her head in disbelief, she answered, "You cannot know what this means. Thank you!"

"No problem, Mrs. Garlow. We'll get to finishing now."

"Of course. Thank you again. Thank you!"

He lumbered down the basement steps and left her silently jumping up and down in the kitchen. She couldn't believe it! She stood for a moment longer beaming, then grabbed her lunch and headed for school.

The weather was harsh but not unexpected for January in Cleveland. That and the moment she took to chat with the contractor made Melinda exactly two minutes late picking up her charge. Despite the inclement weather, Miss M was on her stoop and at the ready when Melinda pulled in. She caught a tiny bit of hell when they got in the car, but only for worrying Miss M because she was never even a minute late before. Melinda apologized profusely and dropped her boss at the front door, then pushed through the snow and ice to the back parking lot and trudged into the rear entrance of the building and up the back stairs. Her unfettered joy carried her effortlessly up to the sixth floor, where the breakfast buffet was being tapped before the Monday meeting.

As she bounded into the room and shook her coat off, the rest of the staff snapped to attention to see what force had delivered her to them.

"Sorry if we're late," she blurted. "I had a meeting with the contractor."

The lot returned to their conversations and breakfast plates. She wiped her dripping nose with a napkin she grabbed on her way to hot coffee, and Kitt squeezed a cup in beside hers.

"A quickie with the contractor, huh?" she teased as Melinda filled her friend's cup before her own.

"Yes, Kitt. I didn't have time to get to every man on the crew like I usually do of a morning, so I just laid the head guy."

"Anything to get the job done, honey!"

"Speaking of which, I've got news on that front."

Kitt leaned in.

"Not now. You free for lunch?"

"Tiny's?"

"Oh, yes!" Melinda quietly cheered. "I will keep my egg salad sandwich for tomorrow. We're going to Tiny's!"

"Let's go ladies," Deidre hurried the women from the urn. "We're all drinking coffee this morning."

The two shrunk and grinned, then vacated the spot for the rest to pour their share. When all the plates were filled and everyone was seated, Miss M began the meeting with a new enthusiasm that almost rivaled Melinda's.

"Good morning all," she began. "Ike, before you get down to business, I just wanted to say a few words."

Ike nodded and offered an outstretched hand for his mother to proceed.

"Arriving at this time in history has long been a personal goal of mine. But I must confess, I never truly thought I'd live to see the year 2000. What a crazy thing."

The expressions of those around the table exhibited agreement.

"And it's not just a milestone for me, but for all of us. Through all the changes in Cleveland… in the world, this institution, begun by my wonderful husband and continued by our beautiful children, has stood the test of time."

Those of her children present exchanged looks of wonder while the rest of the staff waited for the other shoe.

"I know whatever Deidre and Ike came up with for our numbers this year, we're going to live to fight another day at the Cleveland Business Academy. You will finish the rest of the year strong."

Deidre and Ike nodded in accord.

"But you will finish without me."

The breath of every soul in the room stalled in their chests. They were frozen in place. That was indeed the other shoe.

As usual, Kitt was the only one with courage enough.

"Miss M, are you retiring?"

Nodding, she answered, "Yes, Kitt. I will use these last weeks before my ninetieth birthday to conclude my business as the academy's senior board member, then Ike, Manny, Sam, and the rest of the family will carry on. It's been a long time coming. I'm ready."

Melinda reached for the old woman's hand without thinking.

"Miss M, what will you do?" she asked.

She patted the girl's hand as a devilish grin overtook her face. "Anything I damn well want!"

A nervous laugh trickled out of the collective and Miss M winked in Melinda's direction, then encouraged the rest to proceed with the meeting.

No one at the school could have imagined this turn, but it was all they could talk about the rest of the day. Lunch at Tiny's with Kitt was highjacked by the topic until just before she and Melinda got back to their classrooms.

"Oh shoot, Melinda," Kitt remembered. "What were you going to tell me about the contractor?"

"Oh nothing," she lied. "It's no big deal."

Kitt shrugged and held the door open for her students to enter ahead of her, rolled her eyes at her friend and charged, "Back into the fray!"

Melinda hailed her on and got back to it herself. She wasn't able to stay engaged for long before she started to mull over everything that had transpired that morning. She set her students to auto pilot by assigning in-school reading to free herself up for deep thinking.

She was ready to confess to Kitt that she too would not remain at the school beyond the end of the month but hadn't even fathomed mustering the courage to tell Miss M. Now though, with the queen's revelation about leaving, maybe the timing was perfect to officially tender her resignation as well. They could make a grand exit together.

"That's it!" she exclaimed to her silent students, who startled at her outburst just as the bell sounded for their dismissal. "Sorry! Questions at the end of the chapter for discussion tomorrow. Thank you!"

The last class of the day wasn't much better. Her mind kept wandering to a life beyond the snowbound winters on Lake Erie, to the beaches of the Atlantic with Brady. In her mind's eye, she pictured the images from the tampon commercials of women in white pants and oatmeal sweaters splashing in the wake of the breaking waves, picking up shells and holding hands with their men. She could be that carefree girl on the beach with Brady. White pants and all, she could be there in a couple of weeks. How cold does it get on the coast in the dead of winter? She didn't care if she had to wear her heaviest coat, hat, and gloves; she was going to put on her white pants and take off her shoes and socks and walk right into the water… in just a few more weeks.

Careful not to jinx it, she decided she would wait until the work was officially completed to call the realtor and to tell anyone at the school that she was leaving. If they really were done by the middle of the month, that would be a solid two week notice and that was more than professional enough for the Cleveland Business Academy. The next two weeks of school would be hard to manage without giving herself away. But how was she going to get through the rest of the photo album project alone with Miss M without telling her?

She'd just have to.

"Now more than ever, Melinda," she told herself, "It's only temporary!"

"Quite the announcement, Miss M," Melinda declared as she greeted her friend at the end of the day.

"Did you like that, girls?" Miss M teased Kitt and Melinda before taking their arms and trudging out into the slushy lot behind the building.

"Could have knocked me over with a feather, Miss M!" Kitt admitted. "We all thought you'd die at the helm and here you are retiring just as you're getting to the good part, Ha-HA!"

Miss M laughed too.

"Precisely my point, dear. I want to do something besides reporting to work before I die."

"Like what?" asked Melinda.

"Any damn thing…"

"Any damn thing she wants!" chimed the two younger women in unison.

"Yes!" Miss M agreed.

"I know, but seriously, what do you want to do?" Melinda pressed.

"I don't know yet. Read? Write? Travel?"

Kitt deposited them at Melinda's car and took her leave. "It all sounds good to me, Miss M. Good luck!"

"Thanks Kitt. Good night!"

Melinda helped her into the passenger seat and got to the other side before they could continue.

"It does sound good to get to do what you want after all this time. I'm happy for you."

"Thank you, my dear. I truly feel like it's what is supposed to happen next. It feels right."

"Then it must be."

"Let's get home and get back to work on those albums. My birthday party is in a few weeks."

"I know it, ma'am. Just a few more weeks."

A pot of tomato soup and grilled cheese sandwiches and the coffee was put on to brew.

"That has to be the best grilled cheese I've ever had in my life!" Melinda declared, wiping the buttery crumbs from her face with her bare hand.

"Real butter, real cheese, and hard crust Italian bread," Miss M stated. "And never butter the bread. Always melt the butter in the pan; even between flipping."

"I'll never make them any other way."

Melinda washed and Miss M dried and put away the dishes and pans. Miss M grabbed the mugs from the cabinet and directed Melinda back upstairs for the next box of pictures.

The young woman obeyed and climbed to the same room she had dozens of times over the past few months. Where once had been a mound of carboard cartons stacked precariously to the ceiling in all directions, now was an orderly bank of photo albums lined up and standing knee high against the far windowed wall, and the few boxes left they hadn't yet examined. She took note of the wool rug in the center of the floor that had revealed its pattern one square at a time. It was a deep teal background with swirls of greens and blues upstaged by clusters of big, pastel, and dark pink peonies. She made a mental note to run the vacuum once it was totally free of its cargo.

She stacked two of the remaining boxes on top of one another and carefully descended the stairs.

Miss M was already seated with the coffees and ready to begin.

"We're getting down to the nitty-gritty up there, Miss M," Melinda said. "You should go up and see the progress you've made. You can almost see all of the rug!"

"Really?" she asked. "I can't even remember what rug is down in that room?"

"Peonies."

"Of course. That was the girls' room." Miss M began the story without a photograph to describe, only her memory of the space. "I bought the rug after Hildy grew out of the nursery. I was pregnant with the twins and moved her into the peony room ahead of delivering them. Peonies were my mother's favorite flower. Dad befriended a Chinese grocer who had them for sale in his shop and presented Mother with a bouquet on their first date. She was so impressed. She'd only seen drawings of them in biology class, but they were exquisite to hold in your hands and their scent was honey sweet. The very next day, he returned to the grocer and bought seeds to cultivate his own, so she would always have peonies. When we came to Cleveland, he built flower boxes under the south-facing windows in the apartment so she could have them here. He could grow anything."

"I envy that," Melinda confessed. "I have a brown thumb!"

Miss M laughed, "You? I can't grow anything but mold on my shower curtain!"

That made Melinda laugh out loud and her friend laughed at her laughing.

"I know the building still stands, but are the flower boxes still there, Miss M?"

"Right after we were married, Isaak secretly bought the building. He wanted me to decide what happened to the shop and our little apartment. After Dad died, he told me what he'd done, and I was simply stunned at his generosity. He knew it would be hard to let go of my father and the last place we were a family together, all in one fell swoop."

"Isaak sounds like a fine human."

Miss M smiled at the bittersweetness of the memory.

"So, to answer your question, I don't know if the flower boxes are still there. I didn't do a thing with the building when I could. Now it's just a husk of a place. Probably no good to anyone. I should have rented it to a new family or sold it to another barber. That would have been the thing to do."

Melinda watched as a shadow of regret covered the old woman's face and circled back to the story she began before.

"So the peony room?"

"Oh, yes. I can remember Hildy climbing onto what little lap I had left, out to here with twins, and asking me to tell her the story of Mother and the peonies over and over again in that room. We'd stare down at those flowers and swear they were real. We could almost smell the sweet scent of the blossoms. Hildy pretended there were ants climbing in and out and all up and down the stems."

Miss M sat still and beamed with the glow she surely possessed all those years ago, a young mother tenderly caring for her tiny daughter in that room, on that beautiful rug.

"What a sweet memory," observed Melinda.

She shook her head clear and returned to the present. "I hope we come across a picture of my parents' peonies. I would love to put those in Hildy's album."

"Let's get looking."

As they had since the first box left the peony room, Melinda and Miss M waded through the images on squares of yellowing albumen and glossy scalloped-edged prints. They came across sepia tins and instamatic snapshots alike. A century of recorded lives with all the details elaborated upon by this woman whose memories narrated the show.

"Here we go!" Miss M cheered when she came across an envelope of more recent prints. "These will mostly be Sammy."

"We really haven't had as many of him as the others."

"Hey, listen, he was the youngest of the bunch. Do you know how busy and tired you get after five kids and two of them at once?"

Melinda giggled.

"He's lucky we remembered to get any pictures of him."

She flipped through and handed them off one by one to her secretary.

"Little league, he was eight, so 1957."

"Cute," Melinda commented as she placed the picture and recorded the date.

"This is school crossing guard in fifth grade. 1960."

"Look at his chest puffed out! He's so proud!"

"He was. Ike and Manny teased him about being a man in uniform. But he was so proud of himself for being chosen. You had to have good grades *and* show you could be responsible."

"It was a big deal at my school, too. I never wanted to do it. Too much for me."

"You know, he actually saved a little girl from being hit by a speeding car once."

"Really?"

"Yes! They did a writeup on him in *The Sun*. 'Local Patrol Boy Saves Schoolmate'," Miss M framed the imaginary headline with her hands above her head.

"Wow!"

"It was near the end of the first week of school his fifth-grade year... probably a *Thursday*..."

Melinda smiled.

"She was a first or second grader and she was straggling behind a group of older kids crossing. The driver saw the other students nearing the other side and didn't even brake.

But Samuel saw the little thing dart out and he tackled her back to the curb. The car clipped his flagpole and snapped it in half!"

"Oh my God!" Melinda gasped and pressed her hands to her guts.

"It terrified me. I wanted him to quit right away. It was just too dangerous, I didn't care how heroic it seemed. That was my baby boy!"

"What did he do?"

"He got a new flag and went right back out there."

"Really."

"His dad sat him down and told him that a hero is someone who *does*. Doing *something* is always better than doing nothing."

Miss M lovingly smiled at the boy in the photo.

"Not all the chances he took ended so heroically. The first girl he married was a medical student who left him for her preceptor. His second wife is a gold-digger with the IQ of an old tire. He hunted for bear in Alaska and lost two toes to frostbite. And when he tried to write his novel, a freelance editor stole it and made it into a miniseries."

"Oh no," Melinda sighed. "He started out so strong."

"Hard to believe he peaked just after this picture was taken, huh?" The two shared a sympathetic glance.

"Aww. That's not quite fair. So he had a bunch of do-overs. Hey, that's been the story of my life. There's something to be said for that kind of tenacity."

"You're absolutely right, Melinda. He is my tenacious one. He doesn't know the meaning of the word *quit*. Put 'Hero Patrol Boy 1960' under this one."

They finished the two boxes Melinda retrieved, virtually filling Sam's album, and instead of going for another, Miss M opted to retire to the living room to finish their coffee and talk by the fire.

Melinda ignited the gas logs and curled her feet under her on the sofa opposite her host.

"This is nice."

The two were comfortable in the company of one another.

"I love sitting by the fire again, since you lit it that first night, Melinda," Miss M confessed. "You reminded me of how nice this place felt with the warmth of a fire… and a friend."

"Miss M, I'm glad you see me as a friend," began the younger, "I think of you that way too."

"Don't get all sappy on my now, girl," Miss M frowned.

Melinda laughed, "Of course not. What are we, a couple? It's just lovely to have made a friend in you, that's all. I'm grateful."

"That's nice to hear."

Once Melinda's cup was empty, she stared at the flames another minute, then rose to make her exit.

"I could fall asleep if I sit much longer. I need to start for home. Can I get you another cup of coffee before I go?"

"No thanks. I'll take my time finishing this one, then head to bed myself. Thank you for coming again tonight, Melinda."

"My pleasure, dear. Good night."

Miss M waited until she heard her friend leave by the kitchen door, then she rose to lock it and dump the rest of her coffee in the sink. She listened to the sound of Melinda's tires slush through the street until it trailed off to silence. Busying herself setting up the percolator for tomorrow, turning off the fireplace, and the rest of the downstairs lights, took up the last few minutes of Miss M's day. When she finally headed past the stairs to her room, she stopped at the newel post and looked up for a moment.

"I *would* like to see the progress we made," she admitted to the empty halls.

But in the next moment she acknowledged her fatigue and decided not the risk the stairs so late and alone in the house. She dropped her head and stared at her slippered feet.

"I never thought a single thing about that before, and the day I announce my retirement, I suddenly feel afraid to walk up my own damn stairs." She scolded herself aloud, "You lily-livered chicken shit."

She shook her head and put herself to bed.

Melinda wrote the money order out for the full amount, having deposited the last three overtime checks Brady mailed from Delaware. They had more than enough to cover the rest of Caldwell's fee and were looking at a small surplus they could use to pay for the move. He walked her through the updates and assured her that there wasn't a bank in Ohio that wouldn't approve a loan on the place now. She clamped both her hands over his when they shook on it and thanked him profusely for a job well done.

Once his truck cleared the driveway, she looked up the number of Home At Last Realty and made the call.

"Hello, Mary? It's Melinda Garlow. We're ready!"

Mary Rutherford wasted no time getting a sign in the yard and submitting the listing for the paper that Sunday. She had the description ready, including the selling points 'new furnace and all new electrical' even before the renovations were done.

Melinda waited for Brady's Friday night call.

"Hello!"

"Oh, how good it is to hear your voice, honey," he breathed. "I've had a helluva week!"

"Lot's going on here too, baby."

"Really? What's the old bat up to now?"

"No, not with Miss M," Melinda reassured him. "Well, she announced her retirement, but no, not with her. With *us*!"

"*Us?*"

"Caldwell's done, Brady!"

Crickets...

He couldn't make a sound.

She worried.

"Brady? Babe, are you there?"

"Did you just say that Caldwell is done?"

"Yep. I paid him off this afternoon and called Mary Rutherford immediately."

"You're kidding right? He wasn't due to finish for two more weeks! How the hell is he already done?"

"When you wired in the box downstairs for the dryer, you must have done some of the stuff they thought they'd still have to do."

"I'll be damned! I guess I did something right, huh?"

"You sure did, babe!"

"Well... so... what did Mary say?"

"She came over with a sign just after calling in the ad to *The Sun* for Sunday!"

"There's already a sign in the yard? Damn, Mary Rutherford does not mess around!"

The couple giggled with excitement until Melinda remembered the 'helluva week' her husband mentioned at the start of the call.

"Wait, what's your helluva week?" she asked.

"Oh yeah! So Riffle came down to the floor after lunch and said they were posting a supervisor's job opening on the body paint and prep floor and said I should sign up for it. He knew that was the department I started in at Ford and said he heard they were hoping to find someone with experience. So I went to talk to the foreman about it and got myself an interview Monday morning before my shift starts."

"Oh my God, Brady, that's amazing!"

"Wait, honey, that's not even the *best* news," he cautioned. "I think I found us a new place!"

"What? Where? What's it like?"

"Slow down, slow down. I don't have it yet but it's between me and another guy at the plant, but he's single and the daughter of the old lady that's selling it says her mom wants it to go to a family."

"Aww. That's so sweet. Well, where is it? Have you seen it?"

"Yes, of course. I rode out there with Johnson last week and looked it over. It's three bedrooms all on one floor with a screened-in porch out back and a big backyard, that's mostly sand and pebbles but a little grass, and some nice creeping myrtle trees. The house needs some love but they want someone who can rent to own and I'll be damned if that's not us, right, honey?"

"Brady, it sounds perfect. I can't wait to see it."

"Now that you bring it up, how long do you think we'll have to wait?"

"Right…" the wind escaped her sails, and she tried hard to hide it from him. "I just need to write up my letter of resignation and then I can start the countdown, I guess."

"You *guess*? You guess!"

She felt his temperature rising through the phone and headed him off. "No. I mean, I'm writing my letter and delivering the news at the Monday morning meeting. I will work out my two-week notice, Brady. That much I owe these people."

"Whew! I thought for a minute there you were getting cold feet. *I guess*. You scared me again, Melinda Jo."

"I *told* you I would be ready when the time came, Brady." That came out sterner than she meant it to, but she didn't retreat. "I know you're busting your ass over there, but I've been doing everything I can, too."

"I know, honey. I didn't mean…"

"I am the one who has lived with the mess and the noise, and the adjusting to full-time teaching, and the politics of that place, and all the guilt that we got stuck unloading this debt in the first place!"

"Honey…honey….easy," he cooed. "Easy does it, Mrs. Garlow. We're a team, remember. I know you've had it tough alone back there, while I've had Roger and Charlie to keep me company and all the overtime to keep me busy. Believe me, every spare minute I wasn't working, I thought about you and what you're doing to get us out of there."

She settled herself with a breath and returned the gratitude.

"And I can only imagine how hard you've been working, regardless of whether or not you had company when you were off. Maybe if you get this supervisor position, you won't have to work so many hours."

"Fewer hours and more pay!"

"Brady, that would be the very best ever!"

Their hackles relaxed, the couple returned to neutral ground and spent the rest of the call fantasizing about the kids they'd fill those three bedrooms and that screen porch with when the next chapter of their lives began.

⚶

Although Reynolds had been back to work since right before the new year, Ike was instructed to busy him elsewhere away from Miss M. She insisted that until she purchased a new vehicle, she was content to share the commute with Melinda. This only helped to increase the family's suspicion about their relationship. Melinda was caught up in the sport of it and her own anticipation of Miss M's big reveal grew with every passing day. Driving to pick her up on the morning she would tender her resignation though had the young woman anxious. She practiced on the way there.

"Miss M, I have good news! No… great news, Miss M!"

She sighed heavily and attempted another approach.

"Miss M, we've become so close, I feel I should let you know before we get to school that I have to tender my resignation."

She sat at a red light and listened to that one play back in her imagination.

"Hmm. Do I have to say the part about us becoming so close? That's a given. She won't want to hear a bunch of superfluous jibber-jabber. Keep it simple, Melinda. Miss M, I'm tendering my resignation this morning. The house is done and we're ready to move on."

That was the one. Simple. Short. Succinct.

She went over it aloud again a couple more times before she reached the big house and put on her blinker to turn into the drive. She stopped short just before the carport because a shiny, new, 2000, pearl white Cadillac stood directly under the canopy with dealer plates and fresh tire marks trailing behind it in the snow.

"Wow," she said flatly and parked.

She made it to the stoop just as Miss M was coming out the door.

"Morning Melinda," greeted Miss M as if nothing were different.

"You ready to go?" asked the young woman.

"Of course. Why wouldn't I be?"

Melinda gestured to the new car and Miss M all but ignored it.

"Oh that. That doesn't mean a thing."

Melinda took her elbow, and they carefully navigated the steps to the drive.

"When did you get it?"

"Ike found it Saturday and sent Sammy and Reynolds over here this morning to deliver it."

They were inside Melinda's car now.

"Reynolds came?"

"Sam drove the Caddy and Reynolds followed him in *his* car. I suppose he thought I'd let him drive me this morning.

But I said, no thank you sir! Melinda and I have things to discuss."

"We do?" Melinda checked, already dreading what she had to talk about. "What things?"

"The party, of course! Oh, and I got you something."

Melinda drove on and glanced down at her passenger wrangling something from her tote bag. When she stopped at the next light, she turned to see Miss M holding up two new photo albums.

"They're for you and Brady!"

Melinda's eyes relaxed and glassed over with a thin layer of tears.

"Oh, Miss M!"

"One for your past and one to start you out going forward."

The light changed and rescued the women from a moment too sentimental for the time they had left in the car.

"That is truly the sweetest thing. Thank you."

"No, dear. Thank *you*! I couldn't and probably *wouldn't* have gone through my picture boxes without all your help and encouragement. I am really looking forward to presenting the albums to the children. It has truly become a celebration to me now that I have something of value to share with them."

"They're going to love it! Do you think they suspect anything?"

"How could they?" the old woman giggled. "I like the secret part. Oh, they know we're up to something, but they have no clue what it is."

Melinda shook her head thinking about how devious this old girl was, then came the ambush.

"So, what's with the for sale sign in your front yard, Melinda?"

Melinda's spine straightened in her seat and sent her braking foot hard to the floor, jolting the car to a violent stop in front of the school. The two women reached simultaneously across the seat to catch each other in the moment.

"Shit!" grimaced Melinda. "I'm so sorry, Miss M."

"I'm ok. What was *that* all about?"

"I was going to tell you this morning on our way to work. But here we are and you already saw the sign? I wanted you to know before the meeting this morning…"

"You've chewed it up, kid. Now spit it out!"

"I'm quitting!" Melinda blurted it out and then exhaled and put the car in park. "The contractors are done, so we can finally list the place. Brady found a little house in Delaware and he is up for a promotion. We're moving. I'm turning in my two weeks' notice today."

"Well now, see? That wasn't so hard, was it?"

Melinda looked confused for a second, then admitted, "No… it wasn't."

"I don't know why everyone is always afraid to tell me things," Miss M wondered out loud. "Have a little courage. No one is truly fearless. Even *I'm* afraid of some things. Being courageous means knowing you're afraid and going ahead in the face of it. It's never as bad as you think."

Melinda was spellbound. She expected a fit, a tantrum, or even a good cussing. Instead, this once hardened old soul met her with compassion and kindness.

"Thank you for understanding, Miss M. I guess I felt bad for leaving you to the mercy of Reynolds' driving again, so I dreaded telling you."

"We'll finish together in two weeks. We'll celebrate at my party and who knows, maybe if I need a ride after that, one of my kids might volunteer to take me."

"I like the way you think, ma'am!"

Once the breakfast meeting commenced, Melinda watched Miss M for a sign to interject with her news. When the old woman nodded, she went forward with it.

"I have something to say," she started, then cleared her throat to continue. "I am sorry to say, I am giving my notice today." She took in the faces around the table and handed her resignation to Miss M.

Deidre's eyes rolled beneath their swollen lids and she muttered under her breath, "That didn't take long."

Kitt frowned in her direction and took the letter as Miss M handed it down the table toward Ike's end. "*I* will be sorry to see you go, Melinda."

"We will *all* be sorry to see her go, Kitt," Miss M agreed. "Jeannie, why don't you dig up the other resumes that came in when we hired Melinda and see if we can choose someone without advertising again?"

"Or maybe there's a senior who just left we could hire?" offered Manny.

"That's actually smart," Sam agreed. "Job placement for a graduate *and* filling the staff position."

Melinda was pleased that her leaving wouldn't leave many ripples and even though she felt a little too replaceable by their nonchalant reaction, she had already started to separate herself from the place in her head. No one uttered a word about her quitting after they concluded the meeting, but she and Kitt talked about one last lunch at Tiny's and staying in touch on the way down the fire stairs. They were each glad to say they'd made a friend in the other.

Melinda would miss lunches at Tiny's and Kitt, but the others hadn't bothered themselves to bond with her. They would probably be like her ex-coworkers at the library, barely remembered.

But Miss M was another story.

Miss M had endeared herself to Melinda in a way that no one else had; not her mother, or Aunt Helen, or even Brady had imprinted as much as Mrs. Emalina Malloy Maxwell. And even if she felt like she was already leaving the others behind, she was sure she'd never forget Miss M.

She lamented leaving her friend the rest of the afternoon and just before the bell to dismiss for the day, Manny and Sam came knocking again.

She advised her students on what they'd need to do for homework and walked out into the hall and closed the door.

"What's up, fellas?"

"Quite a bombshell you dropped at the meeting this morning, Melinda," Manny began. "Had Jeannie scurrying around all day to call those other people for interviews."

"You're worried about Jeannie?"

"No. Of course not," Sam answered. "That's what she does. We're worried about our mother!"

Melinda blinked at the puff of air that accompanied Sam's urgent intent.

Manny placed a hand on his brother's arm in an effort to soften their approach. "We are worried that you two have become so close and with her retiring and all, we're just hoping you can let us in on what you two have been doing all those nights and weekends you're spending together."

"How do *you* know I've been over there in the evenings?" Melinda played. "Just kidding. I don't care if you've been spying on us. We're friends, boys. I *like* your mom. She's funny and smart and she's seen so much in her lifetime. I love hearing her stories, you know?"

The two stood stock still, trying to recognize any portion of the woman Melinda was describing as their mother.

"Stories… right," Manny agreed. "So, is she telling you stories about our family? Private stories?"

"Nothing that hasn't been in the papers!" Melinda kidded with a wink and an elbow.

The men grabbed each other and shared an expression of mild shock.

"Nothing personal, jeez!" she explained. "Just family stories of when you kids were little and before you were born, when she and your dad got together. Nothing scandalous, I assure you." She studied their faces and then she thought she got it. "Oh! You're worried that I'll go away and talk shit on everyone here, aren't you?"

The men recovered and began shaking their heads in unison.

"You have nothing to worry about. I wouldn't tell a soul what she shared with me. You won't have to worry about the IRS coming after you for something *I've* heard, scout's honor!"

She crossed her heart with two fingers, kissed her fingertips, and held them up to avow her discretion to the pair.

The dismissal bell rang. BRRRRRRRRRRINGGGG!

"Great!" said Manny nervously and turned his brother at the shoulders to leave her in the hallway to be swallowed by the mass exodus of students ending their day.

She called out after them, "She's going to share it all when we leave!"

They barely caught her last words over the clamor in the hall. The men took the back stairs up to the sixth floor, where an informal board meeting was taking shape in the conference room. Ike, Marta, and Gus waited for the spies. Only Hildy, Farmer, and Miss M herself were absent from the official roll.

Manny and Sam blew in and Gus slammed the door shut behind them and begged, "What did she tell you?"

"She said Mother's been talking about the *family*!" Manny panted in a sweat.

"She said nothing *private*, nothing the *I... R... S* would need to know about!" added Sam.

Marta snapped her fingers. "It's the money!"

"We don't know that, Marta," Ike cautioned. "And even if it is, what *is* it about the money?"

They all guessed at once.

"Where it is!"

"How much is left!"

"If it's all gone!"

Ike put his hands up in surrender, "Alright! That's just about enough." He turned his attention back to his brothers. "Did she actually use the word 'money' at all?"

They each replayed the conversation to themselves while their breathing returned to normal, looked at each other for confirmation, and shook their heads.

"No," Sam said. "But she said, 'she'd share it all when we leave'."

"When who leaves? *Mother*?" asked Marta.

"Melinda."

"*Melinda* would share it all when Mother leaves?" asked Gus.

"No! Melinda said *Mother* would share it all when Melinda *leaves* and Mother *retires*."

They all thought about it for a moment. Then Gus broke the silence.

"Well, what the hell does *that* mean?"

The group fell into wild speculation about the cryptic message their mother's only friend left them to decipher. They lingered over the possibilities well after the street lamps were summoned to light the dark mid-January streets.

Everyone would have to wait two more weeks.

🌱

"Yes, Miss M, I agree with you," Melinda stated. "But in this case, I think you'd be better off going with the flow, as they say."

"Who says that? Riverboat captains! It's *my* birthday, and I wanted to celebrate on my *actual* birthday!"

"You know how much trouble they've gone to. Saturday was the better choice for a party of this magnitude. No one wants to book a hotel ballroom on a Monday night."

"I didn't ask for any of this extravagance. This is all Ike and his snotty wife. This isn't me!"

The old girl was losing sight of her mission and Melinda was the only one who could reel her back in.

"Miss M, you need to be gracious and let the children celebrate you. I know if you had your way, you'd be in your lounging pajamas in front of your fireplace giving them your gifts like some Christmas past scenario, and if you want, you and I can celebrate just like that day-after-tomorrow. But just be nice and show them you appreciate it."

Miss M sat dressed to the nines, arms folded, pouting in the spacious back seat of her new Cadillac next to Melinda, also in her best eveningwear, as Reynolds carefully drove them to The Renaissance Cleveland.

She showed little signs of lightening up and Melinda knew she was just nervous about how things would go, so she tried once more before they turned down Superior Avenue.

"I read there is supposed to be a lunar eclipse on the night of your actual birthday."

The old woman allowed the hint of a grin to turn up the corners of her mouth.

"I'll come over after work and bring hoagies from Tiny's and you and I can stay up all night and watch it. It will be our big finale. Deal?"

Miss M turned to the girl and reached for her hand across the seat.

"I can't think of any better way to celebrate."

The car came to a gentle stop and Reynolds parked in front of the towering e-shaped building. The doorman helped Miss M out of the car, only to be sharply ordered to bring out the bellboys and start transporting the boxes in her trunk to a secure location just outside the ballroom where the party was to take place. Melinda would stay with the cargo and arrange it for the presentation while Miss M was escorted into the hotel and deposited with Ike and the others.

All of Cleveland's small business owners had been invited to the event. Miss M was taken to a chair in the center of the head table and a few at a time, all the merchants took a turn coming by to reintroduce themselves and their spouses and wish her many happy returns.

Miss M assumed she would hate all the attention, but what she found was something akin to what she uncovered while completing the picture project; her connection to all these kind people had been weakened and faded by the time she spent with her head down and her forward momentum in running the school. She met sons and daughters of the bakers, cobblers, tailors, and florists that used to thrive downtown, who had long since buried their parents but still kept some piece of their livelihoods afloat. The Select Pastry family moved their operation to the mall when the old lady died. The East Side Florists sold their building on Murphy Street but expanded their greenhouse just outside of town and distributed to all the supermarkets and flower outlets in the greater Cleveland area.

Her town wasn't dying. Just like the academy had for decades, it was just reinventing itself for the next generation. She was channeling Isaak all night. She could feel his diplomacy and good will flowing through her and their children. This wasn't just a celebration of her life of ninety years, but a tribute to her family's mark on the community in which they'd lived and worked. With every handshake and old story shared, she felt more and more endeared to those around her, and her confidence grew in the gifts she made for her children to be the pinnacle of the evening.

After dinner was enjoyed, Manny and Marta escorted their mother around in front of the head table while the beautiful room filled with toasts and then singing as the band played and the catering staff wheeled in the cart bearing the cake ablaze with candles. The rest of the family gathered in around her and together they blew the fire out to the great hall, erupting in cheers. She symbolically cut into the cake and vogued for the photographer from *The Sun Press*.

Melinda sat at a table with the rest of the academy staff and watched her friend for the signal.

Miss M winked at the girl as they moved the cake aside to cut and serve, and Melinda excused herself and darted for a side door that lead to a service entrance just outside the ballroom. There a line of hotel staff stood with carts of the photo albums neatly stacked and covered with crisp white linen tablecloths.

Melinda radiated with excitement as she led the way toward the front of the room while Miss M was preparing the crowd for the unveiling.

"I am overwhelmed with gratitude for this heart-felt display of love and respect from all of you tonight," she began, lifting a glass of champagne. "I'd like to propose a toast… or two, this evening, if you'll bear with me."

A collective laugh.

"To Cleveland! This place can be hard and demanding. It can stink to high heaven and still come out smelling like a rose. It can sink you and at the same time encourage you to rise up and overcome the worst life has to throw at you. But to each and every one of us here tonight, Cleveland is our home. Where our people were buried and our babies were born. She is our lives and our livelihoods. And I love her. To Cleveland!"

The cheers and applause echoed in the great hall like it was midnight New Year's Eve. Everyone was on their feet, lauding one of the most powerful fixtures in their community. She hushed them, waited for them to sit, and kept on.

"My next toast is to my family." She batted at the shoulders of the closest ones to her and urged them all to stand and be recognized. "These beautiful people are mine. Their father and I brought them into this life with love and hope that they'd be good for us and indeed the world they lived in."

The grown children braced for what they weren't sure
would come next.

"Ike, Manny, Gus, Marta, Hildy, and Sam," she raised her
glass. "Three cheers for the best damn kids a mother could
ever ask for!"

The motley crew stood flabbergasted at their mother's
praise while all of Cleveland's business elite hailed them
alongside her.

"Hip, hip, hooray! Hip, hip, hooray! Hip, hip, hooray!"

Once again, Miss M called to quiet the crowd, and she
gathered Melinda up under her wing.

"And to this little girl, Melinda Garlow. Many of you knew
her people. Not only is she from excellent stock, but she
herself has proven to be made of the best stuff these last
five months."

Melinda's shoulders caved in a little under the attention and
she felt the heat rise up her neck to flush her face.

"Melinda came to work for us at the academy in the fall
and she has helped me with a special project very close to
my heart. A reward of sorts for my children and all they
mean to me and have done for me."

Ike and Gus exchanged hopeful looks. Marta grabbed
Hildy's hand, and they all held their breath.

"Melinda, will you help me?"

The girl signaled the white jackets to wheel the carts out in front of the head table and wait behind them while Miss M gathered her children around her once more.

Melinda stepped back out of the way and gave her friend and her family center stage.

"Children, Melinda and I have gone through every photograph your father and I had and made each one of you your own personal Maxwell family albums to have and keep for yourselves and your families!"

The linens were pulled from atop all the carts to reveal the dark blue and black chronicles Melinda and Miss M had so painstakingly sorted and compiled in the first long, dark weeks of winter.

The Maxwell family stood stone still in the vacuum of the grand ballroom of The Renaissance Hotel, flat and unimpressed.

Another round of applause burst forth from the crowd, only to die down to a muted dissonance when those closest to them read the disappointment on the faces of the clan.

Then it began to unravel.

Hildy snorted out a quiet giggle… then she began to laugh out loud… then she slapped her hands together repeatedly in a slow, deliberate show of contempt.

"Brilliant, Mother!" she exclaimed. "Look at them. They're shocked. They all thought they were getting a check tonight. And instead you're giving us pictures of our childhood? I *love* it!"

"Marta, shut her up!" seethed Gus, who was too far from his drunken sister to reach without drawing attention.

Marta grabbed at her wrist, but she tugged away and staggered back to her place at the table, leaving the rest of her siblings to fend for themselves.

"Thank you, Mother!" Manny stepped forward to save face. "This is a delightful surprise."

The crowd began shifting in their seats. Melinda sweat and wrung her hands while she watched helplessly.

"No, Manny!" Marta charged in, shaking her head. "Hildy's right, Mother! If we've been so good for you and the world, where is our cut?"

"Marta, shut up!" Ike reacted before he could check himself. "Not here."

Miss M stood frowning in disbelief.

"Why not here, son?" she asked. "You afraid of what all these people will think of you and your money-hungry brothers and sisters? You afraid of making a bad impression on all these important people?"

Sam and Gus moved in front of their mother to quiet her, and Hildy chugged another flute of champagne, then started her slow clap again.

"Hip, hip, hooray, Momma! Hip, hip, hooray!" she mocked.

"Get away from me, you spoiled brats!" the old woman seethed, her voice straining against the combination of anger and grief.

The children closed their circle tighter, and Manny signaled the band to resume playing to divert the crowd for the moment.

Ike put his arm around his mother's shoulder and squeezed to physically drive her out of the spotlight and away from the view of the crowd.

"Let go of me, Ike!"

She leaned away from his body, and he pulled her back.

"Is that what you want? Do want the money? Melinda!" She tried to look over the guard of her children for her friend. "Melinda, give them the goddamned books! Give them the books!"

Melinda started toward her, and Manny cut her off.

"Let the family handle this now, Melinda," he hissed at her.

She stood back in horror as they manhandled their mother back behind the table again and then one more flail of her tiny body and… they lost her!

The men dove to catch her just after Miss M tugged free and fell through the banquet chair onto the floor with a terrible crash, pulling the table setting and her purse to the ground with her.

"Melinda!" she called out, clutching her chest.

"Mother!" Ike screamed and looked around for his brother. "Manny, get these people out of here and go get help!"

Manny walked toward the guests and, waving his hands toward the exits, directed them to leave quietly and thanked them for coming, apologizing for the display as they left.

Marta pushed through her brothers and took hold of her mother's hand.

"I'm here Mother," she faked. "We're all right here. Are you alright?"

"No, I'm not alright, goddamn it! I want Melinda!" she pushed at her daughter. "Melinda, give them the books!"

"Forget about the fuckin' books, Mother!" Gus barked. "Are you hurt?"

They fussed and crowded in on the old bird while she fought for the space to breathe, clutching her chest tighter and wincing in pain.

Hildy laid her head down over her outstretched arm at her place at the table and looked over at the frozen Melinda.

"You better go," she urged. "You're being summoned."

Melinda stared at the drunken woman, too afraid to move, when she heard her friend call out to her one more time.

"Melinda!"

Then she darted for the old girl. She pushed past Marta and Gus and knelt down on the floor right next to her friend.

"I'm here, Miss M," she said. "You're going to be alright."

Melinda was terrified. Her perfectly coiffed hair was tousled in her eyes, her face contorted with pain, losing color by the minute. The young woman looked around to see the contents of her friend's purse spilled all around them and wished she could take her compact, freshen her makeup, and put her hairdo right for her. The old woman hated to be undone. And to be undone in front of this crowd of people. Melinda was choking on the shame, sure to be smothering her friend.

Miss M held tight to Melinda's hand and pulled her closer. She raised up to whisper to the young woman and Melinda cradled her head to help support it.

"I feel like I have to shit," she whispered.

Melinda's eyes widened, and an awkward smile crept onto her face.

"You what?"

"I feel like I have to poop, Melinda. Get me up and take me to the bathroom."

"Miss M, we can't move you. You have to stay put until the ambulance comes."

"I don't want to go anywhere in an ambulance. Get me up or I'm going to shit in my pants, I tell you!"

"Then just do it," said Melinda without batting an eye. "If you feel like your bowels are going to move, then just do it. Shit your pants full, Miss M. Who cares?"

Now the old *woman's* eyes widened, and she giggled at the prospect of embarrassing Ike and his snotty wife just one more time tonight by filling her pants at The Renaissance Hotel.

"Here they are!" Manny announced as he led the men with the gurney toward his mother.

The others backed away to give them room to assess her.

She kept Melinda close to her until they pulled their hands apart.

"Give them the books, honey," she said one final time before they rolled her out of the ballroom and out of the hotel.

"Somebody get Hildy," ordered Ike as he followed the gurney out the giant French doors. Gus and Marta each hooked one of her arms over their necks and pulled her free from the table, then dragged her out a side door of the hall.

Melinda looked at Sam and Manny and pleaded, "Please take the books. That's all she wanted to do tonight was give you something meaningful."

"We need to get to the hospital, Melinda," snapped Manny.

Sam knelt next to where his mother was, gathering her spilled purse and barked, "You take the damn books!"

Melinda stood surveying the damage in the empty ballroom while the family departed… without the books. She looked down at where her friend had been just moments before. She didn't feel it, but her legs bent out from under her and she suddenly found herself on the cold, glossy marble floor. Her head swam with the images of the night and her throat tightened with tears she couldn't hold back any longer.

"My friend," she cried. "My friend."

She held her hands tight against her eyes and wept, broken-hearted and afraid until she was spent. She hadn't even noticed that the concierge had returned and was standing over her, trying to give her the moment.

She opened her eyes with a start.

"Oh!"

"Oh, no miss," he started. "Please, I'm so sorry. Is there anything we can do for you?"

She wiped her face and moved to all fours to get herself vertical but stopped dead when she saw it.

Max Factor Red Rose #3.

It must have rolled under the table when she dumped her purse.

"Miss?" he asked, not knowing how to help her to her feet.

She reached for the lipstick and sat back on folded legs for another moment, just looking at the label on the bottom of the tube and picturing the state her friend was in when she left her ninetieth birthday party.

"If she just could have put on her lipstick."

"Miss?"

She shook her head clear and reached for the concierge to get herself off the floor, clutching the lipstick tightly in her hand.

"What should we do with her books?"

Melinda took a deep breath and decided.

"I'll take them with me."

"Do you have a car out front?"

In the next moment they heard the echoing opening of the enormous doors, and there stood Reynolds.

She smiled. "He can take me."

Reynolds placed the last of the albums in a neat stack well inside Melinda's garage and gently closed the trunk of Miss M's new Cadillac.

"I'm going to the hospital to see if they need anything," he said.

"Can I give you my number?" Melinda asked. "I just want to know if she's ok."

He nodded.

She looked around and spied the yellowing pages of an old calendar hanging just inside the door to the breezeway. She snatched a corner off the first page and grabbed the pencil hanging from a piece of twine that shared a nail with the record of expired reminders.

"Call me if Miss M needs anything, ok?"

"Sure."

"I don't care how late."

He folded the note and placed it in his pants pocket, then nodded again and went for the car.

"Reynolds!" she called after him.

He stopped at the open door and turned back.

"Thank you!"

A kindness spread his across his face, and he smiled.

"Thank you for taking such good care of her all those years," she went on and walked a pace or two toward him. She felt compelled to set him straight for her friend. "I know how hard it was to take her crap. Believe me!"

"Yes, ma'am. You and I might be the *only* ones who know."

"But I also know she was grateful for your help."

"That's kind of you to say, Miss Melinda."

She watched him climb behind the wheel and disappear down the dark street. Standing in the driveway, holding her coat tight over her party clothes, she watched as a silent snow began to fall. Staring up into the black sky, she was mesmerized by the flakes glistening in the light of the street lamps and the glow of the open garage behind her. She wondered if the weather would be clearer in a couple of nights for her and Miss M to see the eclipse. She stood for another moment wondering how it all went so sour, so fast, then she saw headlights out of the corner of her eye.

She watched as the truck pulled up in front of her house and a man got out of the passenger side.

She puffed out a breath of air with his name in it, "Brady!"

She ran down the driveway and he met her in the headlight beams of Riffle's pickup. She jumped into his arms and wept with relief or happiness or grief or all of it. He held her up above the wet street for a moment, then set her down and covered her shoulders with his coat and waved his friend off as he walked her back up the drive.

They closed the garage and made it in to the kitchen when she collapsed in a chair at the table and started related the events of the night. He sat holding her hands and wiping her tears as she cried over the fate of her friend.

She sobbed to a stop and held his face.

"I can't believe you're home, Brady."

He smiled and stared at her.

"Wait! Why are you home, Brady?" she asked. "What's wrong?"

"Nothing, honey," he answered. "Nothing is wrong. It's all really, really good, Melinda."

"*What's* really good? What's going on?"

"I got the promotion, and the company is giving me this week to get us moved."

She looked stunned. Could this really be happening? Are they finally getting out?

"Brady, that's wonderful," she said, her posture failing a little from the weight of the last year resting on her bones. "I thought this day would never come."

She teared up again, and he caught the first drop with his fingertip.

"I *told* you, honey. I *promised* we'd be on our way sooner than later."

She inched across the table and wrapped herself around his neck.

"Thank you, thank you, thank you," she whispered again and again into his hair.

He rose from his chair, cradled her in his arms, and walked her up the stairs, under the new trim, and into their room. He placed her on their bed and laid down beside her to hold her and comfort her like he wanted to all those nights they spent apart. She rested her head on his chest and drifted off to sleep with the sound of his heartbeat in her ear once again.

Barely an hour ticked off and the phone rang, waking them both with a start.

"That's Reynolds!" Melinda slurred and lunged for the phone. "Hello?"

Brady sat up and put his hand on her knee and waited, watching her face.

She didn't say another word. She let her hands fall to her lap, still holding the receiver.

"Honey?" he said. "What is it?"

She hung up the phone and stared blankly into the dark room.

"My friend is gone," she said. She heard the words escape her head just before it filled with the deafening din of grief that crashed in on her.

Brady wrapped around her again and held her in her pain while she mourned.

⁂

Melinda stayed in bed all day Sunday while Brady fielded phone calls from Kitt, Jeannie, and even Deidre. She didn't want to talk to anyone. He made sure she didn't have to. She refused to eat all day until he insisted around dinnertime when he brought her some soup and crackers.

"Just a few bites, Melinda, please."

"I'll try," she relented. "I'm just not hungry."

"I know, honey. But you have to get something in you."

She sat up in bed, and he placed the tray over her lap.

"I'm half sick to my stomach," she admitted.

"I'm sure it's from not eating."

She nibbled on a saltine and shook her head.

"I don't think so, babe. I feel sick."

"Just try for me, please."

She waved the cracker in his face and he shot her a pointed look, then left her alone.

The next morning, Brady opened the door to retrieve the Monday morning edition of the paper to find Mary Rutherford on his stoop about to ring the bell.

"Mary!" he said with a start. "Did we have an appointment?"

"Good morning, Mr. Garlow!" she began.

"Please, call me Brady. I was just coming for the morning paper."

She knelt to pick it up and handed it over as she invited herself past. "Mind if I come in?"

He made a hole for her to enter and lead her to the living room, where he offered her a seat.

"I'm sorry, Melinda isn't up yet," he excused. "She lost a friend over the weekend and she's taking it pretty hard."

"It wasn't Mrs. Maxwell, was it? It's all over today's paper. She and I served on the Committee for a Better Cleveland. Just short of her ninetieth birthday. What a shame."

Brady glanced down at the front page spread dedicated to Miss M and her contribution to the community. He smiled when he thought about Melinda finding a place of honor in the family Bible for the story.

"Well, I don't need Melinda for this visit, Brady." She beamed and clasped her hands together under her chin to announce the news, "I just wanted you to know that I've already had several calls about the house and I have three couples scheduled for tours tomorrow and four Wednesday. And I still want to stage an open house!"

His eyes narrowed, and he leaned toward the woman. "No kidding?"

"No kidding, mister. Isn't that exciting?"

"Oh, Mary, you have no idea!"

"Well, I can't stay," she said as she popped to her feet. "Just wanted to let you know it's time to polish up this old girl so we can impress one of these potential buyers. The cleaner the better."

"Yes, ma'am!" he cheered. "I'll go over everything with a fine-tooth comb. She'll be spic-and-span. Thanks for letting us know."

He showed her out, and they exchanged their 'see you tomorrows' then he bolted up the stairs to his wife.

She heard his bounding footsteps and cringed about the time he would have crashed into the trim, but heard no hesitation, no splintering wood.

He made it to the door, panting and all smiles.

"I didn't hear you bash into the trim, Brady. Are you finally getting the hang of it?" she asked.

"That was Mary downstairs."

"Mary Rutherford? I didn't hear the doorbell?"

"She didn't ring it," he puffed and crossed to sit next to her on the bed. "She came by to say she has buyers coming tomorrow and Wednesday. Seven couples are already lined up to tour the place! And she hasn't even scheduled the open house yet!"

"Brady!" she squealed and grabbed his sleeves. "That's awesome! Oh my God, wait!"

Her expression changed from smiling to stunned and his to a frown.

"No, no, no! No *wait*, honey. There's no more waiting!" he cautioned.

"No, I just mean we have a lot to get done."

He sighed with relief. "*Cleaning*. Yes, she said we need to get it shining to impress the buyers."

"Let's get going!" Melinda urged.

Brady jumped from the bed and asked, "Are you sure you're up for it?"

"I'm still sick to my stomach today, Brady, but I'm ready. I literally have nothing and no one keeping me here anymore. Let's get this house sold!"

He clapped his big hands together and waited for her directive.

"I'll start up here and you get the sweeper going downstairs," she dictated. "We can pack as we clean, throw me up some empty boxes from the garage before you get started."

The couple went into hyper-drive to accomplish their tasks. Melinda pushed through despite her nausea and had the upstairs bathroom and bedrooms clean, dusted, and vacuumed in a couple of hours. She was packing their summer clothes when she stopped to come down for more boxes and spied the paper on the coffee table where Brady left it.

"Happy Birthday, old girl," she said under her breath.

She sat for a moment and read the writeup. Someone had taken great pains to include all the best things her friend had accomplished, her education, her part in the academy, her membership in business associations and seats on civic committees, her children and grandchildren. They mentioned her immigration to America as a tot and her parents and their origins. But nowhere in the entire article did it mention one friend. Melinda didn't expect to be named but felt it odd that no one else was mentioned either. Not one nod to any one person she was close to outside her immediate family. The piece ended with the funeral announcement which read '…private family service to be held at Cummings and Davis Funeral Home.'

She felt hurt that she wouldn't be afforded the chance at a proper goodbye. She stared at the picture of Miss M taking up the top third of the paper and spoke to it as if she were in the room with the grand dame herself.

"Let'em have their private family service, Miss M. I've got a much better sendoff planned for us."

Melinda sent her husband to Tiny's for the hoagies they'd pack for the late night celebration. Then the couple milled around, packing a few more boxes and stacking everything in the garage to get the mess out of Mary Rutherford's way. They watched the eleven o'clock news and when the weatherman said it would be clear the rest of the night, they smiled at each other and jumped from the couch. Melinda put a sixpack of Miller High Life in a cooler bag and bundled up before meeting Brady outside in the warming car; the trunk stuffed with lawn chairs and blankets.

"It feels weird sitting in her seat," she confessed.

"Do you want to drive?" he offered.

She shook her head.

They drove through the frigid January night the same route she had taken for four months with Miss M. Melinda's head turned when they passed her darkened house on the way to Merrifield Road. She remembered shimmying down into the basement, discovering the pictures, every cup of coffee, every mundane Thursday, and all the other tiny details of her friendship with Miss M. She smiled, knowing that she alone knew that version of her friend.

Brady pulled down an alley across from the academy that wound around the back of the barbershop where Miss M grew up. He parked and looked up at the zig-zagging fire escape stairs that clung to the old bricks.

"You sure you want to do this, Melinda?" he checked one last time.

"Positive. I promised."

They got out of the car and approached the building. Brady jumped for the ladder and waited for it to descend before climbing with the chairs hooked over his shoulder and the blankets under his arm. Melinda waited until he was clear and hung the cooler bag over her shoulder and made her way up. They ascended the rusty metal stairs, switching back at every landing to make it to the next floor. They passed the porch boxes Miss M told Melinda about, now rotten and decaying. Melinda pictured them brimming with sweet peonies and her friend delivering the cut blooms to her ailing mother. She imagined Isaak waking from his stupor to find Emalina's note. She envisioned the teenaged version of her friend spying on the gangsters talking shop in her father's barber chair downstairs.

The two made it to the roof and Brady helped Melinda hike her leg up over the ledge and onto the safety of the horizontal surface. They both puffed out great clouds of wet breath from the effort.

"You ok, honey?" he asked.

"I need a minute to catch my breath, Brady," she answered. "I feel so tired."

The man waited by his wife's side until she could take a full, deep breath, then he led her away from the edge to a spot near the center of the roof. He looked up to survey the view and decided where to plant the chairs.

"How about right here?"

"This is fine. I just need to sit."

"We did too much today, Melinda," Brady relented. "I shouldn't have let you work so hard."

"I'm not tired like that, babe. It doesn't feel like I'm worn out from working too hard."

He bundled the blankets around her.

"I feel a deep fatigue," she kept on. "Like I could fall asleep on my feet."

"We did a lot today, Melinda. And I think you're run down from the emotional weight of the past few days. You *have* to be feeling some kind of way about all of this."

She nodded and wiped her dripping nose with the back of her glove.

"I'm feeling so many things right now, Brady."

He opened a beer for them both and handed one off to her, then placed her sandwich in her lap and retrieved his from the bag. They held the bottles between their knees and unwrapped the hoagies to eat.

"I'm heart-broken for my friend," Melinda started, eyeing the best first bite to take. "For the disappointment I know she felt. She wanted so much to reconnect with her family before she died. I wonder if she felt afraid in her last minutes, surrounded by those ungrateful assholes."

He tipped his beer up and washed down a mouthful. "You don't know, honey. They might have reconciled in the final moments. Don't start torturing yourself with what-ifs."

"Right, right," she mumbled with her mouth full of hoagie. "But I'm also feeling truly happy that I got to know her. I mean, *really know* who she was as a person."

"From everything you've told me about her, I'd say she loved her time with you, too."

Melinda smiled, drank from her beer, and nodded.

"I think she did."

The couple laid their heads back and took in the round white wonder of the full moon above them. They talked and ate and celebrated Miss M as the night wore on and the earth began to hide the light.

"It's starting!" Melinda announced.

Brady slouched down and letting his head hang off the back of his lawn chair, folded his hands behind his neck for support.

Melinda drew her feet up under her and folded an elbow under her ear to get comfortable.

"Did I tell you there was a lunar eclipse right after Miss M lost her mother?"

"No. Really?"

"Yep. Her dad brought her up to this very roof to watch it. They listened to the radio to stay awake until it started and then they climbed up here and talked and snacked and watched the whole thing together."

"That's so cool."

"She said he told her that we don't really have any proof that we're here in this place in the universe until we see our shadow on something around us. And when the earth casts its shadow on the moon, we see we're truly here."

"That's beautiful," he said and reached for her hand.

She took his and said, "I think he was trying to tell her that her mother would never really be gone because she had made an impression on her daughter. That is the proof we were here, whatever memories we've left behind in the people we loved."

The couple fell silent in the awe of the night. Watching the earth's silhouette float across the face of the moon until nothing but an orange halo remained, they held on to one another, safe in the belief that they were indeed part of the living world at that very moment. They counted. And everything they had been through to that pointed counted too.

Their parents counted.

Their babies counted.

Aunt Helen counted.

Miss M counted.

☀

The day they left Cleveland, Melinda found it easier than she imagined leaving behind the house and all the living they had done in it. She was feeling beat from the frantic cleaning and the loss of her friend and all the upheaval she'd been through. Brady helped her up into the cab of the U-Haul and she took one last look.

The place looked happier somehow. Maybe she imagined it appreciating the renovations. Maybe she imagined it glad to be rid of them. Whatever it was, the place looked happier, and that made Melinda smile.

Mary Rutherford stood at the front door waving the keys above the 'open house' sign as the first cars started pulling into the driveway.

Brady climbed aboard and waved back.

"Good luck," Mary called out. "I'll call you!"

"Thanks, Mary!" he answered, and turned to his wife. "Ready, honey?"

"I *really* am."

"Want to stop at Tiny's to get some hoagies for the road?"

"Ugh! I can't think about anything that heavy on my guts yet, babe," she grimaced. "But I will be *inconsolable* come lunch if we don't get them now. So... yes!"

This made him grin.

"Could you drop me somewhere while you pick them up?"

"Where to? You name it!"

She cut her eyes at him, and he knew in an instant.

He pulled up in front of the purple door, pitching to a stop with the full moving truck and her Probe in tow.

"I should have known we wouldn't get out of town without one last visit to Clara's," he said.

"I won't be long."

"Take your time, Melinda. I'll be back with the sandwiches in a flash and be right here when you come out."

She bounced across the seat and kissed him, then climbed down to the street and through the purple door.

When she got to the top of the steep stairs, the door to the outer room was open. The chairs were folded and leaning in a clump with the potted plants and Clara was around the corner tediously peeling the lettering from the glass on the door.

Melinda was surprised and confused.

"Clara, what's going on?"

"Morning, Melinda," she said. "Oh this? I'm giving it up."

The seer's head and hands fell, and she fiddled with the sticky letters she'd managed to remove.

"Giving it up?" Melinda asked.

"Yes. My brother offered me a job at the lumber store, and I have to take it. There's just no one left around here that wants their fortunes read."

"Clara, that can't be true."

"Everyone is so depressed about the present state, they can't imagine things getting any better."

"Well, *I'm* here," Melinda smiled. "Just about everything you've ever told me has been spot on, Clara. Brady *did* go away. I *did* go back to where I started and here we are on our way out of town to a new place. A better place. And you knew all of that was coming my way."

The woman managed a weak smile and shrugged.

"I've packed up all my things… but… I guess I *could* do your numbers again one last time if you want."

"Yes, please! After all, that's why I come here."

Clara closed the door to the stairs and lead Melinda through to the inner room as she had so many times before. This time, the fluorescent overheads were on. The darkly painted ceiling looked cheap and ugly without the sheer aubergine drapes and the twinkle lights. The purple walls did not show well in the light either. Clara took the candles and incense out of the boxes she'd already packed and placed them where they usually sat atop the chest of drawers, then lit each one. Melinda felt as if the electricity exposed all the secrets known to the tiny room, and mercifully switched off the lights. Together, the women unfolded the fringed crushed velvet throw and laid it on the table. Melinda smoothed out the creases while Clara placed the amber bowl in the center. They each grabbed a chair and pulled up to the edge of it to begin.

"As always, I invite you, Melinda, to this space to connect you to the spirit world for all it has to offer. Will you please accept the invitation and light the Candle of Belief to open the channels?"

Melinda complied, then immediately grasped her friend's hands in hers and squeezed.

Clara's face softened, and she held tight.

"We are open, spirits. We are here in heart and mind. What wisdom do you have for this one who seeks to know?"

They breathed in the silent air between them and felt the warmth in their hands and knew *this* was the real energy they connected with every time. This version of love and friendship. This thread of humanity was something that Melinda could count on even when everything else seemed to tell her she would always feel alone.

The flames were still. There was no sound or change in the air.

Melinda squeezed and released Clara's hands and made a suggestion, "Maybe there's no one left with anything to teach me, Clara."

"That's never true, you know that?"

"Let's do my numbers."

Clara nodded and reached back into one of the boxes she'd packed and retrieved her tarot cards and journal. She carefully prepared the deck and opened the ledger to where the pen held the place of the next blank page.

"M-I-N-..."

"No, Clara," she interjected. "Do Melinda this time."

"Are you sure?"

"Yes," she chuckled. "You know Miss M called me everything *but* Melinda for months, and you were right, no one but my mother *ever* called me Mindy Jo and she's been gone for so long. I think my *truest* Daily Name is Melinda."

Clara beamed, "Now we're getting somewhere, friend."

"M-E-L-I-N-D-A, so 4-5-3-5-4-1, so 23, which reduces to the value of 5."

"What is the value of 5?"

"This is you, my dear. The number 5 is all about freedom and change. This is so good, Melinda! The 5 energies root to the need for more, breaking out, searching for adventure."

"We're leaving town today. Brady's driving the loaded truck back to pick me up. We're moving to the beach!"

"That's only the beginning, friend." Clara scratched a few more calculations down in her book and continued, "Five is also associated with balance; half way between one and ten. You don't have to feel like you're lost in the chaos. *You* are the administrator. Return to your center so you can follow your senses and live your life looking forward to change and fresh adventures instead of dreading the next loss."

Melinda took her fortune into her lungs with a deep inhale and realized she felt something new and unusual.

She felt…free.

"Clara, this… you… are truly a gift to me. This is *exactly* what I needed to hear today."

"Melinda, I'm so glad you came in," she answered. "I'm honored that I get to send you off pregnant and free for the first time."

"Me t…" Melinda stopped short and stared blankly into the face of her psychic.

Clara waited for her to finish, then realized her mistake.

"You didn't know?"

"I… I… I haven't felt very… I've been nauseated… I thought…"

Clara giggled, "Relax, love." She rose and gathered her stunned client from her chair. "Brady is waiting downstairs for you to start your adventure."

"But how do you know?" Melinda asked as they walked in tandem to the stairs.

"I heard the truck pull up."

"No, Clara. About the baby."

"I feel like it was over Christmas. That female energy that's been waiting for you is your daughter."

Melinda planted herself and turned to face the seer, clutching her arms and searching her face for the truth.

"I thought it was Miss M. I thought she was waiting for me to finish this gift for her children."

"Any gift you got from Miss M was meant for *you*, Melinda."

These words fell to the deepest part of Melinda's heart like a stone to the bottom of a well. She knew what it meant. She knew what she gained, what she would *always* have because of Miss M. She felt blessed, and now a baby, too.

"How can you be sure about the baby, Clara? You know I've been through so many…"

"It's good this time, Melinda. It's time. *This* is your new adventure. She's *really* coming."

Melinda's eyes spilled over with joy, and she threw her arms around Clara's neck and held on for dear life.

Clara embraced her friend and cried along with her. She cried for her joy, for the new life to come, and for the page that now turned in their friendship.

Melinda released her friend but held Clara's hands tightly to imprint her gratitude.

"Thank you, Clara. Thank you for everything."

"Thank you for *believing*, Melinda. Good luck."

The two held one another's gaze for one second more, then Melinda turned down the stairs and out the purple door for the last time.

Summer 2004

***

Melinda opened the door to Lucy's room and found her face down on the bed.

"Excuse me, Miss Lucy," she interrupted the child's fit. "What in the world are you doing in here on this beautiful day? Maxie has been looking all over for you."

"I don't wanna play with Maxie," came her muffled response from deep in her pillow.

Melinda sat on the bed and rolled the nearly four-year-old over.

"What's up, Lucy?"

"Maxie's a *baby*. And I'm a *big* girl. Big girls don't play with babies."

"Oh, is that right? You know, you're not just a big girl. You're the big sister," Melinda explained. "That's kind of a big deal."

"I know," Lucy said, remaining flat on the bed but folding her arms hard over her chest. "I know I'm the big sister. Max is the brother and I'm the sister."

"Right!"

"So what's the *new* baby going to be?"

Melinda ran a hand over her ripe belly and reached the other one out to her curly-headed daughter.

"Well, the doctor says this one is going to be a girl."

Lucy sprung to her knees and anchored her hands on her hips in a declaration.

"*I'm* the sister, Momma!"

"Come here, beauty." Melinda gathered her close and kissed the top of her head. "Lucy, you will *always* be the big sister. This baby girl is going to love you, just like Max does. You have to help us teach her everything, just like you did with Maxie. She won't know how to talk or walk or feed herself."

"Or poop in the pot?"

"Nope. She's going to need to learn that, too."

"*You* have got to do that part, Momma. I can't go through that again. Maxie is a mess!"

"I know! Boys are a little different."

"It's that *penis*! That thing just doesn't make any sense!"

Melinda strained to keep her laughter from mocking her daughter's wisdom.

"I know, I know. Let's keep that penis stuff between us, ok?"

"Ok."

Melinda held the girl's face in her hands and kissed her forehead.

"Lucy, you are the *best* kind of people, you know that?"

"You love me, huh?"

"Too the moon and back."

"And back to the moon?"

"And back again!"

"And back to the moon?"

She tackled the girl to the bed, tickled her middle, and listened to her giggle as they played on and on.

Brady stood over the parts of the crib, taking inventory before he began assembling. Lucy came darting into the side door and gathered her brother by the hand to draw with sidewalk chalk just beyond the open garage doors in the driveway under the shade of the myrtles. Melinda waddled into the cool space and smiled up at her husband.

"Where was she?"

"Face down in her pillows contemplating her place in life, where else?"

"A little freakout over the baby?"

"I think," Melinda answered. "She's good. How's it coming out here?"

"I have found everything but the hardware. I remember putting it in a Ziplock but it wasn't with the rest of the crib."

"Did you look in your sortie thingy?"

"Yes."

"The big tool box?"

"First thing."

"The *little* tool box?"

"Yes!"

"*Now* you need to look like a woman."

Melinda ambled toward the back wall of the garage where tons of toys, outdoor equipment, and tools hung, stacked, and stood in a semi-organized fashion. She picked up athletic bags and gas cans. She moved ski pants and paint buckets.

"I swear, Melinda. If you find this tiny bag of nuts and bolts, I'll…"

"You'll *what* Brady?"

She twisted around to admonish him and caught a kick to the ribs from the baby. She winced and grabbed at the pain.

"Ow!"

Brady lunged for her, instantly regretting egging her on.

"That's it! I'll find it. I'll look like a woman," he promised, leading her to a lawn chair to rest.

"I'm *fine*. She just got me good when I turned around, that's all."

"That's all well and good, but you're done looking. We've got it. C'mon kids, let's play a game!"

Lucy and Max jumped to their feet, abandoning their chalk art and ran to their father.

"We're looking for a tiny treasure."

Their eyes widened.

"It's a little plastic bag with magic screws and washers inside. When we find it, we can make this pile of wood into a crib for the new baby!"

Lucy clapped her hands and grabbed her brother around the shoulders.

"We'll find it, Dad!"

The kids raced to the back wall and began peeking behind rakes and brooms and under muddy boots.

Brady leaned over his wife and smiled. She was flushed and plump. Not yet swollen and misshapen like at the end of the third trimester. Just healthy, happy, and beautiful. He beamed with joy and she beamed back.

A loud crash woke them from their reverie to find Max on his butt with a cowboy hat down over his eyes and a pile of spilled softball bats scattered on the ground around him.

Brady was quick to his rescue.

"You ok, Maxie?" he asked, freeing his face from the hat and eyeballing him for dents and dings.

"Ok, Dad," Max answered. Brady delivered the boy to his mother, and she felt for lumps on his head. When she found none, she tossed his hair, kissed him, and sent him back into the search.

"What's in these boxes, Daddy?" Lucy asked, uncovering a collection of sealed tubs under a tarp.

"Let's see what you have there, Lucy, my love."

Brady pulled the tarp free and opened the first tub.

"Oh! Books!" Lucy exclaimed. She *loved* to read.

"Well, not books exactly," her father cautioned. He took one out and handed it off to Lucy. "Go give this to Momma."

The girl delivered the prize. "Look Momma, we found books."

Melinda held the album in her hands and stared for a
moment while Lucy stood by to watch her open it.

"Read it, Momma."

"Oh baby girl, these books aren't for reading," her mother
started. "These are picture albums."

"Albums?"

Melinda opened the album and began, "These books
belonged to my friend Miss M. These are all the pictures of
her life."

"Picture books can tell a story too, huh Momma?"

"Yes ma'am."

Melinda ran her fingertips over the photos and their tags,
remembering the hours she spent learning her friend's
story.

"Well, tell us the story of Miss M."

Max joined them to see the pictures too, and Brady
returned to search for the missing hardware.

She began.

"This is a picture of Miss M and her daddy when she was
just a little older than you are now."

"Why is it brown?" Lucy asked of the sepia tone.

"It is very, very old. Long ago, when this picture was taken,
they didn't have colored pictures."

"What's this one?" the girl pointed to another.

"*That* one is the barber shop where Miss M's daddy worked."

"Like where Max gets his hair cut?"

"Hair cut!" Max aped, clipping his fingers like scissors and winding up a bit.

"Yes, like Maxie's haircuts." Lucy and her mother giggled at the toddler's antics.

"Dis one!" Max called out, smashing his chubby hand down on the book.

"Oh!" Melinda reached for him, but not before he pulled the picture free from its corner anchors and loosed something that dropped to the floor from behind it.

"Easy Max! We must be *easy* with Miss M's pictures, son. They are very important to Momma."

"Easy, Momma," Max echoed, handing back the photograph.

Lucy bent to retrieve what fell out of the book and studied it for a moment while her mother eased the photo back into place.

"This is a picture of a man. Is that Miss M's daddy too?"

Melinda held out her hand for the girl to return the object. She stared at it in disbelief, then answered the child.

"No, darling. That's Benjamin Franklin."

"Who's that?"

"He was a statesman from Philadelphia," she answered in mild shock, then carefully pulled one corner of another photo free and found another bill… then another… then another!

"Brady… babe… can you come over here, please?"

"Here it is! I taped it to the underside of the mattress! Now I remember!"

He pulled the Ziplock full of crib hardware free from the mattress and bounded across the concrete floor to his wife's side.

She sat with the pages of Miss M's family photos open across her lap with a pile of folded hundreds stacked in the middle.

He stood frozen in place.

"Is this what I *think* it is?" he questioned.

"If you think it's your lucky day, then yes. It *is* what you think it is?"

"*What* day is it?" Lucy asked.

Melinda answered with a smile a mile wide.

"Beautiful girl…it's just Thursday."

ABOUT THE AUTHOR

Diana Johnson grew up in Fairmont, WV not far from where she currently lives with her husband and daughter. She began her first attempts at storytelling on a used word processor between her sons' T-ball games and loads of laundry; but these works lay incomplete at the bottom of her dresser drawer for decades.

With nearly half her life lived, she decided to answer her calling to write with a resounding 'YES!'. Compiling a bank of stories and characters from all her *other* lives, she began to weave them into her own signature tales of life and love.

Diana writes contemporary human fiction about the third thing between us. No matter how people come together, they create a third thing, competition, friendship, hate, love, lust. She believes our humanity lies in understanding that third thing.

Johnson published her debut work in 2019, the near future, sci-fi, feminist novel *Cold Daughters,* followed by her second, the friendship fiction *Just DIY;* both in paperback, eBook, and audiobook versions. Visit her website at dianajohnsonwriter.com for upcoming projects, blog posts, contact info, and more or simply scan the QR code below to connect with this unique storyteller.

Made in the USA
Monee, IL
19 March 2023

29768799R00194